Shadowplays

Shadowplays

Edited by
PETER COLEBORN
& MIKE CHINN

CONTENTS

THANKS

We wish to thank Peter and Nicky Crowther and all at PS for supporting this project, as well as all the contributors who have entrusted us with their stories.

DEDICATION

To Stephen Jones and David Sutton for their friendship and inspiration which has encouraged me to edit and publish under the Alchemy Press imprint as well as this anthology. And especially to Jan for supporting me in all my endeavours.

—Peter

To Caroline, for putting up with all of this crazy stuff over the years, with the minimum of eyerolls.

—Mike

INTRODUCTION

Peter Coleborn & Mike Chinn

"HOW DO you fancy co-editing an anthology themed around *Unknown*-type fiction?"

There are certain words and phrases that should never be uttered out loud, like saying "Candyman" or "Beetlejuice" too many times; you can never be sure who, or what, is listening. The question was asked at ChillerCon UK in Scarborough, England, in May 2022, so there was always a good chance the gods of genre fiction would have half an ear open. Luckily, it seems they were feeling less capricious than usual at that moment.

For anyone who doesn't already know, *Unknown* was a short-lived (1939-43) pulp fantasy magazine which would become synonymous with a certain style of fiction. Edited by John W Campbell (he of *Astounding Science Fiction* fame), it published fantasy and horror that aimed at more subtlety and humour than was common in the more shocking (for the time) horror-orientated fiction being printed in the major genre magazine of the day, *Weird Tales*. In the very first issue of *Unknown*, HL Gold's "Trouble with Water" was an amusing tale concerning a New Yorker and a water gnome; the first of many to combine commonplace reality with the fantastic.

It was the darker side of the marriage between the commonplace and the fantastic that we were after for this anthology. Additionally, we wanted to reflect the kind of short story that Ray Bradbury wrote, as well as episodes typically featured in the TV series *The Twilight Zone*. Reality skewed. Unease instead of sheer shocks.

Peter and Nicky Crowther were quite taken by the concept, and by the time ChillerCon UK was concluded we were up and running. Sort of.

We had a working title—*Book of the Unknown*—but as the submission call went out, and stories started to arrive in the office, we knew a more memorable title was needed. After much juggling of Shakespearean quotes, famous sayings, song titles and lyrics, we finally settled on *Shadowplays*—because that is exactly what the stories within these pages are: small slices of life playing out in those darker regions where the mundane rubs shoulders with the bizarre and unsettling. Subtle horrors that lurk and play in the shadows only to emerge to haunt us.

So what do we have lined up for you?

Appropriately, topping and tailing are stories about actors— "TOTU" by Stephen Volk and "South Riding" from Reggie Oliver—in which the desire to escape that perennial curse of 'resting' leads the protagonists into very strange territory. And from Ray Bradbury himself, "If MGM is Killed, Who Gets the Lion" is a tale set in a world that is already part fantasy: Hollywood.

Rosanne Rabinowitz's "Damaged but Adorable" is a bittersweet fable about hope and longing which would sit right at home in *The Twilight Zone*. Nancy Kilpatrick's "As Far as Sacred Goes" is a wry tale of cultural appropriation and sacrifice. In "Stigma" by Paul Kane, Gavin learns just why nobody—not even his parents— seems to like him much, and in Robert Bagnall's "The Charmed",

Juliet finds out what it means to be really, really lucky. "Never To Be Told" from Colleen Anderson and Tom Johnstone explores the reality behind the old verse about magpies.

Gary McMahon's "Ever So Quietly, Ever So Softly" is a disturbing tale of a family retreating from reality, and Steve Rasnic Tem's "I Is for Infestation" sees Eric—or rather, it doesn't—overwhelmed by reality. Gail-Nina Anderson gives us a Fortean tale of spirit photographs in "The Fire Ghost", while Tim Jeffreys' "Begbrook" and Marion Pitman's "Echoes, Dying" involve quite different styles of haunting.

Bret McCormick's "Commitment to Truth" has Rebecca literally confronting truth in a bar in Austin. Stuck at a party in Maui, Jack also finds it hard to face his own truth in KC Grifant's "The Pit". Garry Kilworth gives us a slightly tongue-in-cheek revenge story in "The Long Drop Upwards".

John Linwood Grant's "December's Children" is a melancholy tale about those who both work and stay at the Langton hotel. In Wendy Purcell's "The Rosehill Truth Doctor", the suppression of lies brings its own horror. And Joanne Anderton's Japan-set "He Dances Alone" is a reflection on how fiction can shape reality itself.

Nineteen tales from twenty authors. Explorers in the unknown and possibly unknowable. We hope you enjoy them as much as we do, and join us in thanking the gods of genre fiction (in the guise of PS Publishing) for the chance to present them.

Shadowplays

TOTU

Stephen Volk

HER TEETH SANK into it for the fifteenth time, and for the fifteenth time it tasted disgusting. She wanted to retch and her stomach had the same idea, but here she was, with a yummy-yum-yum smile on her lips, grinning into the lens of the camera shortly after hair and make-up stepped away, her belly really protesting now, giving a spasm as the seeping greasiness of the previous take rose up in her gullet.

"Cut!" the director said, and she didn't waste a second in spitting out the mouthful of sliced bread and bacon into the bowl conveniently provided out of shot.

It was embarrassing to watch the trail of her own scarlet saliva dripping away from her lips into the plastic bucket, as if she was a contestant between rounds in a boxing match, but serve her right for signing up to appear in a ketchup commercial. Faced with, of all things, a bacon sarnie. Her a vegetarian, having to spit out after every take.

Izzy was a pro (or thought she was) but by the end of the day she felt lightheaded with the sheer physical effort of enduring the salty oil slick on her taste buds. That, or with the sheer moral hypocrisy. She wasn't sure which.

The things you do for art, love.

Mercifully, it was the last set-up of the shoot, her close-up before the pack shot, the big smile on her freckled face selling the garish product. She knew now why they liked her at the audition. That big grin of hers. And her expression of near-orgasmic pleasure. That, presumably, did the trick too, she thought, as she wiped the last of the gooey red sauce from the side of her mouth.

In the loo, afterwards, she hugged the throne for ten minutes, hoping to bring up whatever had made its way to her digestive system. No such luck. As a result she found herself walking to the Tube slightly unsteady on her feet, thinking she might bring it up at any moment, which filled her with dread. She imagined passers-by thinking her a reeling alcoholic after a night on the tiles, or a bit of fluff who'd had a long, boozy lunch with some gropey manager who wanted to get in her knickers. She realised she was spinning all sorts of dubious scenarios in her head because that was what it had felt like. Dubious. Yet it was what she had chosen to do, for money. Nobody had forced her.

Maybe the sick feeling in her gut was merely her guilt speaking.

Anyway, it was over. That was the main thing. Nobody had died, she told herself as she arrived back at the flat, eager for nothing more than bed. A meal—even a healthy one—was out of the question. She didn't even want to think about food, but Moon already had mushroom soup warming on the stove. At the smell of it, her heart dropped. But bless him, of course.

He came bounding out like a puppy dog with poodle hair and a long-sleeved Dennis the Menace top, panting to know how it had gone. Shooting a commercial! Professional crew! Must be exciting, right? Well, no, actually. Actually it was *work*. But she didn't say that, even as the cascade of questions came at her thick and fast before she'd unzipped her boots, walking in her socks to the fridge and grasping the neck of a bottle of cheap white from within. Freezing at the object she saw sitting on the work surface. Ticking. Its second hand moving. The minute hand going clunk.

Her heart dropped further. Through the floor this time.

Oh no. Not again.

But he was already talking. The super-fast "speaking in tongues" she was used to, yet thought was in the past now he was on his latest medication. The rat-a-tat enthusiasm that used to intoxicate her—part of what made her fall in love with him—but now filled her with dread. She wanted to cut it off midstream with a hand over his mouth or two hands on his throat because she couldn't bear it anymore.

"A submarine clock. Look, with a submarine design on it! In the shape of a porthole. Maybe it was a porthole. A porthole turned into a clock! How cool is that? I'm not kidding, they were giving it away. Giving it away! And Russian. Look, Russian lettering! So it must be the real thing. Sitting there on the market stall, I'm telling you, they have no idea what they're selling, they have no idea of the *wonders*, honest to God," her boyfriend was saying, forehead creased with seriousness, like it was the Ark of the Covenant. He'd found the Ark of the Covenant on Portobello Market.

"Moon, Moon." She held up one hand and told him to think for a minute. "If you were on a submarine, would you need a picture of a submarine on the clock, to remind you where you were?"

"I don't know."

"Like, 'Oh, yeah, shit, I'm on a submarine!'."

"I don't know! I'm not Russian!"

"No, you're a genius."

"What is that supposed to mean?"

"Nothing. Nothing."

He said he was going to put it up for auction. He was going to make hundreds. This was going to be the easiest five hundred quid he ever made in his life. No, seven hundred. No, nine! It was fucking sweet, and she would eat her words. Wait and see.

"Like the others," Izzy muttered under her breath, seeing him refuse to look up, like he had blanked her. "I said, 'Like the others'. Hello! Do you have any idea how many friggin' clocks you have cluttering up the bedroom right now that you haven't sold? Twenty? Thirty? Ding dong merrily on—"

"I'll try another auction house. There's a guy in Notting Hill. A specialist. You've got to move things around. It's an art. As much of an art as acting."

"Oh, thank you."

"I didn't mean—"

"Yes, you *did* fucking mean," she said, turning away. "You did."

"I'm only trying to do right by us." He stood up off the stool and put his arms around her. "I'm investing to speculating." He didn't even make grammatical sense anymore, and there was that telltale saliva on his lips, close to, which meant the manic phase was well and truly in force. "I'm using my God-given initiative, Iz. Don't you see this is going to pay off? It's going to bail us out, big time! Why can't you see the big picture? This is the potential catalyst for a business empire. And that is not hyperbole—that is fact. And yes, I used our joint account. What else am I going to use? I'll pay you back at the end of the month."

"Oh, like last month?"

"Sorry. Silly me. I thought we were in this relationship together. Why can't you cut me a bit of fucking slack for once instead of criticising everything I do?"

"Do what you want," she said flatly, the fight deserting her. "Honestly. Do what you fucking want. I'm going to bed."

He shouted after her that they were going to be minted.

Izzy Achilleos lay on her bed and wailed. It had all been building, but now it came out. She couldn't stop it. Part of her wanted Moon to hear her crying, and come in, and sit on the bed and say it would be all right, but she knew deep down he couldn't. He was flying. He was Superman. Superman doesn't say sorry for his superpowers, he just saves your life.

If only.

After two hours she knew she wouldn't sleep, and her throat felt as raw as burnt canvas. She wrapped her dressing gown around her and walked to the kitchen, filling a glass of water from the tap. The bottle of Blue Nun stood where she'd left it. She put it back in the fridge, then took it out and filled the empty glass.

Moon was sitting in the living room in the dark, and came to the door jamb, sleeves tugged over his hands.

She looked at the label on the Russian clock. "That's my acting fee for the whole day." She didn't need to point out to him it was the only fee she'd had all year. Even in the self-engrossed state he was in, he knew that. "It doesn't even tell the right time. It's slow."

"That can be fixed. I know a guy."

She closed her eyes. Heard it, seen it, a million times now. She wanted to sleep and get away from it. Sleep forever. That money was meant to pay the rent, which was already late and the landlord had read them the riot act. He was now well within his rights to sling them out in the street. And who could blame him?

"We can't go on living like this," she said. And before he said he couldn't help his illness, she said she knew that, but he could do something about his pills. The problem was, when he felt great, he thought he didn't need them, and didn't take them, and now, here they were again, in exactly the place she didn't want to be. Stuck. Frozen. Trapped. With no way out. She'd tried to claw them both out, but he'd dragged them back in, and she couldn't deal with that anymore.

"I love you so much," he said, but she knew the sorrow and shame of old. They were his bedfellows.

"I know you do," she said. "And it's not all your fault."

Which was true. She couldn't lay all the financial troubles at manic depression's door. She hadn't been properly bringing home the—ha ha!—bacon for years. What had she done? The odd voiceover. Bit part in a horror film shot in Spain. Maybe it was time for her to snap out of her *own* delusion. She was an aspiring young actress running on empty, not getting any breaks. Artistically driven and in love with her craft, but getting exactly nowhere. At what point do you say, enough is enough? That nagging feeling inside told her it was high time for a reality check. Perhaps the ridiculous enterprise of the ketchup advert had been the last straw—but also a wake-up call.

"I'm going to jack it in," she said. "It's not working and it'll never work. There are thousands of actors on the dole and I'm not going to be one of them anymore. It's too soul destroying."

"No," he said plaintively. "You're talented. Don't throw it away. Don't destroy your soul."

"The business has done that. It doesn't want me. The writing is on the wall. I just chose not to see it, for aeons. And life's too short. I don't even feel bad about it, now I've said it out loud."

"I do," Moon said, kissing her neck. "I'm gutted. I want to see you on the big screen. I want to see you in Hollywood."

Izzy smiled. "Cricklewood, more like."

"I love you."

"You said that."

"I said it again," he said, and hugged her tear-reddened cheek to his Dennis the Menace top. He believed in her, and that gave her a warm glow, for all his faults, which were plentiful. He believed in her, even if she didn't.

Next day, new beginnings, she visited a local bookshop—no need of part-time staff said the creepy geezer in Steptoe gloves—and a Lebanese restaurant where she received a theatrical shrug from a short man with a forest of ear hair. The minimarket was her next, ignominious, port of call, but there were no shifts available, though the Hindu lady couldn't have been nicer, baby asleep on her lap as she rang up the till. Izzy bought a Galaxy bar to take the edge off her disappointment. Not wanted as an actress. Not even wanted as a shelf stacker.

Great.

She phoned her agent from the phone box under the brooding arch of a concrete flyover. Not the ideal place to do it, but she thought she may as well bite the bullet and tell Belinda she was through. Old bossy boots would probably be all too relieved to get her off her books. She'd probably hang up at the end of the call and not have a single thought about her for the rest of her life.

Having deposited the requisite coins in the pay phone, Izzy stood listening to the ringing tone at the other end, calculating the money she'd save by not having to have her photo and contact details in *Spotlight* every year, and it brightened her mood and toughened her resolve. She didn't know why she was nervous. The casting agent scared her a little bit, but she should at least have the courage of her convictions. After all, it was her own life, not anyone else's.

"Darling!" Belinda yelped perkily, taking her aback. Lady B had picked up the receiver herself and recognised her name instantly, which was a shock in itself—and before Izzy could tell the matriarch of Levinson & Associates she was knocking it on the head the woman was already in full flow: "I swear, this must be mental telepathy at work, darling, because I was literally mentioning you *literally* seconds ago."

Izzy thought that was probably the most blatant flannel. "Really? Well..."

"I know we haven't spoken in a while. Not really spoken. I mean, that commercial was a disaster. But never mind. A job has come in. Pukka TV company. One of the ITV regions. Not one of these Johnny fly-by-nights. Just came off the phone to them. Terribly nice people. No idea who they are, of course. Nor do I care, sweetheart, as long as they sign the cheque." Izzy heard a fist banging the desk and imagined the flamingo-drinking-water toy quivering. "So get over there this minute—44 Berwick Court. Off Berwick Street. Do you know it? If you don't know it, find it. You have an *A-Z*, I'm sure."

"What's the job exactly?"

"Television! I have no idea, darling. Series. Repeat fees. You'll find out when you get there. They wouldn't tell me. All very hush-hush. 'Totu' is all they'd say. Good-looking actress. Good figure. One with a bit of pizzazz. They're looking for something special."

"No riff raff."

"Definitely no riff raff. Though I'm sure you could do riff raff at a push. Weren't you born in Dalston?"

"Dawlish."

"Same thing." There was the snap of a cigarette lighter. Izzy heard the smoky exhale of a Benson & Hedges. "Let me know how it goes. It'll go marvellously. Be yourself. Expect the unexpected. 'Bye!"

It'll go marvellously. Be yourself.

How often had she heard that? Belinda's mantra. Always gushing from the corner of her fag-holding mouth as she ushered you out of the door while the phone was ringing. Always fitting you in between other clients who seemed to be fantastically more important and successful. Or so Izzy's self-doubt told her as she'd hobbled down the narrow, uncarpeted staircase in Poland Street so many times, past the film and theatre posters of movies and shows that Belinda and her cohorts had had a hand in setting up.

Was this one such an opportunity, she wondered, as she stepped out of the phone box into the cold air? Would her name and her face be on one of those posters some day? Was this the one?

It was probably ridiculous, but just when she'd resigned herself to the fact it was all meaningless to her, and her fantasy career was all a hiding to nothing, she nevertheless found her heart beating a little faster. Not in celebration exactly—no, of course not—but in celebration of the *possibility*.

She knew Berwick Street well. The heart of Soho, home to the British Film Industry and the heart of the London's red-light district, which didn't seem entirely alien from each other at times. She'd attended enough auditions to know that sometimes the plight and desperation of an actress, especially a young and pretty one, could flirt hideously close to being part of the sex trade, or was expected to be, in terms of favours, albeit couched in a cloak of innuendo. Which was why she approached even this one with a degree of caution.

The market traders were barking their calls and whistling, twirling their brown paper bags into knots, nudging their caps off their foreheads. A few wolf whistles came in her direction. The long legs and mini skirt made it inevitable. The sway of her hips as her high heels negotiated the cobbles drew a few winks in her direction, too, but she knew it was mostly harmless. Men mostly were, and the boisterous catcalls really only served the purpose of asserting their manhood to other men. She wondered if they did

it when there were no women in the street, and the idea brought
a smile to her lips. The kind of sketch Benny Hill might do. Not
that she liked Benny Hill much.

She found the door to number 44 without difficulty. Pressed
the buzzer next to the flat marked "TOTU" and gave her name.
What was it? An African name? She supposed she'd find out soon
enough. A female voice told her to come up to the third floor. The
door buzzed open as she pushed it and clanged shut after she'd
entered, cutting down the noise of the market. The smell of rotten
and discarded fruit somehow still exuded into the narrow, dingy
passageway and accompanied the footfall of her leather boots as
she climbed the stairs.

By the time she reached the third floor much of the exterior
sound had receded and the top of the building—if it was the top—
felt stuffy and airless, like an underground bunker or the sort of
pillbox used in WWII, not that she'd ever been in one. Fresh air
was lacking and she was slightly out of puff.

The girl who greeted her didn't give her name but happily took
care of Izzy's coat and scarf, draping them over the wire coat-
hanger in her hand, telling her almost as an afterthought to go
straight ahead. "They're in there. They're waiting for you."

"Are there any pages? ... Pages?"

"No pages."

"Can you tell me about the part?"

"They'll tell you everything you need to know."

The door in front of her on the little landing was off-kilter, as
if the subtle movement of the building over decades or centuries
had shifted it off its axis and it didn't quite fit the frame. The
creamish paint was chipped. A small handwritten sign was
Sellotaped to it reading "TOTU"—that word again. The word she
didn't understand.

She flattened the front of her skirt with her hands, took a deep
breath, and turned the handle.

Two men in suits sat behind a desk and she immediately
thought of school and teachers. One had a large belly and the
aspect of an overbearing public-school headmaster or defrocked
priest. Under the desk, she could make out the extent his slate grey

socks reached high up his shins and the pale flesh, like uncooked chicken skin, between where they ended and his trousers began. The other one looked more like a geography master, the sort with patches sewn onto his elbows and a crust of snot surrounding his nostrils, which in this case were spectacularly wide. What disturbed her greatly was that he sported virulent and unruly eyebrows. If they'd been much longer they'd have needed to have been swept back with a comb. Under which the scrawny man's eyes were hooded, his expression seeming both supercilious and somnolent.

There was no chair for her to sit in, just a cross made from gaffer tape on the floor. Which she imagined she should stand on—her "mark" as they called it on set—so she did, clearing her throat before assuming her best and most radiant smile. She imagined they'd speak first but they didn't. They didn't even say her name, so she did.

They still said nothing, as if the exercise they were undertaking was to examine her unease. But she wasn't having that and decided to fill the silence herself

"Have you looked at my CV?"

"What would we find on your CV?" asked the skinny one.

"Facts."

"Facts?"

"That I was born in 1956. That I'm twenty-two years old. All the boring stuff."

"Are you boring, then?" The fat one eased his bulk forward slightly.

"No. I hope not."

"Your agent assured us you weren't. She was singing your praises quite effusively."

"Was she? I'm glad someone is."

The skinny one with the eyebrows interjected. "You don't seem confident of your talent, Izzy, if I may say so."

"Don't I?"

"But perhaps that's innately your talent. To not know just how talented you are. That's a gift in itself."

She laughed, not sure if that was a joke or not. But neither of them was smiling.

Between the two men on the desk sat a bottle of red wine, the label of which the fatter one was examining closely after revolving it towards him. Beside it lay a red rose with a long, thorny stem. Next to that, a pack of unusually large playing cards with an elaborate and Baroque-looking design on the backs.

As the fat one poured himself a glass, the younger man stood up and handed her the pack of cards. "Shuffle them. Vigorously." While she did as he asked, he turned to a straight-backed dining chair positioned to one side and took off his trousers, which he folded neatly over the back. He wore shorts—not underpants or Y-fronts, but the sort of baggy shorts footballers wore—and his legs, she saw now, were covered in thick black hairs, though his bare feet were small and delicate. "Place the pack back on the desk, please. Tap it three times with the index finger of your left hand, then divide it in two."

She obeyed his request, thinking this, and the trousers, another stupid test. Some sort of game to see whether she would be horrified or not. Either that or he suffered a constriction in the crotch area that needed to be relieved—and that didn't bear thinking about. Or this was a prelude to . . . no, that didn't bear thinking about either.

Tap, tap, tap. Two piles. *There.*

"Now put one pile on top of the other."

When she had, the skinny one took the top card and showed it to her. The illustration upon it depicted a skeleton with a plague-ridden landscape in the background and the word DEATH at the bottom.

"Of course, Death doesn't mean Death. Death means change. The end of one state of being and the beginning of another."

"Thank God for that." Izzy emitted an all-too-obvious nervous laugh and cleared her throat again. She wasn't sure if there was a cloying smell of damp in the room or if she had trodden in a discarded piece of vegetable from a market stall and trailed it up the stairs with her. Either way, it made her feel sick.

The fat man rolled the wine around his mouth and swallowed, punctuating his enjoyment with a *pah*. "What's your ambition, Izzy?" the glistening lips uttered.

"To work. To work on this series or whatever it is that—"

"No. No, No… what's *your* real ambition, deep down?" The ruddiness of what he'd imbibed seemed to eke over his whole features. "You know the best performances come from a point of honesty, and that's what we want here. The *only* thing we want here. *Honesty.*"

In spite of her nervousness and her urge to flee, Izzy found herself thinking about the answer, her honest answer, and why she was avoiding saying it, because she'd never said it aloud before. She wasn't even sure she'd truly thought it before that moment. "To be noticed," she said. "That's right. That's all. To be noticed. To be seen. Isn't that what everybody wants?"

"Not everybody. By no means everybody. But if that's what you want, we can make you noticed by millions."

"That's why you're here," said the other, with icy conviction.

"It's a non-dialogue part, by the way."

"That's fine," said Izzy quickly.

"Is it fine? Are you sure about that?"

"Yes, of course. It's all a learning curve at the very least."

"Why 'at the very least'?"

She became flustered and didn't want to show it. "A, well… a lot can be achieved by physical acting. Look at the silent comedians. Look at Marcel Marceau."

"Marcel Marceau." The fat one rolled the four syllables over his huge, bulbous tongue as he had done the red wine. She wasn't sure if it meant she was being ridiculed or admired for her filmic erudition. She couldn't believe it was the latter.

"Can we see how you move, do you think?"

"How do you mean?"

"Can you just walk up and down for us, moving naturally? Being natural is the hardest thing to do, of course."

There was an angel fish in an aquarium and it seemed to be looking at her too.

Flight or fight was waving a flag—not because of the angel fish but because of *everything*—but this was her last, best opportunity, and she didn't want to go to her grave knowing she'd flunked it. Ran away, because of some—How was she going to say that to Moon without her seeming like the weakest, most pathetic...No, she'd do it. Do it, and *was* doing it, walking five paces to her left, turning on her heel, and walking back with a faux-confident swish of her hips.

"Again. With a little more attitude, if you please."

Right.

The sashay became a tad more catwalk. The shoulders dipped, the chin swung. Her eyes fastened on those of the men as she changed direction. *Screw you*, she thought with every step. *Screw you. Screw you. Give me the job. Give me the job. Screw you.* The torch song of every audition she'd ever been to. What she said in her mind to every leering male face that dared to assess her, chew her up and spit her out. *Screw you.*

"Now put your hands above your head. Snake them in the air a little bit."

"Use your fingers. That's the stuff."

"Don't think about us. Think about your body. Think you are a snake being charmed by a snake charmer."

"Turn three hundred and sixty degrees."

"That's perfect. Perfect."

She didn't look at them because she didn't want to see what they were thinking. She didn't want to see what they were feeling. She wanted her nice warm bed, and Moon. Mad, Bad Moon—the man who loved her. The man she'd bail out if only she got this part, and their lives would change forever.

"Thank you."

She stopped, catching her breath, and stood to attention, facing them.

"Now we'd like you to take your clothes off."

I beg your pardon?

She searched their faces for any betrayal that this was a sick joke, but could detect nothing. They were not leering as men usually leered. The wine glass was empty except for a dribble like a tear on the inside. They were staring at her like accountants.

"Not here. Of course, not here." The fat schoolmaster grinned.

So it was a joke? Was it? "In the next room. If you could strip down to your underwear, please."

"As part of the audition?

"You've got the part," the thin one said. "This is no longer part of the audition."

What is it then?

The priest-like one pointed a chubby hand towards a second door. Not the one by which Izzy had entered. This one was painted black. Its handle was gold. The woman who had met her at the top of the stairs was standing next to it. She was no longer wearing the tartan skirt and chunky Fair Isle sweater she'd worn earlier. Now she was adorned with a trouser suit that made her vaguely resemble an aircraft flight attendant. She said nothing but opened the black door for Izzy.

"When you hear the music, just dance," said the geography-teacher-looking one, shuffling the deck of Tarot cards idly. "That's all you have to do. Just move the way the music compels you."

"Will you be filming?"

"We will be watching."

"Everyone will be watching," said the fat man, rocking back in his swivel chair. "Don't worry."

Izzy rested her hand against the door jamb. The wood was warm. The woman was gone and the person holding the door handle was herself. She felt grease and ketchup conspiring in her digestive tract.

"Tell me about the part," she said in a whisper, as if to a father confessor. She thought of her dad. His love of red wine. The death of him. Wine buff. Gambler. Liar.

You're alone. You're afraid. You're trapped. You are vulnerable to the buffeting forces of fate.

But there's the wheel.

"The wheel?" she said.

The wheel of life. Ever turning. Never ending.

"Like the windmills of my mind?"

Something like that.

Are you ready?

"Ready for what?"

Ready to do your piece?

"I don't have a piece."

Yes you do. You know you do. You've always known your whole life there'd be a moment when you could truly show who you are to the whole world. Well, this is your chance.

She took off all her clothes except for her bra and panties, left them in a heap at her ankles, and stepped through the door.

The room was the size of the bedroom she had when she was a child. A place of lullabies and pillows and waking and wishing. But there was no bed, no furniture she could see in the gloom. There was just her. And she almost loved that darkness, the darkness of sleep where she was safe, but a light came on, a bright light from a pinpoint on the wall and it bathed her and blinded her. She reeled back at the assault of it. And the loud, jaunty music that hit her in the head...music like a sinister fairground ride...the theme of a ghostly hurdy-gurdy...something that might accompany dancing skeletons in a joyous but nasty danse macabre.

When you hear the music, just dance.

And she knew she had to dance. Dance as she would with Moon when they went to see a band at The Lyceum. Dance as they would at a party when they'd taken pot and downed several bottles of Mateus Rosé. Dance and dance as the wheel turned. As the Tarot cards marched by. As the red wine was poured. Whether they were watching or not. Whether they were filming or not. Because this was where fate had taken her.

She stretched her arms above her head, twining them around each other like snakes embracing each other, dipping one knee then the other, revolving her hips, swaying from side to side in lugubrious abandon. Losing herself in the tune. Possessed by a force stronger than any tarantella, any fit, or seizure—because it was her dream come true.

The first time the music ended she thought it was over and walked to the door handle, but it wouldn't turn. The second time the music played she shouted for help. The third time she screamed at the top of her voice. The fourth time she hammered on the door. But by the twentieth time her hands were bleeding and she knew nobody could hear her, or if they could, they didn't care.

The music played on.

She danced because she had no alternative and didn't know what would happen if she stopped.

She didn't eat because they didn't give her food and didn't sleep because they gave her no bed. It made no difference.

She still heard the music.

She still danced.

By the seventh day it occurred to her that her distress caused them pleasure so she called them all the names under the sun, and a few that would have made the sun blush. It did no good, and soon she resigned herself to let the music wash over her again, and again, and again, and again...the hurdy-gurdy...the fairground danse macabre.

Until the tears dried on her cheeks and the memory of her life began to fade. Everything she'd ever loved faded.

Only the music remained. And, again, it came.

She couldn't escape it, the passing days, weeks, months soon told her that. The constant loop of merry-go-round, Tarot cards, wheel. When would it end? It wouldn't. *She* wouldn't.

That was the immortality they promised her, she now realised. The promise to be noticed. To be watched by millions. Well, now she was. Her perpetual night—her perpetual disco—trapped in the dark behind the television screen. Eternally and inextricably part of one of the most iconic drama series of all time.

TOTU

Tales of the Unexpected.

The show everyone remembered. And even if they didn't remember all the stories, they remembered her.

The swan-neck arms coiling in space. Her figure duplicated across the screen in the 1978 choreography nobody could forget. Her shape posterized into primary colours, into slinky, sexy anonymity as the title sequence played out at the start of every episode.

When you hear the music, just dance.

She did. She would. Forever.

And they hadn't lied, you see.

You're alone. You're afraid. You're trapped. You are vulnerable to the buffeting forces of fate.

And Death didn't always mean Death. It could mean a change to another state of being.

And so she danced, and is dancing now—somewhere, where a TV set is switched on, where a channel is showing repeats somewhere on the globe ... or in the next street to you ... or on a DVD you have in your collection ... and will go on dancing, dancing on your TV screen, at the beginning of every repeat of *Tales of the Unexpected* you watch, floating, almost swimming, lost in that haunting, twinkling, transporting music.

Watched, watched a million times, watched and sometimes even noticed. Even if no-one hears her screaming.

IF MGM IS KILLED,
WHO GETS THE LION?

Ray Bradbury

"**H**OLY JEEZ, DAMN. Christ off the cross!" said
Jerry Would.

"Please," said his typist-secretary, pausing to erase a
typo in a screenplay, "I have Christian ears."

"Yeah, but my tongue is Bronx, New York," said Would,
staring out the window. "Will you just look, take one long fat look
at *that!*"

The secretary glanced up and saw what he saw, beyond.

"They're repainting the studio. That's Stage One, isn't it?"

"You're damn right. Stage One, where we built the *Bounty* in
'34 and shot the Tara interiors in '39 and Marie Antoinette's
palace in '34 and now, for God's sake, look what they're doing!"

"Looks like they're changing the number."

"Changing the number, hell, they're wiping it *out!* No more
One. Watch those guys with the plastic overlays in the alley,
holding up the goddamn pieces, trying them for size."

The typist rose and took off her glasses to see better.

"That looks like UGH. What does 'Ugh' mean?"

"Wait till they fit the first letter. See? Is that or is that not an H?"

"H added to UGH. Say, I bet I know the rest. Hughes! And down there on the ground, in small letters, the stencil? 'Aircraft'?"

"Hughes Aircraft, dammit!"

"Since when are we making planes? I know the war's on, but—"

"We're not making any damn planes," Jerry Would cried, turning from the window.

"We're shooting air combat films, then?"

"No, and we're not shooting no damn air films!"

"I don't see . . . "

"Put your damn glasses back on and look. Think! Why would those SOBs be changing the number for a name, hey? What's the big idea? We're not making an aircraft carrier flick and we're not in the business of tacking together P-38s and—Jesus, *now* look!"

A shadow hovered over the building and a shape loomed in the noon California sky.

His secretary shielded her eyes. "I'll be damned," she said.

"You ain't the only one. You wanna tell me what that thing is?"

She squinted again. "A balloon?" she said. "A barrage balloon?"

"You can say that again, but *don't!*"

She shut her mouth, eyed the grey monster in the sky, and sat back down. "How do you want this letter addressed?" she said.

Jerry Would turned on her with a killing aspect. "Who gives a damn about a stupid letter when the world is going to hell? Don't you get the full aspect, the great significance? Why, I ask you, would MGM have to be protected by a barrage—hell, there goes *another!* That makes *two* barrage balloons!"

"*No* reason," she said. "We're not a prime munitions or aircraft target." She typed a few letters and stopped abruptly with a laugh. "I'm slow, right? We are a prime bombing target?"

She rose again and came to the window as the stencils were

hauled up and the painters started blowgunning paint on the side of Stage One.

"Yep," she said, softly, "there it is. AIRCRAFT COMPANY. HUGHES. When does he move *in*?"

"What, Howie the nut? Howard the fruitcake? Hughes the billionaire bastard?"

"*That* one, yeah."

"He's going nowhere, he still has his pants glued to an office just three miles away. Think! Add it up. MGM is here, right, two miles from the Pacific coast, two blocks away from where Laurel and Hardy ran their tin lizzie like an accordion between trolley cars in 1928! And three miles north of us and *also* two miles in from the ocean is—" He let her fill in the blanks.

"Hughes Aircraft?"

He shut his eyes and laid his brow against the window to let it cool. "Give the lady a five-cent seegar."

"I'll be damned," she breathed with revelatory delight.

"You ain't the only one."

"When the Japs fly over or the subs surface out beyond Culver City, the people painting that building and re-lettering the signs hope that the Japs will think Clark Gable and Spencer Tracy are running around Hughes Aircraft two miles north of here, making pictures. And that MGM, *here*, has Rosie the Riveters and P-38s flying out of that hangar down there all day!"

Jerry Would opened his eyes and examined the evidence below. "I got to admit, a sound stage does look like a hangar. A hangar looks like a sound stage. Put the right labels on them and invite the Japs *in*. *Banzai!*"

"Brilliant," his secretary exclaimed.

"You're fired," he said.

"*What?*"

"Take a letter," said Jerry Would, his back turned.

"Another letter?"

"To Mr Sid Goldfarb."

"But he's right upstairs."

"Take a letter, dammit, to Goldfarb, Sidney. Dear Sid. Strike that. Just Sid. I am damned angry. What the hell is going on? I walk in the office at eight a.m. and it's MGM. I walk out to the commissary at noon and Howard Hughes is pinching the waitresses' behinds. Whose bright idea was this?"

"Just what I wondered," his secretary said.

"You're fired," said Jerry Would.

"Go on," she said.

"Dear Sid. Where was I? Oh, yeah. Sid, why weren't we informed that this camouflage would happen? Remember the old joke? We were all hired to watch for icebergs sailing up Culver Boulevard? Relatives of the studio, uncles, cousins? And now the damned iceberg's here. And it wears tennis shoes, a leather jacket, and a moustache over a dirty smile. I been here twelve years, Sidney, and I refuse—aw, hell, finish typing it. Sincerely. No, not sincerely. Angrily yours. Angrily. Where do I sign?"

He tore the letter from the machine and whipped out a pen.

"Now take this upstairs and throw it over the transom."

"Messengers get killed for messages like this."

"Killed is better than fired."

She sat quietly.

"Well?" he said.

"I'm waiting for you to cool down. You may want to tear this letter up, half an hour from now."

"I will not cool down and I will not tear it up. Go."

And still she sat, watching his face until the lines faded and the colour paled. Then very quietly she folded the letter and tore it across once and tore it across twice and then a third and fourth time. She let the confetti drift into the trash basket as he watched.

"How many times have I fired you today?" he said.

"Just three."

"Four times and you're out. Call Hughes Aircraft."

"I was wondering when you—"

"Don't wonder. Get."

She flipped through the phone book, underlined a number, and glanced up. "Who do you want to talk to?"

"Mr Tennis Shoes, Mr Flying Jacket, the billionaire butinsky."

"You really think he ever answers the phone?"

"Try."

She tried and talked while he gnawed his thumbnail and watched them finish putting up and spraying the AIRCRAFT stencil below.

"Hell and damn," she said at last, in total surprise. She held out the phone. "He's *there*! And answered the phone *himself*!"

"You're putting me on!" cried Jerry Would.

She shoved the phone out in the air and shrugged.

He grabbed it. "Hello, who's this? What? Well, say, Howard, I mean Mr. Hughes. Sure. This is MGM Studios. My name? Would. Jerry Would. You *what*? You heard of me? You saw *Back to Broadway*? And *Glory Years*. But sure, you once owned RKO Studios, right? Sure, sure. Say, Mr. Hughes, I got a little problem here. I'll make this short and sweet."

He paused and winked at his secretary.

She winked back. The voice on the line spoke nice and soft.

"What?" said Jerry Would. "Something's going on over at *your* place, *too*? So you know why I'm calling, sir. Well, they just put up the aircraft letters and spelled out HUGHES on Stage One. You like that, huh? Looks great. Well, I was wondering, Howard, Mr. Hughes, if you could do me a little favour."

"Name it," said the quiet voice a long way off.

"I was thinking if the Japs come with the next tide by air or by sea and no Paul Revere to say which, well, when they see those big letters right outside my window, they're sure going to bomb the hell outta what they think is P-38 country and Hughes territory. A brilliant concept, sir, brilliant. Is *what*? Is everyone here at MGM happy with the ruse? They're not dancing in the streets but they do congratulate you for coming up with such a world-shaking plan. Now here's my point. I gotta lot of work to finish. Six films shooting, two films editing, three films starting. What I need is a nice safe place to work, you got the idea? That's it. Yeah. That's it. You got a nice small corner of one of your hangars that— sure! You're way ahead of me. I should *what*? Yeah, I'll send my secretary over right after lunch with some files. You got a typewriter? I'll leave mine here. Boy, How—Mr Hughes, you're a peach. Now, tit for tat, if *you* should want to move into *my* office here? Just joking. Okay. Thanks. Thanks. Okay. She'll be there, pronto."

And he hung up.

His secretary sat stolidly, examining him. He looked away, refused to meet her stare. A slow blush moved up his face.

"*You're* fired," she said.

"Take it easy," he said.

She rose, gathered a few papers, hunted for her purse, applied a perfect lipstick mouth, and stood at the door.

"Have Joey and Ralph bring all the stuff in that top file," she said. "That'll do for starters. You coming?"

"In a moment," he said, standing by the window, still not looking at her.

"What if the Japs figure out this comedy, and bomb real Hughes Aircraft instead of this fake one?"

"Some days," sighed Jerry Would, "you can't win for losing."

"Shall I write a letter to Goldfarb to tell him where you're going?"

"Don't write, call. That way there's no evidence."

A shadow loomed. They both looked up at the sky over the studio.

"Hey," he said, softly, "there's another. A *third* balloon."

"How come," she said, "it looks like a producer I used to know?"

"You're—" he said.

But she was gone. The door shut.

DAMAGED
BUT ADORABLE

Rosanne Rabinowitz

HAZEL FLEES THE office before Vicious Valerie (never Val) can have another go at her.

As she walks, a turning of her heel reminds her that the sole of her shoe is worn down. A new pair of trainers, that's what she needs. That should cheer her up. And what better place to find them than Takky Max?

But she still feels sick as she walks into the shop. Anxiety wraps its wires around her chest and tightens them, an inner garrotting. People stride up and down the aisles with their deep, plastic trolleys and she starts to feel like she's in their way. Some irritating tune spews out of the Tannoy. A petite young staff member with bunched be-ribboned hair carries a box almost half her size. But she is half-smiling and surprisingly serene, given the load she is carrying.

Hazel wonders what could be in that box. Seeking distraction, she wanders to the Home section behind the girl and watches her fish out strings of dinosaur fairy lights and set them up along a shelf. There's a T-Rex and a stegosaurus and that big vegetarian one with the long neck.

It's amazing how the wires around her chest loosen when she imagines them decked out with those twinkling green dinosaurs. She releases a deep breath and looks about in hope of finding further solace.

This may be the Home section but it resembles no home she knows. Who shares a house with a squad of gangster angels wearing shades, like those across the aisle? She walks on until a gleam of silver catches her eye.

It's a bell with crab claws and legs.

A crab bell. Her mother kept such a bell on the reception desk of the seaside B&B she ran for years. When Hazel was little she could just about reach up and *ding* it. It was always so satisfying to hear that *ding*.

Hazel, what are you doing? You'll break it!

Mum didn't like it when she rang that bell. But now Hazel remembers how she sat behind the desk, greeting guests with such graciousness. Hazel thought she was the most glamorous, welcoming woman in the world. Her smile never faltered, even when guests became a rare occurrence.

The gleaming surface of the crab bell blurs in her sight; she gives her eyes a furtive swipe. Her mother died over five years ago so she's not sure why it's upsetting her now. There's no reason to be sentimental about that crab or the B&B.

They were poor and worked all hours. She had bitter arguments with her mother about going away to university. She fought to get an education and a good job in media, working for a charity, everything she wanted.

The bell is twelve quid. They must be kidding! Her mum probably got her crab bell at a jumble sale, the sort of place where most of her tat came from. But anyway, Hazel came here for trainers. She makes her way to the shoe shelves.

Hazel wants shoes she can wear to work that will also get her *away* from there fast. Therefore, those pink things with rhinestone buckles and feathers won't fit the bill. Neither will the orange ones with smiley faces and green-rimmed glasses.

She still thinks fondly of a beloved pair of Ecco shoes that cost a mere £15 at this very shop. They were both smart and comfortable. A good find from Takky is something to be treasured. She earns well enough to go elsewhere now but doesn't see the sense in paying £80 or more for plimsolls.

You need to be methodical. The best ones are often wedged in between the worst, like those leopard ones over there... When she comes closer, she sees that more than one animal went into making this footwear.

The upper part of the trainer consists of furry leopard print fabric, with a border of shiny gold faux leather, then furry black stuff. And the soles—wide, streamlined, futuristic—are black-spotted like a Dalmatian dog. A very awkward mating must have taken place. They're so bright and ridiculous she must try them. She picks a pair off the shelf. Then she hears something beneath the jingle jangle of the shop radio that makes her put those trainers down and stand to attention.

Surpassing the ring of the door alarm, the chirp of phones... a familiar *ding*.

Someone's ringing the crab bell. She can't explain how she can hear it from here, a whole floor away, or how it differs from any other bell. But she knows it's the toll of the crab bell. Someone is touching the crab bell, someone likely to take it away. There is only one. She should've bought it on the spot!

She rushes up the escalator and stampedes into the Home section. She peers at the shelves, seeking its gleam. Instead, she encounters a host of other creatures. They might have been there for months but she only notices them now. They shout for her attention, as if they've seen her for the first time, too.

A gorilla bears a lamp aloft; a table stands on slender legs with *chicken* feet. She has to laugh, which brings such a rush. Hilarity bubbles forth into a deluge. Just look at that!

What a strange noise she's making. Hooting like a monkey, just like one of those grinning simian soap dispensers on the shelf a couple of aisles down.

She thinks of the multi-pelted trainers she almost tried on. Leopard and Dalmatian ... She can hear those animals yowling in their passionate coupling now.

But she wouldn't want to hear from *all* these creatures. She eyes the cherubs dancing attendance on either side of a full-sized doorless doorframe. Very fat ones, all with little potbellies and thimble dicklets. Ghastly creatures.

And what about those two floor lamps standing on each side of the empty doorframe? Their bases are swollen like pregnant bellies, with two little arms reaching out above them, fingers splayed, searching for an absent bulb and light shade.

"Hieronymus," Hazel says to herself. Hieronymus, as in Bosch. He could've designed those lamps. Imagine having one of them in your living room. Yes, indeed. Now she wants one. Or both? Shouldn't they come together, like sibling kittens who can't bear to be separated? The thought makes her laugh again. And between gasps of laughter the harsh strip lighting turns warm and peachy.

Hazel's in a haze again ... that's what people used to say about her.

"Are you okay, madam? Can I help you?" It's the young woman who'd set up the dinosaur lights. "Madam" sounds so formal, coming from someone who appears too young to be working in a shop. Her name pin identifies her as *Fiona*.

Hazel leans down and rubs the belly of one of the headless lamps. "Do I need to buy these together?"

"It's up to you." The girl shrugs. "But I do have a feeling it would be a real shame to separate them. I've got fond of those fellas."

Fiona pats the belly of the other lamp and smiles.

She sure does seem to like her job, Hazel thinks. She clasps the grasping hand extended by the lamp. The metal is cool under her fingers. *I'm looking for my head!* Those little fingers seem to tighten but Hazel leaves her hand there. Imagine being a lamp without a light.

"I see you like those lamps too!" Fiona nods. "Like I said, those guys grow on you. Go on. Treat yourself!"

But Fiona's sales pitch only reminds Hazel of what she really came here for.

"I'm tempted. But I already have a treat in mind. I'm looking for the crab bell."

Fiona nods as if she knows exactly what Hazel is talking about. "Someone else was looking for that crab bell..."

"Oh, were they? I better get over there... *thanks!*"

Hazel isn't entirely sure where "there" might be, though she remembers a bunch of gangster angels. But when she locates the angels there's no crab bell to be found. She rubs her eyes and examines the shelf again, just to be sure.

A young man is watching her. "Have you seen a crab bell?" he asks. "It was here just a moment ago." He blinks and frowns as if he has just emerged from a dark tunnel.

"I was looking for it too," says Hazel.

He has a pleasant, open face, if somewhat shiny. He's wearing a suit and manages to look prim and dishevelled at the same time.

"Maybe it's been moved to another shelf with other silver decorations. Where bells go." She suggests this though she's not sure if they're collaborators or competitors.

Then she does spot a bell one shelf down. It's not a crab but a turtle with a cracked shell. "Damaged but adorable" says a round orange sticker attached to it. Other objects on the shelf show similar afflictions. A peacock covered with blue-green fake velvet and glitter suffers from a severed tail, its jagged Styrofoam rump sore and exposed with stringy feather remnants jutting around it. A mirror with a unicorn head, but its horn has been snapped off. Is the thing crying? Hazel thinks of her mother though the animal looks nothing like her. Its head hangs to the right at a peculiar angle, as if it wants to hide. Let it have some peace, let it nurse its wounds. She pushes it behind a sheep lacking an ear and a fairy without wings.

On the shelf below, a giraffe is missing both of the bumps on its head. And there's a globe holder without a globe. She picks up the bracket, notes its emptiness. She puts it down. Why does this upset her, too? A world is gone, leaving empty space.

Someone says: "Those little things get to me, too. They might be pieces of plastic or plaster but they're also symbols. And symbols always stand for something, don't they? Something real."

It's the young man who'd asked her about the crab bell.

This time she smiles. She's glad to see him despite that initial suspicion. A fellow searcher! Perhaps they should start a group for it on Facebook. She shakes her head. "A unicorn without a horn... what kind of symbol is that?"

"Don't laugh! I've heard about a gang that goes around doing shit like that... breaking arms and legs off fairies, decapitating dinosaurs, de-horning unicorns."

"That's terrible..." she murmurs.

She picks up half a bauble, the edges ragged. This "damaged but adorable" item goes for £3.00. She's tempted to give the poor broken thing a home.

She picks it up and makes her way to the cashier.

D arren buys DVDs at the charity shop to cheer himself up after the failed job interview, then drops in for further consolation at the Max. He usually goes to the food section for its selection of posh mustards for non-posh prices.

He passes through the Home section as the day's interview replays in his mind. He'd been wearing his suit and couldn't stop worrying about how he looked while he answered their questions. He can't believe they still ask applicants to "discuss your strengths and your weaknesses" without a trace of irony. *Yup, I'm a perfectionist*—even though he was stone cold sober he couldn't keep from cracking up.

The panel regarded him. Shouldn't he welcome the attention? People usually *didn't* notice him, even when he spoke up or offered to do things. Sometimes he wonders if he'd died without realising and turned into a ghost.

I'm a perfectionist, he said again, and managed not to laugh this time.

Didn't they ever see *Trainspotting*? Yes, it's an old film but plenty of young people watch old films. Now he wants to look at himself in a mirror. Like one of those over there. Reassurance, maybe? Or to remind himself of how he fucked up. The solemn plaster face of a giraffe regards him over the mirror he chooses. There's another mirror next to it that's adorned with a smirking unicorn. He gazes at himself in both.

I'm a perfectionist, yeah.

"Describe a situation where you overcame adversity at work," asked HR bot number one.

He has seen plenty of adversity. Like, all those times he didn't hear instructions because he's slightly deaf in one ear due to years of standing in Tinnitus Corner at gigs . . . that bit near the stage and just in front of the speakers.

He just can't get comfortable in the charity-shop suit. It was as good—or as bad—as new when he bought it. New jeans or socks are one thing, but a whole suit of newness? Even when it comes from a charity shop it feels stiff and unnatural.

That unicorn seems puzzled at the sight of him. He sighs. Giraffe, mirror, unicorn . . . why? There are also picture frames featuring unicorn heads. Why? Who thinks of such things? Did some guy or girl sit at a drawing board and think, okay, how about a giraffe head above this mirror? Why not a unicorn at the top of this picture frame? That's what people need . . .

He really *does* need a giraffe head on *something*. Photo frame or mirror? He picks up the mirror, puts it down again. Then the picture frame. He does have a few photos in a drawer that he could bring out into the open. Presented by a giraffe, of course.

Under the giraffe's gaze his face appears pale, the path between his eyes creased with a frown. "Later," he says. "I'll come back later."

He turns and begins walking, further into the novelty section where a wedge of see-no-evil monkeys watches over another shelf of glitter-eyed plastic skulls fringed by gangster angels. He picks up a skull and drops it because the plastic is softer than expected, almost spongy and kind of *warm*. But he bends down and puts it back on the shelf. Nah, it's only latex . . .

Something catches his eye, a gleam next to the angelic gangsters. It's a bell, with claws. A crab bell. The claws are remarkably detailed. He touches one. The dinger's on top, isn't it?

The crab stands on its eight legs, claws extended, ready to pinch. Shining in silver. Like, why a crab bell? Why not a duck bell, why not a chicken bell? Or even a lobster?

Chuckling, he hits down on the bell. A loud *ding* resonates through the shop. The children scampering around the toy section turn to look at him. A woman dragging a trolley-basket draped in tiers of plaid and polka-dotted garments jumps in alarm.

Darren dings the crab bell again. Did one of those big pinchy claws move? What a sound! Clear, yet complex if you listen long enough. The teenage girls checking out make-up turn towards him, smudge-circled eyes suspicious and newly applied lipstick shining.

"Sir . . . " A staff member approaches him.

He's got to hit that dinger one more time. Ding! The claws twitch, surely.

"If you hit that bell again . . . "

"But listen," he protests.

"Young man, you must . . . "

All those people stare at him, just like the interview panel. Except they aren't all people here. Rows of ceramic cats with big open mouths and spiky teeth gape from a table in front of him. Panic moves a finger down his back and drags its dread up and down inside him.

There's laughter, there's music on the PA. He's cruising in the Max, for Chrissakes. What's the fuss about him ringing a bell? It's not like he's sitting in church or attending a solo recital of organ music. He tries to ignore the staring people. He turns, only to be confronted by a formation of bearded guys in snowflake sweaters flashing two red-rimmed rows of square-shaped teeth. Hovering nearby are smiling pigs in tutus and moustachioed geezers with straight rows of rolled white curls and flowerpots hats.

My name is Legion, for we are many. That pops into his head. Something from the Bible. Or does the demon say that in *The Exorcist*, way before "your mother sucks cocks in hell"? Another old movie he's watched many times, up there with *Trainspotting*.

He's feeling dizzy. The ornaments are grouped like soldiers who've had too much to drink on leave. Their lines bend and converge as if spelling out a message. Are they closing ranks and do they want him to leave?

No way. He'll go when he feels like going. Just to emphasise that notion, he reaches over to ring the crab bell again.

But it's gone. Bastard! Who took his crab bell?

He's already thinking of it as *his*.

A tired-looking middle-aged woman is peering in his direction as if she wants to ask something. But he's answered enough questions for the day. So he asks one first... about the crab bell. The glorious thing that was here a moment ago. She tells him that she's looking for the crab bell, too.

In his agitation he bumps into a display where lots of little figures jiggle on hooks. One brushes by his face and he jumps.

A stuffed, velvet-clad clown with the head of a zebra. The critter is wearing a velvet, rust-coloured onesie, along with fluffy brown gloves and boots. A double-ruff flares out from the onesie, one part burgundy, the other leopard-print. Shiny gold scarf, zebra head. Its lips are drawn back in a grimace and well-ordered teeth fill its mouth. Crowning this thing is a top hat of tinsel.

He always imagined zebras to be peaceful animals, so why is this one snarling? Teeth. All these guys show a lot of teeth.

He's gotta go. Get home. Eat dinner. Watch one of his new but old DVDs. It'll be a Cronenberg. *The Fly*. Maybe he'll watch the ancient Vincent Price version after that. The zebra-clown has put him in the mood for it.

When Hazel faces Valerie at work the next day, her nit-picking comments about yesterday's copy don't seem to matter so much. That clenching core of worry has unwound... for a while.

Is this what therapy feels like? Well, a visit to Takky's costs less than engaging a therapist. She'll need to make those expeditions more regular.

Hazel keeps her head down, churns out the work. Just get on with it, that's best. But relief doesn't last long. An email pops up in her inbox with Val as the source. The subject: *Volunteer Work*.

Val writes that she is looking into a group fundraising project for an allied charity. She's found one that involves maintenance work at a local wildlife reserve. *Wouldn't it be good for the team to do this together?*

Followed by a *smiley face*.

Hazel has volunteered in the past...at the local foodbank, collecting clothes for refugees. But she refuses to do unpaid work in her actual job. She considers a reply: *Shouldn't they be paying staff to do that?*

She's seen such things before. The meetings. The pressure— you don't *have* to but you'll be a spoilsport if you don't. Discussions at her next supervision under the category of "attitude" (a bad one) and "team player" (*not*). Worst-case scenarios keep unravelling, distracting her from her actual work.

Valerie is young and obnoxiously keen. Hazel was once young herself, but she's sure she was never keen in that annoying way. It's not an age thing, she decides, just a self-important, self-righteous twit kind of thing.

She stays on later just so she can get a piece of work off her desk and leave it clear for tomorrow. She's always been a bit compulsive about that. As Hazel finally leaves Valerie's head pops up from behind her screen.

"Oh hi, Hazel. Leaving now?"

What does it look like?

"Yes, I'm leaving," She gives a sharp nod towards the clock. "It's getting on."

Val goes back to tapping on her keyboard. "I still have things to finish. You received the brief for the next project, didn't you?"

Of course . . . and it's the longest brief I've ever seen, Hazel thinks. But she nearly gives herself whiplash when she nods "yes".

Hazel knows where to go when she leaves. It's on her way home, after all. The portals of Takky Max welcome her and she steps in.

Today she spots a new denizen, a disgruntled dragon occupying an object that could be a throne but really looks more like a toilet. She goes on to contemplate a chimp in a Beefeater outfit and another in astronaut gear, both surrounded by owls, some ceramic and others soft and stuffed. A grey vase with a slender neck opens into a gleaming set of huge, pouting stylised lips, these glazed deep gold. She has to catch her breath at the sight of those lips. Someone—surely not a staff member—had placed several sprays of artificial daisies between them. Another vase sports random lips all over it. She touches her own mouth and feels an odd kinship. *We have lips.*

Hazel had joked with the lad who talked about symbols. *What kind of symbol is a unicorn without a horn?* Indeed, is it even a unicorn?

But those definitely are lips and this is definitely a pig, a peach-coloured pig in a tutu. She places peachy piggy on the shoulders of an astronaut chimp and sighs. Not quite right. She can arrange the owls, of course. And add that ceramic cat having a stretch with its bottom in the air, complete with a little hole under its tail. Maybe it's meant for burning joss sticks.

Then Hazel spots a diverse flock of parrot lamps further along the shelf. Green ones are most common. But there's also an orange one and an alarming bright pink cockatiel. There's a red parrot candle holder with a fruit-like fixture on its head. A bronze parrot bearing a pineapple. Normally she hates parrots. Mum kept a stuffed parrot in a glitter-encrusted cage overlooking the reception desk. She never could stand the thought of that bird flying around—and someone had killed it and stuffed it.

"But you've never turned down your roast chicken. You're not exactly a vegetarian," said Mum when she complained about the creepy stuffed parrot glaring at her from its cage—especially when she dared to ding the crab bell.

But here the creatures are porcelain, plastic, aluminium or rubber. Their artifice is cheering. Many of them *do* something; they even shed light if you put in a bulb.

She still isn't sure what that pink cat is meant to do but she does know what it needs. She takes two of the fake daisies from the pouting lips and sticks them in the hole under the cat's tail. It's like Bosch again, that section in the *Garden of Earthly Delights*, where a man cavorts in a peculiar game of Twister with a bouquet of flowers up his bum.

The shop staff let her alone—they normally do—as she goes on to place parrot lamps at each corner of the formation. A green one, a red one that looks like it's melting and lost a leg. *Damaged but adorable.* The parrot with the pineapple head-dress and a shy purple one with dinosaur teeth and talons. The round owl eyes that watch her reflect each other. *Who … who.* Round like the letters that spell out their sound. The pursed golden lips frame the sound too—and the daisies that spring from its pout quiver with it as passing shoppers stir the air.

She takes a photo of her garden of plastic and porcelain delights on her phone. At the *click* the assembled creatures fall into place, the right place for them. And there is an answering *click* as if eyes (and mouths) are opening and breath drawn that has no need for lungs.

This photo satisfies her as no piece of work at her job has done for a long time. She feels so much better. It will look good in the Facebook group.

But they all need the crab bell.

D arren adjusts the cuffs on his suit. He loves his new cufflinks, bought on his last visit to the Max. Maybe they're supposed to be beetles but they look more like roaches with sparkly carapaces. They remind him of his sanction-happy "coach" at the job centre, who he now calls the *job roach*.

He's been here at the Max a couple of times since he first discovered the crab bell. Today he hopes to find one again.

He's taken to wearing his interview suit on the pilgrimages. He thinks of it as good luck because he'd been wearing it when he discovered delights far beyond exotic mustards. But he always wears a favourite t-shirt with it; today it's *Pulp Fiction*.

"Hi Steve," he says as he walks past the zebra-clown. Yes, he didn't like the zebra-clown at first but now he's used to it. It just looks like a Steve. Or perhaps an Ed, but that's the name he's given to the unicorn on the mirror because it reminds him of Mr Ed, the talking horse from an ancient TV series his uncle showed him on YouTube. It had been on the air well before his time. It even dates well before his uncle's time but he can appreciate why Uncle Joe loved Mr Ed. Fun to watch with a spliff.

He nods at the other searchers and seekers. He can spot them by raised eyebrows, half-smiles. An intense way of examining the shelves, furtive photos. In fact, he's just joined a Facebook group for people who seek what matters in the Max. Just this morning he saw a post that heralded a new shipment of crab bells.

A young guy in the aisle grins, making pincer motions with his hands. Darren does the same. "All hail," he says, then they both snort with laughter.

"Hey, I hear that crab bells were found downstairs near the checkout. Sometimes they turn up in odd places." His crab-seeking comrade speaks in a low voice. "I'll check it out."

Darren nods goodbye. Then he spots a certain *something* peeking out from under the dress of a long-lashed pig with puckered lips. A claw. A crab claw. His heart starts whomping.

He lifts the pig's skirt and yes, there it is! A crab bell.

Some speculate that the bells would lose their aura, their specialness, if more crab bells flooded the market. But that's a fucked-up attitude. Everyone who wants a crab bell should have one. As he takes the crab bell out from its hiding place, he is moved to ding it. He can't resist. He places it on a shelf shouldered by worried crocodiles, then dings. He hits the bell again. He's so happy with his discovery.

The woman he met after his interview comes running. Hazel. The last time their paths crossed she said hello and introduced herself. She seemed starchy and scary at first but he started to like her. Beneath that more respectable exterior he sees his own panic. He can't say they're the same, only that they discovered common ground on excursions to the Max.

"I heard that ringing!"

"Yes, I found a crab bell!" He holds his find up. "Isn't it exciting?"

"It is..." Hazel says. Her eyes are brighter than he's ever seen them, like she's on drugs or about to go on a long-delayed holiday.

She clears her throat. "And...do you understand? That crab really is mine!" She snatches it away. She's so fast and so brazen about it that he's too gobsmacked to respond. He thought she was a friend. Okay, a friendly acquaintance.

She presses the bell a few times. "You see, I *remember* that sound. It brings back the lobby of my mum's B&B...Lingering scents of overcooked breakfast, an overstuffed aroma of old chairs and cantankerous gas fires. Of course, I hated the place. But now I find the memory comforting. It's completed something. It's a missing piece of puzzle."

"Sorry Hazel...what does that have to do with me and my crab bell?" *Surely she doesn't mean to take it from me*, he thinks. *She only wants a look. Maybe she'll be fine if I invite her to visit.* He can't imagine that she'd want to see him or sit in his squalid little room in a shared house. But she'd be able to see the crab bell and ring it and contemplate the memories it brings.

Some of the regulars are standing around, watching them. He recognises a few. One guy is wearing new trainers with clashing leopard and Dalmatian-dog patterns; he must really be dedicated to maximum Maxness. And he must want the crab bell, too. They all must, though they keep a respectful distance. The deference makes him uneasy, more than if they formed a circle and shouted "fight, fight, fight". He could suggest to Hazel they share the bell. Take turns with it. Why not?

Hazel hugs the crab bell to her chest. "You don't understand. You're just a kid. This bell is part of my childhood. It's just a joke to you. It's ironic, like beards and cocktails in jam jars..."

"I don't know what you're talking about. I've never had a cocktail in a jam jar. I don't even drink cocktails. I don't even eat jam, so why would I have a jam jar"?

"I just need this crab bell," Hazel insists. "Even if it brings back sad memories, looking at it makes me feel able to laugh, able to imagine life without being stressed and miserable."

"But I found this one first, and you just snatched it."

Hazel doesn't answer. She's looking down, towards their audience. Maybe she's distracted by the Dalmatian-print trainers. *She's away with the fucking fairies*, he thinks. *So fuck this!* He darts forward to grab *his* crab bell. But if Hazel seems vague, her reactions are speedy. She whips it away and her foot shoots out and gives him a wicked kick on the shin. And it hurts. Deep pain radiates from the place where her sturdy boot connected.

He lunges forward and grabs a handful of her long hair. She has nice, shiny hair but it feels odd in his hands. Kind of slithery, like thick liquid through his fingers. He pulls and she loses her balance and skids. The hair winds out of his hands. When she jumps forward at him, he panics and lashes out with his fist and punches her in the mouth. That smarts. He's forgotten how punching can hurt the puncher almost as much as the punchee if it's not done right.

The circle of people watching them is hushed, expectant. It generates an electric hum like the song of a pylon, one that moves through his body rather than his ears. Is it only a fight they're waiting for? Something in him shifts under their gaze but he's not sure if he likes it. "What are you watching?" he shouts at them. "Who are you rooting for, huh?"

"What we think doesn't matter," someone says. "The crab chooses."

"And it wants to come home with me," says Hazel.

How does she know? Enough of that. No more silly hair-pulling. He's gonna grab that crab. He must've been chanting it to himself because he hears whispers from the crowd. "Grab the crab, Grab the crab."

"It was my *mother's*," Hazel asserts.

"So your mum had one like it. But this crab was made in India. It's new!"

He gestures at the tag hanging from a claw. And when Hazel glances towards it he reaches forward again, seizing the crab by the claw. In the tussle something snaps. He's holding a claw while Hazel holds the rest of the crab, grimacing in shock. "Now look what you've done," she says. "You broke it, you mutilated it! I'll have to ask for a reduction."

Hazel stalks away with her prize, leaving Darren with his somewhat smaller one. The claw feels surprisingly whole in his hand, comforting in a way. It's terrible that it broke off, yet he can't deny that he feels calmer to hold onto a piece of it. Perhaps it'll bring him luck at the next interview.

People are drifting away. He's surprised that the security people haven't ejected either of them, until he realises that they were part of the group watching the battle. And now he's back to being peaceful and minding his own business. With the surge of adrenalin gone, he begins to feel like he didn't fare very well in the fight. Hazel is a couple of decades older but she looks like she works out. There was power behind that kick. His entire lower leg is aching and bruised. His head hurts, too. He doesn't remember getting hit in the head but maybe he missed something. And his arm feels sore... knuckles grazed. Must be that ill-advised punch. *Darren, you are a tool.*

On his way out he spots a lamp with a giraffe at its base. The giraffe is missing its head bumps and there's a hole where its tail had been. *Who did that to you, old feller?*

Damn, his leg hurts. He's dragging it. What did that woman do? He remembers pulling her hair. He got *forceful* himself. But nothing he did warrants the pain and weariness he feels now.

The other shoppers are settling back into the usual routine. People examine tat, try it on, compare one ridiculous object to another, dither about whether to buy.

This feels familiar. This feels like home, something his actual room and household will never be. He might as well find a place to sit down. He can go to one of the seats scattered around the shop, like the place where he used to park himself when he came here with his girlfriend—*ex*-girlfriend. It seems like such a long time ago, when the Max was just a shop where Ellie picked up bargains and he came here with no real knowledge of what lurked within. He tightens his hand over the crab claw as he sinks into the chair.

It's in a quiet little corner, but he's able to watch a woman and a man trying on suits and parading for each other. He feels a twinge of envy. Soon it's overshadowed as the physical aches and pains from the tussle distract him. But this time he welcomes them. They feel *right*. As if he always carried them about with him and they're part of who he is.

He's tired, so tired, a weariness that grinds in his bones and crawls in his flesh. The room expands as if he is actually contracting. It spins and pulses and he's not sure where he belongs in it. If he could just close his eyes for a minute or two...

He touches his arm as he drifts away. His skin is very soft. Perhaps someone will appreciate it and stroke it some day.

While she's waiting to pay, Hazel has plenty of time to reflect and give herself a good scolding.

What makes me think I deserve this crab? My motive for picking on that lad is bogus, sentimentality for a childhood I loathed. Stuck in that drab seaside town, my mother scraping for customers and income. Back in the day I was weird and out-of-place and picked up my clothes in second-hand shops too. I could've been that young man if I gave in and missed out on uni. I could become an older version if I get sacked.

As the queue straggles forward she decides against buying the prize after all. *I'll give him the crab,* Hazel thinks. *I'll apologise. What got into me? I'm no different than sneaky Valerie with her bullying and undermining ways and notions about people working without getting paid.*

Hazel, you hit someone, just out of selfishness. You should be ashamed of yourself. The boy might still be around. You should at least try to apologise. If she doesn't find him she can keep an eye out and give the crab to him another time. And maybe she'll check out the Dalmatian-leopard trainers. She couldn't help noticing them on a man who was watching the fight.

She leaves the queue and heads to the Home section. Her heart sinks when she sees that the young man is no longer there. She wanders through the other departments, not ready to give up. Then just by chance she sees him in the women's clothing section. Asleep on a seat. She hovers over the sleeping boy and wonders about waking him. But the last thing he'd want to see on waking would be her face. She could quietly leave the crab bell on his lap.

But no... Someone might come along and nick it.

She sets the crab down next to the lad, who is sprawled and snoring on the seat. She sits down herself and leans back. She feels flushed, her face too warm. She just wants to shut her eyes. Just for a bit. The music recedes and she recedes with it. Slipping away... is this like dying? She gasps but the breath flows like normal.

The strip lighting colours her closed lids orange. But she begins to dream of another light and how she will shine it into a darkened room and make everything and everyone bright. She is walking down an aisle at Takky Max, and finds it blocked by a door-frame—this one has an actual door. "That is not for sale," someone tells her but she opens the door anyway.

It reveals a room filled with crab bells. They're climbing over each other and their claws are clicking and the bells are dinging—with no one pressing. She calls to the people behind her: "I've found them! I've found the crab bells!"

The bells keep dinging and she begins to sing, so loud that she is growing small in comparison with all the clamour. It happens so quickly. She's a bird, a *bird* that sheds light all around her. This is what she loves to do but she didn't know it until now. The current runs through her veins, courses out of her mouth, radiates around her head.

The glow makes her happy but something is missing when she closes her mouth. Closing on air, no click. Where *is* her mouth? Does she even have a head? Her perception has a different quality as it extends here, there, everywhere. It flows from her and rests in the circle of radiance that she casts. It's nothing to do with the glare of the overhead strip lights. It's *hers*.

When she looks "down" she sees her claws, gripping a scarlet-glazed branch. She has feathers and scales, part-parrot and part-dino. It's kind of thrilling but suddenly she's very afraid. Who is she? What will she do in this body?

But at least she doesn't have to go to work again.

Fiona starts to tidy up. Time to close. At least it's been quiet for a while. It was a difficult day, especially when that fight broke out. Over a crab bell. Imagine! Fighting over an aluminium crab that goes ding.

Not that she wouldn't mind having one herself.

She straightens the glassware first. Nothing out of order here. When she walks through the aisles she sees that something's been left on a seat. Oh my, she doesn't know whether to laugh or cry. It's a crab bell. It must be *the* crab bell because they only had one. After all the fuss it was left behind. And not only that, the poor thing is missing a claw. She feels a flash of unaccountable rage. They fight over an object, then they break it ... and it's abandoned.

The crab's not alone, though. There's a zebra-clown, sprawled alongside the crab. What's that about? He should be dangling from a hook with the other hanging ornaments. She'd put them together to create a tapestry of the strange and quirky. She's proud of it.

But she's not seen this one before. It's not only a zebra-clown but a blending between zebra, giraffe and something else again. She lets a small smile emerge as she looks at it. This will add nicely to the display—gradations between different animals, different life forms even.

It might give her an idea for a story. Science fiction or horror? Perhaps both.

This creature wears a suit instead of a onesie. Oh, there's a bit of wee t-shirt peeking out of it! Pup fiction? No, it's *"Pulp" Fiction*. But most important, one of the clown's arms is wrapped around an aluminium crab claw. Oh good, the crab might be damaged but at least it can be made whole again.

The velvet on one clown leg is torn though, and beneath it stuffing-fluff bulges out. She lifts the thing by its cord and gently shakes it. One arm doesn't hang right. Something else for "damaged but adorable", though damaged and desolate might be closer to the truth. He looks familiar, a touch of someone she might've met. That's how it is with a lot of this stuff: weird, funny and melancholic at the same time. It makes the day bearable and gives her ideas for stories.

The giraffe's bumps are an odd colour, semi-transparent scarlet plastic. The eyes match. And a glistening emerges from the right eye. Is it wet? Where did that water come from ... the ceiling can't be leaking. No, it is a tear. But it's also plastic, sparkling with fragments of glitter. Those eyes beseech her, moist with an inflamed pink yet bold with a mocking glare.

Then, shining onto all this is a lamp. It has a bulb and it's switched on. And what the actual fuck! Look at the animals holding up the lamp base. The head of a unicorn…she has seen unicorns in all forms and sizes here. Unlike some of its fellow unicorns in this shop it has a fully intact horn. But there's a ring through its nose, the kind that used to be inflicted on bulls. Its brown eyes hint of deep pain and a multitude of troubles.

On the unicorn stands a green parrot—one foot tangled in the mane, the other wrapped around the horn with long, finger-like glass digits. The feathers are individually sculpted in the porcelain, looking more like scales. The parrot feet remind her of the hand-like extremities of rats, combined with an element of sloth-like claw. There is the unmistakeable swell of breasts under its emerald chest feathers.

And it's missing half its beak. Oh no! Damaged but adorable again.

What an odd place to put a lamp, left on a seat with a crab and a bizarre clown. The light is bright enough here you don't need a lamp. But there it is. The three of them belong together. And maybe the lamp does highlight the crab. She picks up the loose claw and places it where it belongs. Superglue? There must be some around.

Maybe she'll take home these three. Staff perks and all that. She'll patch up that claw, she could remove the ring from the unicorn's nose. And she'll catch each and every one of those shiny plastic tears when the giraffe-clown cries for joy.

She wonders where the lamp is plugged in, then sees the flex anchored to the floor socket. It's thicker than a normal flex and glistens like it's alive. She touches it, though it doesn't appeal to her. Feels warm, not as slimy as she thought it might be.

She looks into the glow of the lamp on the crab and the clown. She imagines a silent plea coming from the heart of that light. *Don't…*

Don't what? Fiona shakes her head. A flex should *not* be warm. Must be faulty. Fucking fire hazard. She turns off the lamp and pulls out the plug.

AS FAR AS SACRED GOES

Nancy Kilpatrick

FOURTEEN BOOTED OR sandaled feet plod through the humid thirty Celsius heat, kicking ancient earth into the dense air. The forest they step into is lush with old-growth trees and plants, as well as the wildlife for which this environment is home.

Santos, the guide of the Jungle Tour, halts the procession before one of the countless evergreens that, for centuries, have helped form the mosaic landscape known as The Yucatan.

"This is tree for *las chicle*," Santos says. "He is very old. Sacred to my ancestors."

"Sure don't sound like any scientific name ah ever heard," the tall, slender man comments. Hal, light-haired, just past forty years old, was raised in the deep south of the United States. Something in his tone suggests pride in his heritage. He laughs generously to indicate that no offense is intended.

Short and squat, Santos possesses the broad, silt-coloured

features of the ancient Mayans. He assumes an awkward show-and-tell pose beside the sixty-foot tall Sapodilla tree. His hands, weathered like the wood, caress the bark between the thick vines that use the tree for support.

The group watches Santos remove a penknife from the back pocket of his loose-fitting jeans. He opens it and carefully carves a three-inch vertical gash deep into the tree trunk. Instantly, a milky liquid oozes from the wound.

For a moment, Santos studies the lush growth surrounding him before plucking a sturdy leaf from a nearby bush. Meticulously, he catches on the leaf the grey-white drops sliding slowly down the tree trunk.

"Many years ago, the old Indians, they work and use *las chicle* to wet the mouth. They do not need so much water. Our ancestors, they believe the gods give them this gift to make them happy, and they are grateful to be blessed this way."

"It's just tree gum, right?" Hal says, removing his baseball cap, allowing nervous fingers to create tracks through the hairs on his sweaty scalp.

Santos pauses. "*Si, señor.*"

"Ah knew it!" Hal, grinning, turns to his wife, Peggy, a pretty brunette wearing colourful designer overalls, her face expressing a regret that she did not remain behind by the hotel pool.

"It's hot! How much longer?" she inquires, her shrill voice vibrating with the same distinctive twang as Hal's.

The sound interrupts the call of a multi-coloured bird high above in the tree. *T'uut*, Santos thinks, but he cannot recall the English name and says nothing.

"Ain't this excitin', Hon?" Hal says, squeezing Peggy around the waist. "How many folks get t' explore the jungles of Mexico with a real, live Mexican?"

"All *ah* know is ah'm real hot and dirty and tired of ridin' in *that* thang!" Peggy points a damning finger at Santos' dusty green Jeep which, with the addition of a rumble seat, carried the four men and three women the three hours out of The Fiesta Americana Hotel in Cancun and into the wilds south of Chichen Itza. She uses the tour pamphlet to energetically fan herself briefly, then stops to extract an e-cigarette from her purse from which she inhales.

To Santos she appears to be a woman much like his *Tia* Isabella, who can find no pleasure pressed into a vehicle with strangers.

"Many years ago," he begins again, "your *Señor* Wrigley, he come to Mexico from Chicago in the Illinois." As with the ordinary citizens of many non-English-speaking countries, Santos is unaware that he is lumping his six passengers together. To him they are all *gringos* from the United States. There are, however, two Canadians on the tour, enough to create an anomaly.

Bob and Jean, from Toronto, are sensitive to how their country is envisioned. "Huskies," Bob joked to Hal's query en route, "pull sleds over frozen tundra while Mounties in red uniforms sit proudly on their majestic horses and preserve law and order in the barren Great White North!"

Hal laughed. "That don't surprise me! I been up there in the winter and it sure is hell-freezin'-over cold, let me tell you."

"*Señor* Wrigley," Santos continues, "when he see the Indians, that they use this gift as the gods intend, he takes it back to his home."

"Why, of course!" Hal instructs the group. "Wrigley's Chewin' Gum. And Chiclets, for God's sake! How 'bout that, Peg?" He nudges his wife.

Peggy makes an unpleasant sound before turning away. She stares blankly down the crooked dirt road but does not see it or the Jeep or the pair of iguanas darting across. Even the complexity of the dense foliage that supports and protects a myriad of life does not capture her interest. She glances at her watch, then at her empty clear plastic water bottle, and sighs. "What ah wouldn't give for a drink."

Santos offers her water by holding out his canteen but she rapidly shakes her head *no*.

Raymond, one of the other Americans, sneezes. Peggy, noting the potential for disease transmission, scowls his way.

Santos understands that Raymond and Arlette, the remaining *turistas*, are *not* a married couple. Raymond, bald but well preserved, is a late middle-aged man with a newly grown dark *Mexican Moustache*. Santos overheard him mention to Arlette earlier how several friends had remarked that this newly grown facial hair makes him look "like a devilish, turn-of-the-century rake!"

Arlette, a senior citizen with erect posture, is equally well-preserved. She wears over-sized sunglasses, a slightly angled Tilley hat protecting her head, matching safari pants, and rhinestones around her throat and wrists. She has the look of someone who either had been, or wishes she had been, born a countess. She speaks with the trace of a European accent, only to Raymond, to whom she whispers continually, the words too soft to be understood.

Santos watches Raymond, an avid amateur videographer, plug into his phone a small metal box. He is unfamiliar with this technology.

Raymond, who as a rule speaks only to Arlette, suddenly instructs Santos to "Look at me!" making the tour guide the one exception.

Santos poses, knife in one hand, leaf full of *las chicle* drippings in the other, face impassive.

Raymond films a panoramic while Hal captures the moment in a still photo on his expensive iPhone.

Bob and Jean, pleasantly dressed, looking more like brother and sister than husband and wife, wait patiently and expectantly, preparing pertinent questions and comments that they hope will sound both interesting and insightful, and be politically-correct in Mexico.

When Raymond seems satisfied with capturing the setting of what will end up as a ten-second dramatisation, Santos continues. He dips his thumb into the thick greyish substance from the tree and studies it silently for a moment before sticking his digit into his mouth. He nibbles at what has adhered to thumb-flesh.

"Try!" Santos says, brown eyes shining as he offers the leaf to the group. "Is very good."

Hal recklessly plunges his index finger into the sap and then into his mouth. He turns to his wife. "Try some, Peg."

Peggy shakes her head and stares into infinity as if struggling for patience.

Arlette and Raymond, Bob, and finally Jean, participate in the ritual.

Jean's middle finger skims the remaining liquid clinging to the leaf. She deposits *las chicle* onto her tongue. The moment contact is made, the resin forms a solid that she chews. Some resin remains on her fingertip, rapidly turning hard and greyer. She tries first to bite it off as she'd seen Santos doing, then uses a fingernail to attack the residue, but *las chicle* adheres like Crazy Glue, as if it has become a permanent part of her.

"How strange. It won't come off," she comments to Bob anxiously.

"It tastes like flavourless, sugarless gum," he tells her in a reassuring voice, but his eyes say he is distracted.

Santos catches a bit more of the *las chicle* and extends the leaf once again to Peggy. "*Señora*, please. You join us?"

Peggy folds her arms securely across her chest and tightens her features. She glares at him. Abruptly she turns and takes three steps down the road, mumbling words like "germs" and cautions that others "can take chances if y'all want to, but ahm not touchin' that filthy stuff. *Ahm* not gettin' sick down here!'"

"Hey!" Hal exclaims brightly, "this really is gum!" He has the look of certain men who achieve success because of a deep-rooted *naiveté* which those around them struggle to preserve.

"Fascinating!" Jean comments, her voice relieved now that her finger is clean again.

Bob nods, mopping sweat from his brow.

Raymond chews as he shoots more footage of the verdant landscape dotted with colourful flowers. He hopes his camera picks up the audio of birds in the nearby trees chirping and the subtle rustle of small wildlife in the underbrush. He includes a close-up of Arlette, who chats quietly to him, chewing the gum while attempting to look demure.

"Well, ah'll be darned," Hal chuckles. "So *this* is where old Wrigley got his idea! That man must've been a real genius. Why, he made a fortune sellin' gum."

"*Si, señor*," Santos says. "He sell sacred *las chicle* from our ancestors' trees for many American dollars."

Both Canadians notice the peculiar look in Santos' eyes. They imagine it has something to do with profit and loss but, embarrassed, remain silent, hoping that they have misperceived.

Santos exhales loudly, drawing attention to himself. His features undergo a metamorphosis, which attracts the attention of the group. Suddenly, he appears relaxed and looks like a youth instead of a mature man.

The tourists watch as he gouges another wound in the tree and refills the leaf with resin. His eyes scan the *gringos*. This time he pours all of *las chicle* into his own mouth. Within seconds he is puffing out his cheeks.

Peggy, who has retraced her few steps back to the group mumbles, "Ah'd like to find a ladies room *soon!*" Abruptly, she stops talking and along with the others stares at Santos as if mesmerised.

Raymond—who has finished shooting another brief video— and Arlette, are silent, both unconsciously smiling in Santos' direction.

Bob and Jean watch intensely, grinning uncontrollably like children, dim worries that they might be reacting inappropriately fading fast.

Hal, relaxed, laughs good-naturedly like a boy.

A peculiar calmness overtakes Peggy, surprising her, pushing aside discomfort and frustration and leaving peace behind.

As the sun breaks through the tree leaves, Santos closes his eyes and presents his face to Earth's hot star. He blows a bubble. Big and bigger. Impossibly large. A perfect and beautiful bubble. An *ofrenda sagrada* to the ancient gods, thanking them for this miracle which, in a small way, has altered everyone.

STIGMA

Paul Kane

H E'D ALWAYS KNOWN it was there, if he was being honest.

Had always been aware there was... something. But he'd tried not to think about it, ignored it, pushed it to the back of his mind. Didn't know the name of whatever this was. Just assumed it was one of those things. You know, in life. Something you just had to live with. Gavin Hale used to watch other people and get very jealous, the easy-going way they'd have about them, always able to make friends.

Everyone liking them.

It had never been that way with him. Even from an early age, he was willing to bet even as a baby—and who doesn't love babies, right?—folks had shied away. Family would visit for Christmas, for birthdays; grandparents, aunties and uncles. They'd hand over presents and run like they'd just pulled the pin on a live grenade. Couldn't get away from him fast enough. Wasn't simply that they had nothing in common, no shared frame of reference—as grown-ups they almost certainly wouldn't be interested in comics or playing with toys—it was more that just spending time with him seemed to pain them physically. They didn't even ask how he was doing at school, for goodness' sakes...

School.

That was another thing, how he'd been treated there. At best, the other kids just left him alone, gave him a wide berth. Except for one or two lads who, for want of a better term, weren't the sharpest pencils in the box. Matty Phelps, for example, used to eat crayons; his mouth was always a variety of different colours. And Nev Wylie was obsessed with the matches he used to steal from his old man, who smoked like a bonfire. Last Gavin had heard of Nev, he'd been arrested for arson, trying to set fire to a football stadium after his team lost a match. He wouldn't exactly call either of them close pals.

At worst, Gavin had been the target for bullies. Not unusual in and of itself, a nerd like him, but the sheer hatred they had for Gavin went beyond the usual picking on or beating up. It was like they felt the need to rid the world of Gavin, or something. One particularly vicious bastard called Knowles had even tried to drown him in the boys' toilets once by shoving his head down the loo. That had got Knowles suspended, mainly because he wouldn't apologise to Gavin. Refused, even though the headmaster "Scary Scarsdale" was bearing down on him like he was going to wipe the kid from existence. Though, in the end, even Scarsdale looked at Gavin and shrugged, as if maybe Knowles had a point.

Like maybe he wanted to drown Gavin himself.

None of the teachers really took to him either, though. Didn't give him special attention like they did with some of the students they thought might go far. The puzzling thing to Gavin was that he always did well academically. Studied, worked hard. Was especially good at art, used to sit and draw or paint whatever was put in the middle of the table, as the teacher would wander around looking at the other kids' work and pointing out how it could be improved— walking very quickly past Gavin, usually pulling a face as if he smelled. He didn't, that wasn't it. He washed every single day.

Gavin had been envious, too, as he moved into his teenage years and couples had started pairing off—whether they were straight, gay, bi or whatever. They all made it look so natural, so effortless. Probably wasn't, but it appeared that way to him. No girls would ever talk to Gavin, and the ones he thought about approaching would run a mile if he took one step towards them. Clare Partington, who had been made to sit with him in Maths, for example. Usually he'd be on his own, but the classroom for that lesson was really small so there wasn't the space. The girl had loathed every second of it; would keep her chair as far away from his as possible. Blanked him every time he spoke, even putting up a hand as some kind of fleshy barrier.

He wasn't that horrible, was he? Always tried to be kind; helped old ladies across the street... when they could tolerate it. Wasn't hideously ugly or anything. Why couldn't they—

He wasn't even sure that his parents liked him. Gavin couldn't remember his mother giving him so much as a hug. Not once. She'd put him to bed as quickly as possible, retreating out of the room when he was little, and turning out the lights. Ignoring his protests that there might be monsters in the wardrobe or under his bed. She hadn't given a shit, left him to it—good luck to the monsters, in fact! And his father barely spoke anyway, unless it was to comment on the weather or the cricket. Gavin had given up trying to engage him in conversation by the time his age was into double figures.

When he finally left home, he could see the marked relief on their faces. Why did they even have him in the first place, if that was the case? He'd overheard his mum talking to relatives, about how much she'd longed to start a family; how they both wanted kids. A little brother or sister might have been nice, actually, instead of being an only child, but they'd stopped at just him for some reason. Gavin had to wonder if it was because he'd put them off having more, or perhaps they just didn't want any of their other potential offspring to be around him?

Perhaps they even wished he hadn't been born at all?

On the first occasion he returned home, Gavin discovered that they'd turned his bedroom into a hobby room (his mum liked to make ornaments out of shells she found on the beach a few miles away) and had taken what few photos there had been of him in the house—school uniform ones, for example—down and squirrelled them away somewhere. Either that or burnt them.

"When did all this happen?" he asked them.

"Pretty much as soon as you left," his mother told him bluntly, making sure she was on the sofa with her husband, a good distance away from Gavin. Not even sugar-coating it. Not bothering about his feelings at all.

When he left again, Gavin saw that same look of "Thank Christ!" on their faces. It was like they knew they had to have him over, because he was their son, but on another level couldn't stand to spend an hour or so with him. Couldn't stand to be *around* him.

He'd tried to get into uni, art college even, but always got turned down at the interview stage. On paper, he was the perfect student, but when he met the lecturers in person... There would be those same looks of disdain, of revulsion. He'd even shown up early for one of the interviews and the other girl was late, so they saw him first. You'd have thought it might stand him in good stead, show he had character, respect, but it didn't make any difference.

So he ended up working a few soul-destroying jobs, one in a call centre where he sat in a booth on his own. He'd actually found he was quite good at that, as he only had to talk to people over the phone, but in the end his boss had sacked him for no discernible reason. Stacking shelves at a supermarket had been another, and that had been okay as long as he didn't have to interact with any of the other staff. Just him and the tins. Then there was the nightwatchman's position, which freaked him out a bit whenever he had to patrol the factory he was supposed to be guarding. Too many dark corners for someone with his overactive imagination. Once, when he was passing a window, he thought he saw someone behind him and spun with the torch, but there had been no-one there of course. Just spooking himself.

Gavin would spend hours and hours looking at himself in the cracked bathroom mirror of his basic one-bedroom flat, all he could afford in town on his wages (none of the other residents spoke to him, or had anything to do with him, and the landlord insisted he pay by direct debit so he didn't have to come and collect the rent in person). At first he tried to work out what it was about him people didn't like. Oh, he'd asked them outright in the past; they just hadn't hung around long enough to answer him. Or *couldn't* answer. There was just... something about him.

He'd stare and stare, cocking his head this way and that. Gavin wasn't any great shakes in the looks department, no model or film star, but he wasn't Quasimodo either. Not... repulsive? Just sort of... normal. But he gave up going on dates after a while, especially ones he'd set up online. They'd agree—even appear quite keen in their messages—then walk away once they met him. Some he'd spy approaching the bar or restaurant, through the window, take one look at him and just turn around on the spot. Like he had a neon sign above his head saying "bad date".

Sometimes the light would fade outside as he was spending time gaping at himself, and when it grew dark in his bathroom he felt sure he was being watched. That there was more than one pair of eyes looking back at him in that reflective surface. Gavin always put it down to tiredness, and that overactive imagination once again.

But he'd always known it was more than that, deep down. Always suspected there was... something. And he'd been right to do so. In the end, and at a low ebb, he visited his local GP to see if they could help. All of this was making him very depressed apart from anything else, the loneliness, the—well—the not knowing.

The short woman with a severe fringe had squirmed in her seat as he explained his problem. He'd even brought his sketch book, containing some of his drawings, his paintings, an effort to deal with how he was feeling as an outsider. But as with the people doing those interviews at the college, she barely glimpsed at the images.

"Maybe some face-to-face counselling or something?" he'd suggested, having tried various online options available: wellness meditation; confidence building; finding your inner self.

"F... Face to... face," the doctor had said, scrunching up her own features. Then "hmm" as if she didn't want to put anyone else through such a trial, what she was going through right that minute, being inside a confined space with Gavin. "Perhaps some medication?" she suggested, like she was offering him a chocolate.

But he didn't want to be a zombie, that really wasn't the answer. Didn't want to walk around not feeling anything at all. Feeling numb. Eventually, and probably just to get rid of him, she sent Gavin along to the hospital for some tests. The full range, in case it was something physical rather than mental; an imbalance somewhere. And he'd gone, spent a day there being poked and prodded—getting the feeling that the docs were quite enjoying doing that, might enjoy taking it further like Knowles had wanted to all those years ago. He spent hours inside machines that blipped and pinged. Was sent down south to some specialist place, where they did the same again, with even bigger machines.

One of which actually produced a result. A fancy x-ray device, which they attempted to explain to him, something to do with spectrums or whatnot. Honestly, he stopped listening once they showed him the photographs they'd taken.

And he saw what was causing the problem, what had been causing the problem all his life: there was something on him. That was the only way of describing it: *on* him. Not a mole or welt or even a goitre. But something else on his body, on his shoulder, wrapped tightly around him.

An...*imbalance.* Inner self? He should have been worrying about his *outer self*, as it turned out.

A thing. A creature of some description, though he found it hard to describe, with its dark, shiny shape and bulging, glowing eyes; but the glow might have been the way the machine took pictures, to be fair.

The doctors had a name for it, however. "Stigma," a rotund man with glasses and a receding hairline informed him.

"W—What?" asked Gavin, looking over his shoulder but seeing nothing. Gripping his shoulder and *feeling* nothing.

"I'm afraid you have a stigma attached to you," he said. Gavin was expecting him to laugh then, but he was as serious as anyone he'd ever met.

"W—What?" Gavin asked again. "A what?"

"We call what you have, Mr Hale, a stigma. Oh, you can't see it ordinarily, nobody can. But human beings can sense such things. I can tell just from looking at you right now and—" The doctor shivered visibly. "That's probably been the root cause of your predicaments all these years."

"I...is it dangerous?"

The portly doctor gave a shake then a nod of the head, so Gavin couldn't tell either way.

He decided to be more specific. "What's it doing to me?"

"Nothing much, just living off your lifeforce. Your energy."

"What? That sounds like *something* to me."

"Think of it like one of those watches that uses kinetics to power itself. But your stigma: it's parasitic, you see. It's using you to survive. Or perhaps I should say symbiotic; yes that's probably a better description. *It* exists because *you* exist." He said this like it was Gavin's fault. As if he'd asked for this to happen. He really hadn't.

"How long have I—"

"Probably since birth, or shortly afterwards. It's grown as you've grown. Quite remarkable, really."

Remarkable? Remarkable? He didn't think it was remarkable *at all!* "But..." Gavin had his head in his hands now. "But how can...It's—"

"You're not the first, definitely won't be the last," the doctor told him, which wasn't as much comfort as he probably imagined. "We don't know why this condition affects some people and not others. Why the stigma chooses them. It just does."

"It's not fair," said Gavin, looking up.

The doctor shrugged. "That's life, I'm afraid."

"I don't believe all this. How can something be...be on me that I can't see or touch? How can it be—"

"There are lots of things around us all the time that we can't see, Mr Hale. Germs, for example. But denying them doesn't stop you from catching a common cold now, does it?"

He supposed not. "Is there anything that can be done?" Gavin asked next. "I mean, can you cut it off or something? Laser it?"

The doctor shook his head. "I'm afraid that would result in both your deaths. Like I said, symbiotic. For now, you're just going to have to live with it. Or perhaps I should say live with each other?" He started to laugh, then shivered again. Then he asked Gavin if he wouldn't mind leaving as, frankly, his presence was giving the man the creeps.

When he left the facility Gavin felt sick. Felt like he didn't know what to do with himself, other than just find the nearest tall building and fling himself off. Monsters were definitely real, but they weren't in his closet or under his bed after all. They'd been hiding in plain sight. Or at least one had, with him all these years. Fucking well *attached* to him. And he couldn't get rid of it!

But, as he made his way home again on the train, people moving away from him to sit further down the carriage, he thought to himself that if nothing else this explained everything. The doctor had said as much back there. It hadn't been his fault after all, none of this had. People not liking him, teachers or other students. Girls! Jesus, it totally explained his car-crash of a love life! The...repulsion. It had been down to something he hadn't even been able to see, that he couldn't do anything about; that not even the medicos could, so how was *he* supposed to? But Gavin had known, hadn't he? That there was...something.

Definitely something.

His parents hadn't believed him, naturally. "A what?" his mother had said when he called her, mimicking his own reaction to the news.

"A stigma," he told her. "It's what's been holding me back all this time."

He could hear the information being passed on to his father, who was watching the cricket if the tinny shout of "howzat!" was any indication. Gavin heard a mumbling and his mother came back on the line. "We've never heard anything so ridiculous in all our lives," she told him.

"But...but it's true. That feeling you get when you see me, you know..."

"Oh, that's just..." His mother's sentence tailed off, but he could imagine what she'd been about to say: "That's just you. You disgust us, Gavin. It's nothing to do with some parasite or anything else. It's. Just. You!" Instead, she said that someone was at the door and she had to go and answer it. Gavin was left holding the phone, sighing.

Oh well, his parents might not believe it—sometimes he wasn't even sure if he did either—but that's what the experts had said. That it wasn't him, and he wasn't alone . . . which was quite a poor choice of words when you thought about it.

You're just going to have to live with it. Or perhaps I should say live with each other?

Now, though, when he looked in the mirror he fancied he could actually make out the stigma—especially if he squinted, and if he turned the lights down really low. But peering into the gloom, imagining if not actually *seeing* those huge eyes, freaked him out too. Made him shiver just as much as the doctor had; more so probably. Made him want to have a drink, the only thing that was helping him sleep these days. And even then his dreams—his nightmares—were filled with images of strange worm-like things slipping and sliding all over his body, without so much as a by-your-leave. Once or twice they even burrowed into him, only to explode out of his chest like in that movie with the woman from *Ghostbusters*. The end result was always the same: he'd wake up drenched in sweat and realise it had just been a night terror. Then, seconds later, realise that actually it hadn't only been a dream, wasn't relegated to night-time. Something just as dark and horrific was on him right now, *all* the time, he just couldn't see it or remove it, or—

And you just try telling anyone about it, see what they said. He'd gone to a bar, made the mistake of chatting to a few people, men and women, attempting to explain about the stigma. Those who'd been willing to stick around and listen—after he bought them a drink or several—had the same reaction as his parents. If only the docs had given him some kind of certificate or whatever, but even then it would have looked like something he made himself using a graphics program.

Worst case scenario: it had ended with him getting beaten up again, and the police had been called. Who promptly arrested

Gavin even though he hadn't been the one who'd started all the violence. They let him go again not long afterwards because not even the coppers could stand the notion of him being in their cells. Something about Gavin was just . . . off.

"Yes, it's the stigma. Don't you understand?" he told them as he was thrown out of the station. "It's on me, it's attached to me. You just can't see it, but you know it's there!"

"Fuck off!" snapped one of the uniformed men. "And don't let us catch you causing trouble again or we'll call in an armed response unit next time."

Gavin had made it round the corner from the station and slumped to the ground. Armed response? For what, talking to people? But then he began to think, maybe that wouldn't be such a bad thing. A few bullets and it would all be over, this whole stinking . . .

There were less painful ways though, surely. An overdose? Just go to sleep, never wake up? But there was always a chance someone would find him in time, and those pills might screw him up for life; imagine being in a wheelchair, paralysed, knowing that the stigma . . . Hanging, then? Might hurt a little initially, but . . . Then again, there was always a chance he'd survive that too. Hadn't he read once that unless it was a clean break, you'd end up in agony? He'd only been half-joking when he'd considered that tall building after he first found out about this. Once you threw yourself off then there was no turning back—and very little chance of walking away from it. Literally.

What stopped him going down that road was a call from the hospital. They'd learned of a treatment that had apparently been quite successful abroad, a kind of radiotherapy. Still in its early stages, still quite experimental, and the side-effects varied from person to person, but if he fancied giving it a whirl . . .

Again, they made it sound as trivial as going for a test drive in a new car—but Gavin supposed it was part of their job to put the patient at ease. And anyway, what did he have to lose? What could be worse than what he'd actually got? And if the cure killed him in the meantime, then it would probably be doing him a favour. It would be a blessing, actually, wouldn't it?

So he agreed. Gavin visited yet another facility with yet another set of doctors and nurses, signed *a lot* of forms to confirm he was taking full responsibility for what might happen, and got on with the treatment. Which seemed to involve being strapped down to some kind of bed, virtually naked, and bombarded with lights as everyone else dressed up in hazmat suits and hid behind metal shields which looked as if they could withstand a missile attack.

Gavin couldn't say that he blamed them. Because even after just one dose of whatever the hell this was, he started to feel the effects. The tiredness, the vomiting. His hair began to fall out, though he was assured it would grow back eventually—and in the meantime he was given the option of wearing a wig. Gavin decided to just shave his head.

However, the more times he went the more he began to notice the benefits of the treatment. People were no longer backing away from him, even at the hospital. Folk weren't moving seats if he sat down next to them on the train home, or in the coffee shop at the station he'd pop into before the journey back. Indeed, on one occasion—a very special day—a woman even came and sat with him, bringing her latte over. Yes, it was crowded, but in the past he'd known people to sit outside on the platform in the freezing cold rather than share a table with him.

"Is this seat taken?" she asked and Gavin had shaken his head without even looking up, fully expecting *her* to take it—then go and sit on it somewhere else. But instead she sat down with him, at his table. It was only at that point Gavin looked up from the Americano he'd been stirring since he sat down, just taking sips every now and again in case it made him feel queasy.

What he saw was a lady, a little older than him but not by much, with her hair in a short bob which framed her pretty face perfectly. She was wearing a raincoat, which she undid after she'd sat down and placed her drink on the table, revealing a flowery dress underneath. "Hello," she said to him, holding out her hand—actually holding it out for him to shake!—"I'm Joanna. Jo."

Gavin was aware that his mouth was open, so he tried to close it, but it just fell open once more. Wasn't simply that she was lovely, this woman sitting opposite him. Because she was, she *absolutely* was. It was more that she'd chosen—bloody well *chosen*—to come and sit with him, to talk to him.

Now he was conscious of the fact her hand was just floating there in space. Not creating a barrier, like Clare Partington's all those years ago, but a bridge. Just before Joanna—Jo—could withdraw it again he reached out and grabbed it, perhaps a little too eagerly, and started shaking it. "Gavin," he replied. Not Gav or anything like that; nobody had ever stuck around long enough to affectionately shorten it. And he realised he was still shaking Jo's hand, looked down and let go, then apologised. She just laughed, flapped the newly freed hand, and that had been that.

They talked, the conversation easy-going, natural. It was like nothing Gavin had ever experienced in his life. Like those people he'd been jealous of. It just felt... right. He missed his train but didn't care. Jo said she had to catch hers, but would he like to go out sometime for a proper drink? Gavin hadn't known what to say, apart from, "Er... yes, please. If that's okay?"

She laughed again and gave him a peck on the cheek, before exchanging details and rushing off for her platform. Leaving Gavin touching that cheek. He wasn't sure he was ever going to wash that patch of skin again.

More evidence came in the form of a piece of his artwork that he'd submitted to a small exhibition, and forgotten about, to be honest, getting some attention. A dealer, looking for something different in a few of the smaller towns and villages, had spotted it and not only wanted to buy it but meet the artist. Obviously the money had been welcome but Gavin was hesitant about actually meeting with the man. That never went well.

It was Jo who'd persuaded him to go for it. Jo who, after several dates, was rapidly starting to become a permanent fixture in his life. Certainly someone Gavin trusted and listened to. So he went along and met the man—a fellow called Cameron Mercer, who was so tanned he looked like he was made from wood. He'd taken Gavin out for lunch at a posh restaurant and listened as he'd told him about his process.

"The pain... the anguish, the loneliness: it's all there," Mercer told him. "You're channelling it all into your work. Listen, I'm going to introduce you to a friend of mine. An agent called Wendy Douglas. She represents people like the sculptor Ellis Blare, other artists like Andrew Croft, James Peters..."

So he had, and to Gavin's huge surprise they got on famously. Though whether that was just because Wendy could "make a mint" out of him, as she put it, was debatable. But it didn't matter, no-one had ever offered him an opportunity like this before—and as with Jo's hand, back in that coffee shop, he grabbed it.

Those were good times, in spite of how rough the treatment had made him feel. Gavin didn't care; it was obviously doing the trick. He and Jo became closer—close enough for her to tell him about her son Sam, who Gavin was also getting on well with—he was finally doing what he'd always wanted to do for a living (a pretty good living), and he was even seeing his parents more often. His mother told him once, when he visited, that they were both proud of him, of what he was achieving. Gavin had almost fainted on the spot.

The money Wendy was making from his art meant that eventually he'd been able to get a place with Jo, that they were finally going to become a family. They even talked about marriage, about him adopting Sam—because, let's face it, his real father had pissed off as soon as he'd found out she was pregnant and still wanted nothing to do with his kid. Actually, Gavin and Sam couldn't have been closer if they had been flesh and blood; kind of made up for the fact that one of the side-effects of his treatment was that he probably wouldn't be able to have kids of his own.

So, after all the years, after all that time having to live with...with his condition, it looked like things were at last coming up roses.

Until they weren't.

It took a while, he had to give them that. The treatment ended and Gavin recovered in due course. He and Jo had a good few years of happiness, did the whole marriage thing—on a beach abroad, a lovely ceremony (a very, *very* special day) that all of his friends from the art world attended, all of the family who hadn't been able to stand him before—and Sam officially became Samuel Hale.

Life was good. They were content, the family that he'd been denied while he was growing up, which also now included his old family. His parents. They liked Jo well enough, to begin with, anyway, but absolutely adored Sam, their grandson. Gavin lived his childhood again through Sam, celebrating his successes at school, the recognition he hadn't enjoyed. Father and son, which of course delighted Jo. "I knew it, first time I saw you," she said to him once. "That you were a lovely bloke. That you were someone he might be able to look up to."

Him? Gavin Hale. Imagine that!

Then, one day, everything went... well, it just went. Sideways, pear-shaped, Pete Tong, the lot. He'd gotten too comfortable, too complacent about everything, that was the problem. Gavin had begun to believe it might be this way forever, or at least until they were old, dealing with all the stuff that you do at such an age. But it hadn't waited that long, had come back with a vengeance—and then some.

The first clue had been the rows he started having with Sam. Real humdingers, kicking off over nothing, really, and escalating into full-blown wars. He felt bad for Jo, because she was in the middle a lot of the time; didn't want to take sides, because she loved them both. But he knew, at the end of the day, Sam was her son. There was never really a choice.

Then his work fell out of favour. "It's just lacking that... that certain something now," both Wendy and Cameron would agree, tilting their heads left and right when they scrutinised the canvases on the wall. Might just have been because he was happy, the pain and anguish gone, but in his heart of hearts Gavin knew it wasn't that. Could tell by the way the meetings dried up, both of his biggest champions not wanting to be around him anymore—or spending as little time with Gavin as they could get away with.

The final confirmation came, naturally, when his parents began putting that distance between them. His mother retreating back to the safety of the couch again when he called around, taking the flowers which he always brought and pulling a face. He'd even gone into the kitchen once before leaving and found them stuffed upside down in the bin.

Gavin returned to the hospital, to the facility that had treated him. He didn't really need the diagnosis; he could tell what was happening. That it was back.

The stigma.

He'd been as honest as he could be with Jo about what had happened to him, yet skirting around what had actually been wrong, keeping it vague. For one thing, he thought she wouldn't believe him, or might leave him.

Never heard anything so ridiculous in all our lives...

Didn't matter anymore, because that would happen sooner or later anyway now that he knew for sure.

"But... but I thought you'd got rid of it," he told an altogether different doctor this time, as thin as the other one had been large. Looked like he needed a decent burger or several. The expression on his face was the same, though. Sheer loathing, yet not of Gavin himself, he knew now. Of something else, something that had returned. "Otherwise what was it all for, being sick? Going through all that?"

"Just sleeping, I'm afraid," the doc told him. "Numbed. In a sort of coma, I suppose you could call it. Sadly, it's now woken up—and it's none too happy."

"Not happy, not happy!" shouted Gavin, rising. It wasn't the only fucking one!

"Please Mr Hale, calm down."

Gavin sat again, then nodded. Getting het up wasn't the answer. He needed to know what he could do about this, to get rid of the stigma once more.

"It'll never be gone for good," the doctor explained, cracking his knuckles one by one. "We could try with the treatment again, but I have to warn you it's the law of diminishing returns. It'll be ready next time, bracing itself."

And he'd been right, the treatments just made him sick again but hadn't improved his situation in the slightest. Indeed, things had gotten so bad with Sam he'd said to Gavin, "You don't get to tell me anything, you're not my real dad! I wish you were dead!"

That one had hurt. Really hurt.

Perhaps they even wished he hadn't been born at all?

When it became clear that nothing was having any impact on the stigma, when Gavin was spending hours in front of that mirror again, instead of trying to find work now his savings were drying up—most of which had gone on Jo, on Sam—he came to a decision. Came full circle back to his original decision. About what to do. He'd get rid of the stigma all right—sitting there, all black and ugly and...

Wasn't that horrible... Wasn't hideously ugly or anything.

For now, you're just going to have to live with it. Or perhaps I should say live with each other?

No. He had another option.

It's using you to survive. It exists because you exist.

It's not fair... That's life, I'm afraid.

Or not.

Gavin had gone to that tall building, a choice he'd made quite some time ago before the hospital first telephoned; had gone to the top of it, and stepped up to the edge. Closed his eyes, had been about to walk out into thin air when—

"Gavin. Don't."

Jo. She'd found him. But how...? Then he remembered, he'd told her about his darkest days, what he'd been planning. Hell, he'd even put it into his art. That still didn't explain how she knew where he—

His wife had held up the phone, a twin to the one in his pocket. Both with tracker apps on them so they always knew where the other one was. She'd followed him. "Gavin, please. Come away from there."

He shook his head. "It's for the best, Jo. Really it is. I couldn't bear the thought of you hating me too."

"Oh sweetheart," she replied, looking up at him, tears in her eyes. "I could never hate you. Never."

"You will," he assured her. "Eventually you will. You won't be able to help yourself. It's the—"

"The stigma. Yes, I know."

He turned, almost losing his footing and falling off the side by accident. An... *imbalance.* "What?"

She looked down sadly, then back up at him. "Wasn't a coincidence, us meeting like that at the station. I...I saw you coming out of your appointment. I was there too, you see."

You're not the first, definitely won't be the last.

Not alone.

"You had a stigma?" He couldn't believe what he was asking.

"I *have* a stigma," she replied. "It came back, just like yours."

"But...but I..." Gavin didn't understand, but she said they could talk about it—if he got down from the edge. And then she reached out her hand for his.

Gavin hesitated, knew this time that she wouldn't withdraw it but still he grabbed on, falling into her embrace. They stood like that for so long on the roof of the tall building, just holding on to each other.

Hers had been smaller than Gavin's, granted, and on the other shoulder, but no less nasty. It had been asleep when she came and sat with him in the café, because she was there for her final check-up after treatment and was almost fully recovered herself; hair short but growing back. No wonder Gavin hadn't sensed it, but then again, he hadn't when it returned either—and neither had Jo with his.

"Maybe they cancel each other out or something," she suggested by way of an explanation. Or maybe the couple just hadn't cared, they simply loved each other so much? It explained why her ex had done a runner, once he'd had his fun.

"And Sam...?" he asked.

It was Jo's turn to shake her head. "He doesn't...he's not affected. And it doesn't seem to bother him that I'm..."

"Then why—?"

"Why are you two fighting? He's a teenager, Gavin. It's what they do. He doesn't hate you, and it's not about...Just give it some time, please. You'll see."

So he did, and they did. Got through that and went on to be a family again. Even his parents agreed to try harder, with both Gavin *and* Jo, who they were lukewarm with at best these days. If it meant they got to spend time with Sam, spoil him.

It worked, and they were happy. Happy as long as they had

each other. Everyone else could go jump off a tall . . . Or something like that.

And they tried not to think about the other thing. Never talked about it, if they could help it. Ignored it, pushed it to the back of their minds. Yet would always know it was there, if they were being honest. Would always be aware there was . . . something. Knew full well what the name of it was now, had done for a long time.

But it was one of those things. You know, in life.

Something you just had to . . . no, could *choose to* . . .

Could definitely choose to live with.

THE CHARMED

Robert Bagnall

CHRISTIAN RATTERY WAITED until the coffees had been placed before them, bergs of bronze foam atop white ceramic crucibles with impractical stylised handles, tiny foil-wrapped biscuits balanced on the saucers below. Between ordering and receiving them, Juliet Carwithern had interrogated him, Christian answering straightforwardly and plausibly, and without evasion. He even posed and smiled when she WhatsApp'd his photo. He allowed, almost encouraged, these precautions to such an extent she wondered whether it reflected his total certainty he could physically subdue her any moment he chose, snatch her phone, drag her away into the night.

She thought again. It didn't look likely: he had a vegetarian's pale pastiness, the gaunt awkwardness of somebody who'd never been in a fight. Bouffant hair. He was barely bigger than her. And, if her fears were real, the café staff, including the boy with bumfluff who was sweeping the floor, were in on it. Maybe that was the case. He seemed to know them, to be at least on nodding terms.

"You have magical powers. You are a magician."

He said it so flat, so straight, holding her gaze the whole time, that she choked and blew foam onto the table between them.

The boy sweeping looked up, the broom continuing to oscillate but without conviction.

Christian gazed at the foam blob as it lost its integrity, forming a despondent puddle on the Formica.

"I wanted to wait until the coffee had come. I thought you may find it harder to walk away when you'd tasted it." He raised his voice for the proprietor's benefit. "They make very good coffee here."

"I've hardly drunk any."

"No, you've more snorted it," Christian agreed.

"As chat-up lines go, it's a strange one."

"Oh," Christian said, surprised, "It's not a chat-up line. I meant it literally."

"That I have magical powers?" Juliet sipped the coffee and laughed. She glanced at the door, mentally rehearsing whether she should pull her coat on first or reach for her bag.

"It's good, isn't it? I don't know what they do. I think they may roast their own beans."

"Look, thanks for the coffee, but this is turning out as weird as I thought it would. You're telling me I have magical powers, and not even in a metaphorical I-find-you-alluring way..."

"Alluring?" Christian puzzled. He seemed to take in her outfit, her deliberate, almost wilful anti-style before allowing himself an ironic chuckle. "Oh mercy, no. I'm gay. It has more to do with emotional intelligence. If I wasn't gay, I'd think you'd do well to lose the glasses and let your hair down; maybe swap the old cricket sweater for something else... anything else. Even if it is an attempt at the sexy librarian cliché, with cricketing overtones. Or do I mean trope? Cliché or trope? You are one, though. A magician, I mean."

He returned to sipping his coffee whilst Juliet processed the wall of words, worked through whether she should feel offended.

"You were at the reading, weren't you? Upstairs at the bar. At the back," she asked.

"To be a published author at nineteen. You must be delighted.

I must admit, it sounded...difficult. How did you describe it? A stream of consciousness unreliable narrator epistolary *Rashomon* metafiction with a reverse chronology. Written in the second person. Brave."

"I'm twenty now. And I don't write stories where people suddenly pull guns and explain the plot, if that's what you prefer."

"I didn't follow much of it."

"You couldn't follow *it*, but you did follow *me*? In the dark, through the park. Is that normal for you?"

"We needed to talk."

"To tell me I'm a magician?"

He nodded in response without breaking her gaze, the tiniest of movements; he was so serious about it.

"So, what can I do with these magical powers?" she said, playing along. Juliet had decided she wasn't in immediate mortal danger, and he was right: the coffee was good.

"As little as possible. You're what we call *charmed*."

"Can I make things disappear? Turn water into wine? Pull a rabbit from a hat?"

"Yes—but only if there's a rabbit in there to start with. Conjuring tricks. Apart from the middle one. Jury's still out: maybe he did, maybe he didn't."

"Can I summon demons?"

Christian shook his head. "No, that's black magic, satanism, magick with a 'k'."

"And I suppose you're one of the good wizards?"

He frowned, lost in thought. "I'm never quite sure of my moral compass, to be honest. I tend to do what I feel is right. Try to, at least."

"So, what *can* I do?"

"It's not what can you do, it's what should you do, and the answer is nothing." He leant forward, as if readying himself for a sermon. Or a sales pitch. "You have to understand what magic is. Forget Harry Potter. Forget wands and spells and incantations."

"Harry Potter's not real?" she said with mock-sadness.

"There is only one kind of real magic in the world. People call it by another name."

He paused. Glanced sideways. Without meaning to, Juliet leant in to listen.

*A*uthorities in Oslo have been alerted by a Norwegian shipyard *which has reported receiving an order for a seventy-metre "mega-yacht", paid in full, in cash, in advance. Despite citing "clear red flags", the Norwegian Serious Fraud Office has found no evidence of money laundering, the origin of the buyer's wealth being otherwise inexplicable to outside observers. Sources close to the Pouslen AS shipyard have named the buyer as Tyco Rorschach, a London-based Eastern European of whom little is known.*

—*Associated Press*

Juliet wallowed in the bath, the door ajar, trying to judge whether the dog-ear of peeling wallpaper had worsened since the last time she had been in the tub.

She called out into the hall. "He said, people call it by another name. People call it *luck*."

Kath pushed her way in, shimmied her jeans off below her thighs, positioned herself on the toilet, her knees by Juliet's feet, and urinated.

"Do you think I'm going for the sexy librarian look?" Juliet asked, grabbing her glasses from the edge of the bath, holding them up to her face. "With sporting overtones?"

"He's definitely trying to get into your knickers. Best strategy is not to wear any." Kath followed up her sage wisdom by loudly passing gas. "Who puts an egg in a curry, anyway?"

Juliet snuggled closer to the bubbles' lavender scent and hoped the look of disgust wasn't too obvious. "He said he was gay."

"Strategy."

"He didn't even try to kiss me when he walked me home."

"Strategy."

"You can't respond 'strategy' to everything."

Kath wiped and farted again. "What did he say then?"

"You're an animal."

"He never!"

"I mean, *you're* an animal."

Kath laughed, a round, full Lancastrian chortle. "Oh, I know *that*, chuck. What did he say then? You didn't tell him you bat for both teams, did you?"

"He said I was 'charmed'. That it was incredibly rare. That he didn't think I knew. Which was why he needed to find me and warn me. That I shouldn't use it, shouldn't rely on it."

Kath stood and hauled her jeans back over her pasty, wide thighs. "You think living with me makes you lucky?" And with that, she was gone, leaving behind her the odour of the previous night's biryani and—in its own way, just as unpleasant—a blast of chemical-heavy air freshener.

The water was cooling, but Juliet didn't want to get out, not quite yet. She knew Kath's summation of "strategy" was most probable, but Christian had unsettled her. What if he was right, even if what he had said was unbelievable? Here she was, twenty years old, a published author, all she ever wanted. Was it down to luck—not talent, not resolve, not bloody-minded determination, just dumb luck? Had he pulled back the curtain and shown her how the world worked? That luck, or the lack of it, was something you were born with, something immutable, like being born a citizen of the twenty-first, not the fifteenth century, thus avoiding a lifetime of toothache cut short by death in childbirth? In which case, so what? That made luck her talent. Others had skills; she had luck. Being lucky *was* her skillset.

Unconvinced by her logic, she wrapped the plug-chain around her toes and pulled. As the water drained with a dull gurgle, she wondered whether she'd feel less conflicted, less confused, if she'd simply maced her stalker and carried on walking.

Tyco Rorschach is a new entry in this year's Sunday Times Rich List. *Whilst other multi-billionaires may be camera-shy, the Romanian (or possibly Bulgarian, or maybe Hungarian or Moldovan, accounts vary) Rorschach is anything but; pictures abound of him boarding private jets or disembarking from yachts.*

But what remains elusively out of the picture, as well as where he comes from, is how he acquired his jets, yachts, and Belgravia townhouses. The nearest anybody has come to understanding how, is a less-than-guarded comment from a female associate, who told the Sunday Times *with a shrug, "Every bet seems to come off for Tyco".*

—*The Sunday Times*

The casino was not what Juliet had been led to expect from James Bond movies. It was as though a redundant call centre had made a desperate attempt at glamour by adding thick plush curtains and a stick-on pattern of gold Rococo scrolls. But the curtains were no longer hanging from all their hooks and the swirls had started to peel. It smelt of carpet-cleaning chemicals and cigarettes, despite the ban on smoking, as if past punters had brought it in just by breathing.

Then again, what did she expect from a casino at three on a weekday afternoon on a roundabout on the dual carriageway?

She placed the single chip she had traded for a crisp ten-pound note on the intersection of twenty-eight, twenty-nine, thirty-one and thirty-two, then drew her hand away from the green baize as if it had burnt her.

The croupier—no older than her—turned the wheel and flicked the ball against the spin. As it whirred its orbit and he picked at his late-stage acne, she let her gaze wander up from the potato crisp crumbs on the table and over the room. Two other roulette tables stood nearby, blackjack tables beyond, all in silent shadow. Beyond them, a punter with a paper cup of change graced a slot machine, feeding coins in small, careful movements with desperate concentration, like a sniper facing flashing lights and oh-look-at-me-look-at-me-now klaxons.

The croupier's senior stood to one side, his impassive gaze flicking between Juliet's table and the man feeding the slots.

The ball caught with a clatter, bouncing between slots before settling. The wheel spun too fast for Juliet to see. And she'd forgotten where she'd placed her chip.

She looked down at it, red against the green baize, squarely inside twenty-eight. Hadn't she'd placed it on an intersection? She frowned. Her nervous snatch must have nudged the chip to a single square.

"Twenty-eight," the croupier called.

She looked at the ball, wobbling in its cubby. She was about to say something when the croupier swept up her chip and, in one smooth motion, replaced it with a considerably larger pile.

The ball was in motion again, spinning. The croupier's overseer now only had eyes for Juliette. Paper cup man held no interest. She could feel his stare.

"Place your bets," the croupier broadcast to his audience of one.

Her chips sat where he had left them, on her winning number. She considered snatching them up, cashing in. But what would that prove? Should she move them to other numbers, spread her bets? But if she were lucky, preternaturally lucky, then what was the need? The pit boss' eyes bore into her. She needed to decide— but suddenly she knew how a rabbit in headlights felt.

She was reaching for the chips when she heard the ball rattle and *no more bets* called.

"Twenty-eight," the croupier called.

Ten minutes later she was asked to leave.

Having reached the other side of the roundabout, something compelled Juliet to turn and look back at the casino. In the distance the doors swung open and the croupier was ejected, a push in the back by the pit boss as the now ex-employee pulled on his coat. He turned to remonstrate. There was a brief argument, hand gestures, fighting stances, but no blows were struck, and any words exchanged were lost over the traffic.

Juliet remembered another of Christian's rules: the magician's good luck is balanced by another's bad luck.

my bros bfs sister is like a maid for that Tyco dude. she says he never wears the same thing two times. just dumps it. has a lawndry choote

and just thros stuff down there. when the basements full he sayz
hell just move next door cos he owns that too

—Social media posting

"How did you get this number? I didn't give you my number," said Juliet dumbfounded, standing over sauce-pans on the hob.

"I just dialled a random number, and it was yours."

"And that works?"

Christian sounded exasperated. "You really weren't listening, were you?"

"I went to a casino," Juliet blurted. "I've never gambled before. Not even the Lottery."

"And?" Christian asked, clearly fearing the worst.

"I won almost seventy thousand pounds. I've cleared all my debts."

Christian sounded grave. "I hope you did it subtly. Over the course of an evening. Or a weekend. At different casinos, on different games."

"Took me about ten minutes."

Christian muttered an oath under his breath.

"Listen, I've got some questions," Juliet gabbled, stirring the ragu, heavy on the soya and beans, phone held between chin and shoulder. At the table Kath mimed, *is it him?*

"JK Rowling?"

A pause. Christian had expected more. "What about her?"

"Is she a magician? I mean, is it all down to luck?"

"I have no idea. I doubt it. I hear the books are quite good."

"What about Kim Kardashian? Or Banksy? Or the king?"

"The last one's easy," Christian breezed. "That's just about lineage..."

"But is there anything luckier than finding you're destined to a lifetime of privilege for being first out of a particular womb?"

Juliet found the phone slipping from underneath her chin as it was extracted by Kath. Before she could twist and grab it back Christian had been invited around for dinner.

If there is no credible evidence to support anonymous allegations that Mr. Rorschach has paid and arranged to have cannibals "perform" at his premises, can I suggest we kick this matter into the long grass and avoid letting public curiosity give it momentum.
—*Extract from leaked Metropolitan Police internal email*

An hour later, Christian sat at the too-small table in the too-constrained and mouldy kitchen. He had a jacket on, his black curls nestling on his shoulders.

"...what about lottery winners," Kath probed.

"This is really very good," Christian enthused, holding up a forkful of sauce-laden pasta. He'd brought wine.

"I told you he's very positive about cuisine," Juliet stage-whispered to Kath. "Particularly Italian."

"Have you tried the coffee in the café by the common?" Christian deflected. "It really is very good."

"See?"

"I mean," Kath continued, "lottery winners? Are they lucky, or just...lucky?"

"Oh, you can be lucky without being charmed. But then again, there are those that *are* lucky, and those that *get* lucky," he said gnomically.

Kath nodded, even if her expression showed she wasn't on Christian's wavelength at all. "What about..."

"What about Roy Sullivan?" Christian cut in with forceable bluntness. "Or Frane Selak?"

"Who?" Juliet and Kath said in unison.

"Roy Sullivan was a park ranger. Survived being hit by lightning seven times. Selak survived seven train, plane, and car crashes. Are they lucky? Or would it have been luckier never to have had those things happen?"

"It's not as lucky as winning the lottery, I suppose," Kath volunteered.

Christian took a sip of wine. "Actually, Selak did. A million dollars, two days after his seventy-third birthday."

"Well, there you are." Kath brightened.

Christian waved a fork at her, before she could get too enthusiastic again, and turned to Juliet. "Look, I didn't call you to talk to about JK Rowling or the king or lottery winners. There's somebody I want to talk to you about, something I need you to do. I want to talk to you about Tyco Rorschach."

"Is he lucky?" Juliet wondered.

Christian's face clouded. "I've only ever found two people more charmed than me. Him. And you."

Tyko Rorschachs from outa space
—Graffiti in a London underpass

Streetlights twinkled in the gloaming. Grey cirrus formed stripes over a pink and purple sky. The air had begun to chill.

Christian stood at the gates to Tyco Rorschach's imposing Belgravia townhouse. Or, more precisely, one of Tyco Rorschach's five adjoining Belgravia townhouses.

How did he know Rorschach was in this one? He didn't. Just as he didn't know the keypad combination to unlock the gates. He tapped out a series of numbers, frowned, then added one more. A metallic clunk, and the gate swung open on well-oiled hinges.

"*Thirteen* digits," Christian mused out loud to nobody but himself.

He crunched his way up the short gravel drive, making no effort to hide his presence. Drawing up to the front door he watched a security camera shift angle to follow him. He smiled up into the lens. A red light blinked in apparent response.

The front door clicked open on its own. He pushed and went in, closed it behind him.

Christian found himself in a marble-floored atrium which rose four floors up to a glazed cupola through which the sky showed magenta and ultramarine. The décor was elegant, tasteful, expensive. Almost everything was pearlescent white, from the gleaming ivory telephone stand and the telephone on it—which

Christian guessed was more artwork than functional object—to the snowy umbrella stand and the umbrellas within. Everything, except the sweeping staircase's mahogany banister, the double-height doors leading off to rooms on either side and—standing out like a screaming orgasm during a theology examination—a painting in thick, daubed oils, of a nude woman having intercourse with a horse. It must have been ten feet high, dominating the quadruple-height space, issuing a challenge to anybody coming through the front door.

Christian did not like it. Partially because the horse wore blinkers. But mainly because of the bubble-gum pink background. Too flaunty.

Options. To his right and left were those imposing doors, each with ornate mother of pearl handles asking to be turned. In front of him, below the stallion's legs akimbo, a passage led away into darkness.

Or he could climb the stairs.

He had no assurance it was the right decision. Rorschach may be in one of the reception rooms to left or right. Or in the restaurant-scaled kitchen or banqueting hall, which he judged the hallway must lead to. Or down in his mega-basement. Christian was trusting to luck. And luck had yet to let him down.

On the second floor hung a triptych by the artist responsible for the horse and rider downstairs. The background was marigold yellow; the foreground something physically improbable and morally questionable involving ballet dancers and wolves. Or, possibly, coyotes. At the end of the landing a pair of mahogany doors seemed to call to him.

Christian was delivered into the room equidistant between two huge brown Chesterfield sofas, each good for at least five, as if on a catwalk, with audience cradled snug within the soft leather. Feng shui seemed to want him to stride slowly to the window, hip-swivel, and sashay back to the door. If he had, he would have been watched by an audience of precisely one. Tyco Rorschach. He was smaller than Christian had expected, pudgier around the face. Nobody knew his age—Christian guessed at around fifty, but jowliness suggested older. His black hair had been gelled and swept back; he wore a loose black suit and red shirt, open-collared, tieless. He looked like he should be advertising something.

"Christian Rattery," he purred. "Juliet has told me so much about you."

"Where is she?"

Rorschach shrugged. "Changing, I think."

"I hadn't heard from Juliet since she came here ten days ago. I was worried."

"Well," Rorschach said garrulously, "why don't you get yourself a drink whilst we wait, and then you can ask her yourself." He waved towards an ornate globe with hinged hemispheres, already open to reveal a well-stocked drinks cabinet within. "I'd call for ice but I've given the staff the night off. Just your luck," he added pointedly.

"What you're doing is wrong."

"Offering you a drink?" Rorschach sounded offended.

"There's a cosmic order. And you're ignoring it."

Rorschach made a clicking noise with his teeth, sounding suddenly Slavic. "Cosmic order. Just listen to yourself. Juliet told me you were delusional."

"She's charmed. She barely knows what she is. You know. You have to know."

"Know what?" Rorschach blanked.

"That people like us make our own luck. That we pick an outcome, and that outcome happens. Not because we're lucky. Because it has to happen. People get hurt."

"What people?"

"It's like Newton's third law. Every action has an equal and opposite reaction."

"I get rich. Others get poor?"

"Exactly."

"Your economics are naïve. You're one of those people who can't cope with good fortune," Rorschach told him. "You toss a coin, you win. You want there to be a reason. There always has to be cause and effect. Or somebody to blame."

"With us, it's not luck. It *has* to happen. You have a power. But with great power comes great responsibility—"

"I can never remember," Rorschach cut in, "is that Voltaire or Spider-Man?"

"Hello, Christian," Juliet said, closing the door behind her.

"Mister Rattery and I were discussing... Exactly what were we discussing?" Rorschach feigned ignorance.

"Luck?" she suggested.

It was only when she spoke for a second time that Christian was sure it was Juliet. The glasses had gone, the hair had come down. A gossamer-thin scarlet one-piece dress seemed to cling to her with no obvious acknowledgment of the laws of physics. It was a far cry from jeans and an ex-boyfriend's cricket sweater. She even managed to look taller.

"There's a cosmic order which needs to be maintained," Christian said, turning back to Rorschach.

Rorschach gave a strangled laugh. "Let's say you're right, that we're born lucky. So the universe gives you everything your heart could desire, and you sense a trap. Whereas I take it for all it's worth. Who's the fool?"

"Your good luck is balanced by somebody else's bad luck. You must use your gift wisely."

"You believe all that?"

"Yes," Christian persisted.

"You believe you're lucky?"

"Yes."

"That you're a lucky guy."

"Yes."

"That lady luck has always been looking out for you?"

Exasperation. *"Yes!"*

It happened so fast. Christian saw the glint in Rorschach's hand, wondered where he had drawn the pistol from. Then the bark, the muzzle flash. Not so loud as to scream *firearm*—more like *firework*. And the burning sting under his ribs.

His hand came away smeared red with blood.

"If you don't mind me saying," Rorschach said as Christian's knees buckled and he collapsed to the sofa opposite his assassin, "your entire philosophy is in tatters. Not looking so lucky now, are you?"

"You know," Juliet mused, having sashayed across the room to be with Rorschach, clearly his mistress and muse, "I'm not so sure how lucky it is to be lucky."

Bug-eyed, Christian stared at her in disbelief, as his blood welled around his hand.

"A few weeks ago," she continued, "I was a first-time novelist who thought she'd published the most contrarian, genre-redefining, paradigm-shifting work since *Ulysses*. I had given up almost everything that mattered to live in a garret with my working-class lesbian lover and pursue a dream. Then Christian came into my life. Told me my success was entirely due to luck, that I was a chancer with a manuscript of pretentious drivel, that anything, absolutely anything I wrote, would have been published. That it couldn't have been otherwise. And, you know what? He was right. I wrote the least publishable book ever and got it published first time. It was exactly how he spotted me."

Pale-faced, Christian's eyes flicked between his dripping scarlet hand and Juliet, who was sitting on Rorschach's lap and showed no intention of helping a dying man.

"I can't imagine a worse fate to curse somebody with. Why did you have to tell me? Why couldn't you have just left me alone? At least let me imagine my success was down to me. Don't you understand?" She sneered down at him. "You've just emptied my life of meaning. So I've decided I'm going to write trashy airport novels and sell millions. Make millions, spend millions. And I can't think of anything that goes better with emptiness than decadence."

Rorschach clapped his hands together in delight. "That's my girl."

But Juliet's reaction was to simply stand and swing Rorschach's own gun on him. Christian hadn't seen her hand slip into Rorschach's jacket and take it.

"And I've decided I can do better than a sixty-something billionaire."

His jaw slackened as he looked down the barrel, and then laughed away his initial disbelief. "You're going to need the most incredible luck to get away with this. How the hell do you plan to explain this one away?"

"'Fraid you won't be lucky enough to find out how we do it."

"We?" Rorschach asked, baffled.

Behind her, as changed as Juliet had been since the last time Christian saw her, a fourth person slipped into the room. More voluptuous than Juliet, shorter, fuller, raven-haired, a beautiful vixen. She took in the tableau before her. "By 'eck," was all she said after Juliet pulled the trigger.

The penultimate thing Christian Rattery was aware of was falling through an opening into darkness, onto a soft pile of things, of a jacket button pressed into his cheek telling him he had landed on an ocean of clothes.

The very last thing he was aware of was Tyco Rorschach's body landing on top of him.

Tyco Rorschach, the controversial Eastern-European multi-billionaire, has emerged into the public gaze following several months' absence to reveal he has transitioned genders and now wishes to be known as Katherine Eckersley. Ms Eckersley was photographed dining at Alain Ducasse at The Dorchester, London, in the company of novelist Juliet Carwithern, with whom she is understood to be in a relationship. Ms Carwithern recently announced a ten-million-pound advance for her second novel, which she promised will be a departure from the experimentalism of her first, Embassy Heart Widow Process. *A fellow diner described Ms Eckersley as being "gauchely uncouth". The Dorchester is a short walk away from Belgravia where Ms Eckersley owns a row of adjoining townhouses. Three years ago, she controversially created a 3000 sq. ft sub-basement which, according to plans submitted to Westminster Council, were for nothing more than "garment storage".*

—BBC News website

NEVER TO BE TOLD

Colleen Anderson & Tom Johnstone

A PLACE OUT of time. That's what the texts had said. That's what he told her when his plan had been half-formed. Neither had suspected that it might be so close. *Hidden in plain sight*, Nigel thought. Would they have done it if they'd known the outcome?

The clay-red building, an eighteenth-century, one-storey coaching inn, crouched defiantly anachronistic in the shadow of Heathrow Airport, on the other side of the road from their hotel. The dual carriageway looked impassable until they spotted the pedestrian crossing, the little stick figure beckoning them across with its green light.

The derelict pub had been called The Seven Magpies. Until World War Two the area had been farmland. Then a wayside hamlet, consisting of a country lane with farmland on one side of

Heath Row Lane and orchards on the other, giving way to the concrete, steel, glass and tarmac of the airport which took its name.

Isabella looked both ways before walking, as if still unsure of the direction some wayward driver might come. "Do you really think this is the place?"

"Could be." Nigel squinted at the washed-out sky, wondering if it was the petrol staining the air. "It's a heath, after all," he shouted over the traffic zooming past their backs.

"A blasted heath," she said, wiping wisps of black hair from her face, a faint smile upon her lips, her inviting eyes catching his. The thought of her golden olive skin against the bright white of the hotel room sheets—was this a memory, a wish, a premonition?—made him shiver, but he tried to hide the hitch in his breath.

Right now they were searching. Pleasure, if it was to come, would have to wait.

The pub windows were shuttered in aged wood, the yellow and black sign a faded version of its former glory. They moved around the back of the pub as planes roared overhead. "I've checked a couple of other heaths, but they never matched. Marlowe mentioned the scroll and magpies, so maybe the pub had an earlier incarnation."

"Better start digging then." Isabella pointed towards the pub carpark, buttoning her jacket against the chill autumn wind.

Nigel looked dubiously at the tarmac, then back at her. Not for the first time he wondered if they were searching for the same thing after all. She said she was a rare book historian, but they weren't looking for a book.

He certainly harboured ulterior motives for persuading her to fly over. When he spoke to her, he searched her sloe-eyes for some sign it wasn't entirely one-sided. It was, after all, a long way to come to find a mythical scrap of paper.

She was staring at the weathered pub sign swinging in the chilly breeze. "*Sette gazze*," she muttered.

Nigel saw her shivering. It must be the cold; or that was what he told himself at the time.

They first met, if that was the right phrase, on the Manderbilt forum. Soon, they began exchanging PMs, their mutual interest in supposed magical texts and their off-colour jokes cementing at least the basis of a friendship. They soon escalated to video chats, which often ended abruptly when she announced her husband was due home soon.

"Not that he's the jealous type," she once added hastily. "He's not even interested enough to be...I don't want to give him reason, though."

He couldn't understand why she had sounded so secretive. This was all innocent enough, wasn't it? They were just discussing certain matters of mutual interest. Esoteric ones certainly, arcane even, but that didn't mean she should have to conceal them from her husband, did it?

And yet he had found himself wanting very much to meet her. Maybe that's why, during one of their exchanges, he had casually mentioned that one of the Moebius scrolls was reputedly concealed in the Home Counties.

"Actually, not far from the airport," he added, trying to make his voice sound as nonchalant as possible. He didn't really know for sure then.

"I could fly over!" she said, with far more eagerness than he'd expected or dreamed possible.

There weren't many other people interested in the mythic Moebius scrolls, and usually it was only in the most academic, historical sense. Nigel's had started out that way. *Fairy tales*, one of his friends had scoffed, so Nigel had been careful to whom he revealed his little hobby.

Part of Isabella's attraction was that he knew she wouldn't belittle his interest in the scrolls. Sometimes he felt disgusted with himself, as if he was trying to lure her here with the prospect of the find. But it wasn't like that, he told himself. It was just something he and Isabella had in common.

"**W**here, though?" Nigel scratched his head, turning a slow circle. The day had retreated as dusk approached. "We can't just dig up the whole pub carpark." Indeed, they'd be lucky to dig up any of it today. That would have to wait until morning.

"It's alright. I've got an app for it." Isabella took out her smartphone and tapped the screen a few times, waving it around as if it were a metal detector, or a divining rod.

He shrugged. There were apps for all sorts of things—but finding buried parchment? It didn't matter where she pointed it, they still had to figure out exactly where to dig. Maybe he was just the mule, the brawn to her brains. But it would take a lot of muscle to find the object of their quest, probably a pneumatic drill too.

"What is this—geo-caching?" he joked, but Isabella ignored him, moving forward, stepping delicately over cracked tarmac in her purple high heels. "Or Pokémon Go?"

Her phone led her to the edge of the carpark, over a low crumbling wall and into a patch of waste ground spider-webbed with brambles, spiked with nettles, shot-through with golden rod and rosebay willow herb. At least the ground was, if not exactly soft, a little more broken up.

"We'll have to go get a spade," she said.

"A spade? A pickaxe and machete, more like!"

She tucked her phone back in her jacket and turned, walking toward the pedestrian light.

"Wha—Where are you going?" Nigel yelled.

Isabella punched the pedestrian button then jammed her hands in her pockets. "You don't want to dig with your fingers, do you?"

"**O**ne for sorrow, two for joy, three for a girl, four for a boy, five for silver, six for gold…" he chanted in a rhythmic grunt, squinting in the long shadows of early morning.

"What?" Isabella glanced at the sky, then pushed around the earth he'd broken with his pickaxe. "It's not a treasure hunt." She frowned, as if annoyed at him for not taking their quest seriously enough. To show her own seriousness she'd exchanged yesterday's purple high heels for more practical walking boots. "We're not looking for gold or silver."

He held his breath and smiled at her. It was nice to mystify *her* for once. And it *was* a treasure hunt. "Seven for a secret never to be told... It's just a rhyme about magpies. Don't they have a version of it in Italy?"

"No." Isabella smiled, but not with her eyes, and looked away.

Her terse reply cued him to resume his labours, which he did, while thinking that the name of the pub and the seventh line of the proverb added significance to what they sought.

"We do have an opera, though," she said.

"Oh?" he replied.

"*La Gazza Ladra*," she said. "*The Thieving Magpie*."

"Is that right?" he said, meeting her gaze. There was something playful in those deep, mesmerizing eyes. He felt sure of it. "This is a competition now? You have a nursery rhyme? I raise you an opera!"

She laughed. Ah, there was the humour that had drawn him to her in the forum.

"So tell me about it," he pressed.

"Alright then. But you must keep digging."

As she said this, she touched his wrist, and a vision of her golden limbs twined around tangled white sheets came to him again, more vividly this time; a motion picture rather than a memory or a premonition. More detail, too—his tongue probing between those soft thighs, her ankles at his shoulders while he teased his way inside her... waking up next to her, reaching out for her warmth again—

He blinked.

It couldn't be a memory. They'd eaten together at the hotel last night after their reconnaissance mission, but no matter how Nigel tried to develop a rapport Isabella had been circumspect. She hadn't wanted to chat. An early start to find such a rare antiquity, she'd said. Then they'd both walked to their respective rooms.

Later, feeling restless and lonely, Nigel left his room in search of a quick drink and maybe some company in the hotel bar—as much to stretch his legs as anything else. He certainly got a chance to do that: the corridor seemed to stretch on and on forever. A man at the other end walked away but Nigel didn't see him go into a room. He just walked and walked. Nigel rubbed his eyes—it had been a long day, after all. He decided to give up on the drink.

Returning to his room he felt almost hypnotized by the hall carpet's grey herringbone pattern, which seemed designed to look worn, pre-empting the countless feet and trundling suitcases. Looking up, he'd somehow got turned around and found himself at the wrong end of the endless corridor.

A broken night's sleep didn't help much when Isabella rang him at five a.m. saying they'd start early and catch breakfast later. Yawning, Nigel walked to the elevator, emerging on the ground floor, which seemed to be overrun with black-clad police officers. A large group of about twenty marched towards him, almost in formation, two abreast. They moved like automatons, not talking, all of them swivelling their heads to watch him as he passed.

Waiting outside for her, he saw police vans with the insignias of Kent Police and Devon and Cornwall Constabulary. *Seems a bit out of place in Heathrow*, he thought. Then he remembered it was the weekend of the queen's funeral in London. They must be stationed as part of a related security operation. It didn't make him feel secure as he pulled tools from his car boot.

Leaning on the pickaxe, he remembered the forum's more enthusiastic believers raving that the scroll was real and had power to scramble space-time like an egg. It sounded like a lot of nonsense. All he knew was he would be the toast of the department if he managed to prove it actually existed, maybe get that professorship at last.

"So, *The Thieving Magpie*," he prompted.

Isabella gripped his wrist tightly, reminding him to dig. It also shot a sensation into his cock, a squeezing tightness, and it was all he could do not to gasp.

Just an hallucination.

But nerve endings don't lie, do they? Another part of him objected.

He shook his head impatiently and bent to wedging up black pieces of tarmac.

"It's by Rossini. Gisela took me once. It's about a servant girl who narrowly escapes execution for stealing a piece of silverware."

"So, *she's* the thieving magpie," he grunted between strokes of the pickaxe.

"No, it was a mistake." Isabella furtively looked to the darkening sky, as if she feared something listened. "She was framed by a magpie that flew off with it." Her voice held a certain weight, as if the scenario had a special significance. Or maybe it was just her accent. "There's always a price to pay."

"Who's Gisela?"

"Why have you stopped?" she demanded, noticing him leaning on his pickaxe.

"Just tired, I suppose," he said, wiping sweat theatrically from his brow. "What's the hurry?"

"We haven't got all day," she snapped.

He looked at his watch: only seven forty-three. They did indeed have all day. Why was she so impatient? Perhaps it was her very proficient but nevertheless non-native English that made her voice sound so harsh. A spatter of rain added force to her argument. After all, they didn't want to be digging in the mud. On the other hand, it might soften the ground.

"The sooner we find the scroll, the sooner we can go back to the hotel..." As if wanting to coax now rather than cajole, she spoke in softer tones, her voice a caress, (*...her long fingers with their pointed nails stroking my inner thigh...*) so that he quite forgot what he had been about to say...

"You've stopped digging again," Isabella observed.

"I thought I'd let you do some work for a change."

"Fair enough," she conceded.

"Anyway," he added, "if that gizmo's pointing to where the brambles are, I've been digging over the wrong bit all along. Not much point in carrying on until we've cleared that lot, is there?"

The thatch of thorny brambles and nettles were nature's best defence. Nigel remembered childhood battles with blackberry canes that had left red weals down his arms.

"We need to cut it all back," she said, a long index finger pointing at the thicket of cane. He handed her some secateurs and a pair of thick, thorn-proof gloves.

Secateurs had seemed more practical than the machete he'd suggested. They didn't sell them in the B&Q in Sipson. And even if they had, Nigel would have been too paranoid to carry one near the hotel with so many police around.

"I'll cut; you clear."

He pointed. "You've got the only gloves."

"We'll have to share—one each."

"Careful, though. You don't want to damage those nice, long, purple nails of yours."

"No. Who gets the left glove, and who gets the right?"

"I don't know. Toss for it?"

She gave him a smile that was curiously intimate, her eyes glinting, and he again wondered if they did already share some carnal knowledge after all. Those images of their limbs entwined had been so vivid and sensory. More like flashbacks than fantasies.

Then he remembered what he had been about to say before the last of those visions put him off his stroke. "Are you sure this is a good idea?"

She stepped onto the thicket, taming the branches from lashing upward, and started to cut. "What is?"

"Digging for the scroll."

"Why? Is this the real reason why you've gone *sciopero* on me?"

"*Sciopero*?"

"On strike."

He laughed. "Oh. No, it's not that. It's just..." He couldn't quite put his finger on the source of his unease. Something to do with the other verses of the nursery rhyme:

Eight for a wish,
Nine for a kiss,
Ten a surprise you should be careful not to miss,

Eleven for health,
Twelve for wealth . . .
There was one more line, but he couldn't remember it.

"I think you're just sulking because I had you dig in the wrong place," said Isabella with a lop-sided smile, her berry-like eyes inviting, again suggesting an already shared intimacy. His cock stirred at the sense-memory of reaching towards her warm body next to him in the hotel bed, even though his brain knew they hadn't spent the night together.

He shook his head and resumed without saying anything.

Things had been going a little weird from the moment Isabella had arrived. When he went to pick her up from the airport he felt as if the traffic system had been designed by Moebius, the way, no matter what he did, he kept returning to the same point over and over. He'd forgotten in which terminal her flight was due to land, and there was a bewildering array of them. After three dizzying circuits of the approach roads, he eventually had to pull over onto a side road to check the number of her terminal, only to realise it was a strictly no-parking zone monitored by CCTV.

Once he was sure where to pick her up, he had another problem: the traffic light to this forbidden zone was permanently stuck on red. As if the airport authorities were trying to trap him at the scene of his crime, or at least traffic offence, rather than wait until he returned home and send him a letter with the damning monochrome image of his car caught *in flagrante delicto*, providing incontrovertible evidence of his misdemeanour. This was, after all, what happened before when he'd unwittingly strayed into bus lanes or failed to pay congestion charge on time.

As he had sat there watching the red orb, willing it to descend to amber, then green, time had felt frozen. Eventually he got out of the car and approached one of the army of men in high-viz vests milling around the nearby coach stop, an indication that time was in fact fluid for everything else in the world apart from this infuriating traffic light.

"Does it ever change?" he asked, glancing at his phone where half-a-dozen missed calls from her screamed that he was late for their rendezvous.

The airport worker shrugged and told him to wait in his vehicle. He turned back to the car—only to see the light briefly passing amber on its way back to its default red. He'd missed its vanishingly brief visit to green.

Probably in trouble already, he was tempted to flout the red light and leave. Why not be hanged for a sheep as a lamb? But obedience to traffic lights was ingrained; he continued sitting there in angry silence until a departing coach driver waved him out, shouting from his open window that he could be waiting there forever if he didn't jump the light.

They cut and moved brambles for another hour or more, Nigel momentarily wondering if anyone thought them caretakers for the old building. Even with all the police across the way at the hotel no one approached, as if they were in a bubble.

Fat droplets began to fall as a magpie flew over, cawing, its black and white form disappearing into the dark grey clouds.

Isabella jerked at the sound, looking up, her face pale.

"You all right?" Nigel stacked more brambles.

He wondered if she knew the rhyme, then remembered she'd claimed ignorance of it. Maybe there was an Italian version of the superstition about these single spies of sorrow. If so, it was something else she was keeping to herself.

She rubbed her arms. "Yes, let's go get some food and see if the rain passes."

Nigel didn't express how glad he was to stop. He felt like they'd been digging and chopping and hacking for weeks. He shook his head, checking his watch. Just after ten, but it felt like forever.

They left the tools tucked against a wall of the pub and went in search of food, choosing to avoid the hotel with its swarm of police.

As they sat nursing coffee and a hearty late breakfast of eggs, toast, bacon and hash browns, Nigel couldn't get the events to add up. Had he picked her up yesterday? Was it only twenty-four hours?

Isabella stared out the window at the pelting rain, peering as a gull flew over.

"Who's Gisela?"

"What?"

"You mentioned Gisela earlier."

Isabella seemed distant, turning slowly back to Nigel. "Oh, she was my wi—Is my, how would you say it in English? My wise woman."

He tilted his head. "Your what?" He was sure she was about to say wife. But she had a husband. Or so she'd said.

She waved a hand. "Oh, you know—an older friend who lets me run ideas by her, to see if they make sense." She reached out towards him, but he flinched, jerking his arm away, a gesture she seemed to take as proof he was still sulking about the division of labour between them. She withdrew her hand. "Tell you what, how about I dig next time?"

"No, it's not that." He shrugged, shook his head, unable to put his misgivings into words. "I do know what a wise woman is, by the way," was what he said instead. "You can't pull the wool over my eyes. I don't believe in magic."

"Oh? What is a wise woman then, Mr Know-It-All?"

"A witch by another name."

"Ever heard of the Witch of Agnesi?"

"No, what's that?"

"Ah! Something you *don't* know." Isabella smiled in that infuriating, infatuating way of hers. "It's the cubic plane curve derived from two diametrically opposite points of a circle, named after the Italian mathematician, Maria Gaetano Agnesi."

"And what does that prove?"

"Only how easy it is for someone or something to be called a witch, and how close mathematics and magic are. You see, the Italian word for curve, *versiera*, is also the word for witch. It also proves university professors don't know everything. It was one from Cambridge, no less, who mistranslated 'curve' as 'witch'..."

"I need some more coffee," Nigel muttered, making her laugh at his grumpiness. Rare book purveyor, mathematician... Isabella grew more unfathomable, and more alluring.

He waved to the waitress, but even though she looked directly at him he couldn't seem to attract her attention. His gesticulations became wilder, more frantic, yet still she ignored him. "Bloody hell." He got up from the table and walked to the counter. "Could we have more coffee, please?"

The waitress smiled and brought over the coffee.

Nigel stewed, staring out the window. "So, what happens if we find it?"

"What do you mean 'if'?" Isabella regarded him carefully over the cup's rim. She shrugged. "*When* we find it, we pat each other on the back for a job well done and publish our find."

Despite himself, Nigel couldn't help smiling at her certainty they would be successful. "You mean, co-author a paper?"

"Sure." She smiled back, her lips the richest garnet, so luscious they looked like ripe plums. She was doing it again. Distracting him. Holding out the promise of prolonging their acquaintance by arranging to work together on an academic project.

And yet he very much wanted to be distracted.

Not enough to put aside his misgivings and suspicions entirely, though. "Who gets to keep it, or do we donate it?"

Glancing out the window, she pointed. "Look, the rain's let up. Let's get back to it before we lose the day."

Exhausted, Nigel lay on his bed, trying to muster the energy to shower and find dinner.

What had happened to the day? He didn't remember returning to the hotel. The mud caking his trousers indicated they had returned to dig. Not that he was wearing them. They lay strewn upon the floor with the rest of his crumpled clothes. All of them looked as if they'd been removed and discarded in haste. Nigel wondered if the coupling he'd imagined so vividly had in fact taken place in those lost hours. But he couldn't remember them making love, except in the fragments which flashed into his mind;

and those weren't memories exactly—unless he could have memories of things before they'd happened.

There was one memory, though: of an old leather folio, mildewed and rotting in spots. The sign of a parchment.

He bolted out of the bed, hurriedly disentangling his scattered clothes and pulling them back on. Black lace underwear fell to the ground. His thoughts spun. They *had* been together, and she was going to leave with the scroll! "Damn it!"

He grabbed the key card and rushed out of the room, not even stopping to brush his hair, tearing along the long grey corridor until he reached the lift. There was a man standing in front of the doors, staring at his smartphone, scrolling no doubt. Maybe he was about to press the button but unlike Nigel he seemed in no particular hurry.

"Excuse me," said Nigel, making to get past him and call the lift.

Either the stranger was too engrossed in social media to respond, or he was punishing Nigel for his impatience. Whatever the reason, Nigel was in no mood to be polite. He tapped the man on the shoulder to get his attention.

Or tried to.

The man didn't react. It was as if he couldn't feel Nigel's hand. For that matter, Nigel couldn't feel the man's shoulder, either. His hand plunged straight through to the call-lift button, which he *could* touch. Strange. Was *he* the ghost, or the man?

Sharing the elevator could have been any awkward encounter with a stranger in a tight space; except when Nigel asked him which floor he wanted the man looked up from his phone briefly, his expression puzzled, then returned his gaze to the screen.

Nigel was just grateful they were both heading down. The lift's descent seemed agonisingly slow.

Finally, the elevator arrived on the ground floor. As the doors slid open, Nigel ran out, *through* the unhurried man—who shivered as if chilled.

A row of police stood staring into the lobby, yet not a head turned as Nigel sprinted towards the revolving door. It further hindered his progress, even as the hotel's glass façade revealed the departing figure of Isabella, towing her suitcase towards the taxi rank.

He ran after her, ignoring the chill.

"So, thought you'd sneak off without saying goodbye, did you?" He caught her upper arm, relieved to be able to feel its soft warmth.

"I didn't want to wake you," she protested. "I'm sorry, Nigel, I have to catch my flight back. I must leave before—"

"Not before I—" His lips were on hers, and she responded but broke away. He didn't mind. He was just glad he was able to connect with her, physically at least. Relieved to feel real again. To be able to remember this moment.

Hopefully his ghostliness in the lift had just been a temporary blip. Either that or only she was aware of him now.

"This afternoon was lovely . . . so lovely," she said with a sad smile. "But I haven't got time for this, Nigel."

She looked up towards the sky, where ominous-looking clouds gathered, black and billowing. It looked like rain. *Black as Newgate's knocker*, his nan would have said. Isabella's eyes looked haunted. Hunted, even.

"But I've got so many questions," he said. "Who are you, really?"

She glanced at the taxi rank. The cab was idling, its driver glaring impatiently at Isabella. "They'll have to wait. Message me, Nigel." She shook off his embrace and started to pull her suitcase towards the taxi rank.

"Wait!"

"What now?" She sighed, her eyes looking tight, a ridge between her brows. She seemed to hunch as she peered skyward. Darkness swirled about them—premature twilight, like a solar eclipse.

"You forgot something." He handed her back her discarded underwear with a half-smile.

She laughed at his cheek, despite her impatience to be on her way. "Thanks."

"You're welcome. Now do something for me?"

"What?" Her voice had become irritable again, echoing the cab driver's glowering expression. Perhaps he couldn't even see Nigel and was wondering who the hell his would-be passenger was talking to.

"Can I see it, at least?" he pleaded.

She narrowed her eyes, confused, perhaps even a little playfully, as if he meant something other than the scroll. "But you've already seen it."

There was no time to explain that his memories had flown away like a flock of birds migrating for the winter. "Just one more time," he pleaded. "I need to photograph it. To show my colleagues." He scrabbled for the phone in his pocket.

"Oh." Her look grew hard in contempt and disappointment. "So, this was always just about your career, then? I'd hoped I was wrong about you, but obviously not. Here you are then—here's your trophy to show your university friends!"

"Isabella, you know it wasn't!"

She whipped out the scroll, its brown parchment still soiled from where they'd found it buried, so he couldn't see where the mud stains ended and odd sigils began.

"Go on," she taunted. "Take your little holiday snap. Like you, your cronies might not believe in its power, but at least you'll be able to know it exists."

"But I think I do believe," he protested, feeling as if her scorn was unfair, especially considering he couldn't remember what he might have said about the scroll later in the afternoon. "Things have been pretty weird since you arrived." He told her about the incident in the lift. "What if this scroll can distort reality in some way? Maybe it can warp time like people were saying. I thought they were cranks, but I don't know. After what's been happening to me I'm not so sure. If they're right, maybe it's drawing strength from . . . a big historical event."

"What?"

"The queen dying. Her funeral's the reason there are so many police around here. I know, it sounds like bullshit, but I can't tell what's real anymore. Maybe you can tell me?"

"I can't. I haven't got time to explain it all to you, Nigel." She tugged the parchment from his hand, letting the rotted folio fall to the ground. Her cool aplomb left her. So did the taxi, the driver suddenly losing patience, tyres screeching. "I have to complete the cycle. I have to pay." Isabella looked in despair at the departing taxi, then stared up again at the darkening sky, her expression one of abject terror.

It didn't look like any cloud formation Nigel had ever seen before. It had the fizzing black energy of a murmuration, except unlike one of those it didn't swarm around, at least not yet. He had the curious notion it was biding its time.

Isabella held the scroll in one hand as she hurried towards the taxi rank, as if desperately hoping to hail another cab. But the drivers looked straight through her, like the waitress in the café, but more permanently. One by one they drove off, abandoning her. She stopped for a moment as if considering whether to put the parchment away. Maybe she thought that would make her visible again. But before she had the chance to tuck it in her coat pocket, something swooped.

One for sorrow...

The magpie snatched the parchment from her hand leaving Isabella standing there, empty-handed, suitcase falling over.

"*La gazza ladra!*" she pleaded to the sky.

The blackness plummeted and swallowed her in a blur of wings and shrieking beaks, cutting her to ribbons as Nigel watched.

Then he remembered the final line of the proverb.

Thirteen—beware, it's the devil himself.

EVER SO QUIETLY, EVER SO SOFTLY

Gary McMahon

WHEN CARL ARRIVED home that night the house was dim and quiet. He shut the front door, threw his keys into the bowl on the little oak table at the bottom of the stairs, and drifted through into the kitchen. He was tired, but too wired to even think about sleep. There was a lamp still on in the living room. Its light bled into the hallway and the kitchen just enough for him to move around without switching on the main lights.

As was habitual these days, he went straight to the drinks cupboard and poured two inches of whisky into the tumbler that had taken up residence on the draining board next to the sink. Opening the French doors, he stepped out onto the decking and stared into the neat, simple garden as he took his first hit of the drink. Carl hated working late. It made him feel as if the job had robbed him of too much time. Getting home at this hour, there was nothing left to do but drink and think, and perhaps look out at the night and his moonlit lawn.

He sat down at the little bamboo patio table, placing his glass on the slate coaster, and tried to rid his mind of the facts and figures and dimensions that had dictated his day.

"How was the meeting?"

Polly had come up behind him in silence. He turned around, smiled. "Dull. Looks like we'll finally get the Haye Park project through planning, though."

She nodded, her long black hair glistening in the poor light. It looked, thought Carl, like otter skin. "That's one less problem, I suppose." She sat down next to him, her nightdress lifting up over her bony knees.

"Yeah, but now all the hard work starts. Measuring up, drawing the plans, meeting the contractor." He took another sip of whisky—a small one this time, because his wife was watching. "I foresee a lot more of these long days and late nights in the weeks ahead."

She smiled, but it was a tired smile. One that only went skin deep. "You'll manage. You always do."

He slid his hand across the small tabletop and stroked her ring finger, but she didn't respond. "Would you like a drink?"

She shook her head. "I think I'll go back to bed. I'm so tired these days ... not sure what's going on with me."

"We've had a tough year," he said, hoping that would cover everything needing to be said, along with the things that couldn't be. "You have a right to be tired."

She stood slowly, not making eye contact, and went back inside. "'Night," she called without looking. "Don't stay up too late."

He didn't hear her shut the kitchen door, nor could he discern her footsteps on the stairs. Lately, she seemed to move around the house like a sad phantom: softly, in silence. It was unnerving.

"Shit," he said, realising he'd left the bottle inside and would need to get up to fetch it. But not yet; not until he'd finished this glass.

Before long, he had no choice but to get up and leave the table. His knees ached as he stood, bracing himself against the rickety piece of furniture. He was getting old; they both were. The kids were growing up. His and Polly's jobs were running them down, burning them out. Life never seemed to get any easier. There were always more goals to chase, and additional barriers that appeared in the way of their dreams.

The kitchen was darker now. Polly must have switched off that living room lamp before climbing the stairs to bed. Still, he didn't bother with the main lights. It was cool and quiet in the darkness, and the ambient light from the moon and the stars and the nearby streetlamps was enough for him to go about his business. And sometimes, the habit of drinking was best done in the dark.

This time he added a little tap water to the whisky, just to dilute the effect. As he turned away from the sink he heard a small sound somewhere behind him, perhaps in another room. Puzzled, but not afraid—not yet—he crossed the floor and went out into the hallway.

The sound did not come again.

Standing in the hallway, listening to the tiny groans and creaks and pops the house made at night, he wondered if there had been any sound at all, that he'd just imagined it. At the time it had been like a shoe being scuffed against a wall or a piece of furniture. Now he felt silly for being drawn by it.

He took a sip of whisky. He listened again. Nothing.

Curiosity pulled him towards the open living room door. Inside, the heavy curtains were closed so the room was darker than anywhere else on the ground floor. The dim shapes of the sofa and chairs, the shelves and bureau and television, loomed against the walls but didn't resemble anything other than what they were. Carl had never been an imaginative man; he was rarely afraid of fanciful thoughts in a dark room. What scared him were the grim realities of life—paying bills, maintaining a house, making sure your kids grew up safe and sane and with a bright future.

Was that another sound? Like a single drawn breath?

It had come from the far corner of the room, a wedge of wall between two bookshelves, a narrow niche or cubby hole where the walls met. Softly, he moved in the direction of the bookshelves, smiling a little at his own foolishness.

"Is there anybody there?" He said it in jest; something he'd heard a character say in a table-rapping séance scene in some horror movie he and Polly had laughed through a few weeks ago.

Again, there came what sounded like a short, sharp intake of breath.

He stepped closer to the spot where the bookshelves didn't quite meet. As he came within a yard or so of the exact spot, he began to make out a slightly darker shadow pressed up against the wall.

"What...?" He didn't finish his sentence. In fact, he wasn't even sure what he'd meant to say.

When he got within touching distance he realised there was someone squeezed into that little niche, standing with their face to the wall. Arms pinned to their sides, sleek black hair almost reaching the middle of their back, gossamer nightdress hanging like a delicate cobweb.

"Polly? What the hell are you doing?"

She didn't move.

He began to reach out, meaning to touch her on the shoulder, but for some reason his hand stopped a couple of inches from her body, hanging in mid-air.

"You can't see me," she whispered. So softly and quietly that he could barely make out the words. The only reason he heard them was because it was so still and silent in the room.

"Polly?"

He stood there feeling like an idiot, with his hand outstretched, but for reasons he could not define he didn't want to touch her.

Then, slowly, she turned around—not facing him, because clearly she didn't even know he was there. Her eyes were open but she wasn't looking at him. She wasn't looking at anything. Her eyes looked painted on. Without saying anything more she walked stiffly past him, across the room, and out of the door. He glimpsed the bottom of her nightdress and her small, bare feet as she climbed the stairs, and he heard the bedroom door close, so quietly and softly, as she returned to their bedroom.

There'd been something odd about her feet as he watched them ascend the stairs. It took him a few seconds to process the information, but it was clear to him now that her toes had been clenched so tightly her feet had looked deformed.

The following morning was a Saturday so he deliberately overslept, enjoying the fact that he didn't have to get up for a grinding commute to the office. When he went downstairs Polly was in the kitchen cleaning up the breakfast dishes. Jake was sitting outside at the patio table, pulling on his football boots, getting ready for the morning's game, and little Alice was standing at the sink pretending to wash the dishes.

"Morning," said Polly, smiling. Her eyes were bright. Her face glowed in a way he'd not seen in a long time. "Sleep well?"

"Not bad ... you?" Bracing himself, he waited.

"Pretty good, actually. I can't remember sleeping that well in weeks, to be honest."

He sat down at the kitchen table as she bustled past him, flicking on the kettle. "Tea?" she said, already knowing the answer.

He looked down at her feet. She was wearing a pair of faux leopard-skin slippers so he couldn't see her toes, but she was walking normally.

In the car, taking Jake to his football game, Carl wondered if Polly failed to recall last night's incident, or was simply ignoring it out of embarrassment. He hadn't wanted to ask. It might have shattered her good mood and, God knew, those were so rare these days that he was reluctant to take the risk.

"Dad?"

He glanced at Jake in the passenger seat. The boy looked pale and pensive but, not for the first time, Carl was taken aback by his son's good looks. He resembled his mother, having inherited her dark eyes and button nose.

"What is it?"

"Have you and Mum been arguing again?"

"No ... no, not at all. Why do you ask?"

"I dunno." He paused, as if looking for the right words. "It's just, this morning ... she was in a weird mood. Like, all hyper, and stuff."

Carl took the almost-hidden left turn off the main road leading to the playing fields, the car's tyres crunching loose gravel. "You know she's still taking those pills, right?"

Jake nodded.

"Well, her moods can be a bit swingy, y'know."

"I know. Okay, Dad."

Carl parked next to a big black Range Rover, thinking he could do with an upgrade. The old Ford was getting on a bit, starting to cost him money every time it went through its MOT. These everyday thoughts pushed his anxiety regarding last night to one side, allowing the real world to swallow them up.

"Are you staying to watch the game?" Jake's previous concern was also now forgotten, it seemed, washed away by the excitement of the oncoming match.

"Of course I am, big fella."

Ten minutes into the match, after watching Jake make two spectacular saves to keep his team in the game, his mood was better. He could almost pretend that last night hadn't happened.

The following week went by in a rush of meetings, more meetings, and yet more meetings. The Haye Park project had gathered pace. Architectural drawings were needed quicker than they could be prepared, and the initial design seemed to change more and more in terms of scope and ambition with every day.

He didn't see much of Polly and the kids. Their brief morning greetings in the kitchen, the hallway, or last thing at night, were fleeting and unsatisfactory.

I must try harder, he thought. *Do better. Neglecting my family was part of the problem before.* Polly would never have voiced this accusation, of course, but he knew, deep down inside, that he was partly to blame for her breakdown. He became easily absorbed in his job and often felt himself slipping, sliding. His reality would become warped and nothing else would matter to him but getting a project finished. It made him good at his job, but terrible at being a father and a husband.

So once again he found himself sitting outside at the patio table, a drink in hand. The nights were becoming cooler, the leaves on the trees starting to lose their colour and vibrancy. It was raining more often.

Returning inside, he locked the French doors and switched off the overhead kitchen light. Just as he turned to leave the room he heard the sound of something shifting—perhaps a cup or a plate losing balance on a stack inside one of the cupboards.

He stood for a moment to see if the sound would be repeated. When it wasn't, he found he was unable to walk away. His obsessive nature kicking in again, forcing him to see things right through to the end, no matter what.

Do better. A fleeting thought, one he ignored.

After flicking on the light he walked to the centre of the room. Turning in a slow circle he examined the kitchen. The bare white walls, the tiled area above the sink, the white goods, the standing cupboards and the over-filled shelves.

The door to the cupboard near the dishwasher was slightly ajar, just an inch or so, as if someone had been in there for something and forgotten to close it properly. It was where they kept the random kitchenware that had no real home—strange, forgotten utensils whose function was unclear; old candles nobody could remember buying; dining sets they'd been given as gifts over the years.

Feeling a strange sense of unreality beginning to wash over him, Carl walked over to the cupboard. He watched in a detached manner as his hand reached out and grabbed the handle, then slowly pulled open the door.

Polly was inside the cupboard, crouched down and facing the back wall under the lowest shelf. Not quite on her knees, but huddled into an awkward hunched position that couldn't have been comfortable. She was wearing pink sleep shorts and a black *Friends* t-shirt on backwards, with the logo facing him.

"Polly—what the hell?"

She was motionless. Her arms were tucked up somewhere in front of her body, and he couldn't see her hands. Her feet were bare, the toes curled over like pink claws.

"Please... please, will you come on out of there?"

Around her, at her feet and visible under her backside, were broken plates and cups and saucers. She must have destroyed them as she forced her way into the tight little spot. He only noticed now that she'd cut one of her feet. There was a tiny bit of blood on the thin white skin covering her ankle bone.

"I'm not here," she whispered. Her voice sounded like it was coming from a million miles away, perhaps travelling along some old failing telephone wire, or transmitted on an ancient transistor radio.

Reaching down, he tried to grab her and physically coerce her out of the cupboard, but when he touched her the muscles of her shoulders were as tight as cords, and her skinny arms were unmoveable. Her entire body was tensed, rigid, stuck in place. He realised there would be no way of moving her without causing further injury.

Had she experienced some kind of fit, a muscular spasm that locked her joints so rigidly? Some kind of episode brought on by her medication?

It was too late to call the doctor, and he was too afraid to summon the police or an ambulance. She didn't look to be in any kind of pain or distress. In fact, her voice had sounded calm, serene. He backed up slowly and sat down at the kitchen table, watching her. Wondering what he should do.

Slowly, deliberately, she pushed out a stiff arm, grasped the edge of the cupboard door, and somehow pulled it shut without bending her elbow.

Carl sat there all night, at the kitchen table, watching the cupboard door. No further sounds came from inside. There was no evidence of movement. He nodded off a few times, just for a second, but did not sleep. When morning came, and weak sunlight began to creep into the room, he realised he would have to think of something to tell the children.

Jake came downstairs first. Unlike most teenage boys, he was an early riser. He liked to enjoy the morning, drink orange juice on the patio, and see in the day with open eyes.

"Dad? What are you doing?"

"Sit down, son. I have something—There's something we need to discuss."

Jake pulled up a chair, its legs scraping across the tiled floor. His slight frame looked feeble in a baggy t-shirt and jogging pants—his usual sleeping attire. He ran an oversized, knuckly hand through his messy hair, blinking and yawning. *His mother's looks*, thought Carl, *but my ugly hands…*

"It's Mum."

Jake's eyes became alert. His posture changed, becoming more rigid.

"She's… shit, I don't know. How can I even explain this?" Carl clenched his fists, laying them casually on the tabletop as if they were objects which he might easily discard.

"What is it, Dad? Where's Mum?"

"She's in the cupboard," said Carl, turning his head to look at the door.

"What? In… in there?"

All Carl could do was nod.

Jake stood, moved slowly towards the cupboard and crouched down. His hand strayed to the handle but he didn't open the door immediately. He paused for a moment, his head down, shoulders hunched. Then, finally, reluctantly, he opened the door.

Polly hadn't moved. Not one inch.

"Mum…"

Still, she did not move. She did not speak.

Jake closed the door, gently, with great care, and stood. He didn't turn around. "What do we do?"

"I don't know, son," said Carl. "I really don't know."

But he had to do something.

The ambulance took fifteen minutes to arrive, which was pretty good considering this could in no way be considered an emergency. Carl answered the door to a man and a woman, both shorter and much younger than him.

"This way," he said and led them through into the kitchen.

The cupboard door was already open. She'd stopped closing it after the fifth or sixth attempt, probably registering, somewhere deep within her fugue state, that they wouldn't stop opening it again every time she reached out to pull it shut.

The paramedics seemed unfazed.

"Does she have a history of mental illness?" The woman had kind eyes, a sympathetic manner.

"What medication is she on?" The man was terser, even to the point of brusqueness.

Carl went to the medicine cabinet and retrieved Polly's pills. "She had a breakdown ten months ago, but she's been fine ever since."

"Until now," said the short, terse man.

"Until now," repeated Carl.

They tried for forty minutes to cajole her into coming out, but their attempts met with silence. Both of them remarked that, for a slender woman, she was as heavy as rock, and they admitted that manhandling her out of the cupboard wasn't the way to go.

"Has she said anything?" The woman sat down at the table, scratching her left ear. Her short brown hair had a purple streak in it, and gave her a punkish edge. She was slightly out of breath.

"Just one thing. *'I'm not here.'* She's said nothing more since that. I have no idea what it means."

Eventually, they admitted defeat and left. Before doing so they called Polly's doctor and asked him to come out and see if he could do anything to convince her to move. They didn't want to leave—Carl could see it in their body posture, the way they hung back, talking and talking to delay their exit. But in the end they had no choice but to go. A call came in over their radio that there'd been a big traffic accident on the ring road, and all available emergency services were required at the scene.

Carl walked them to the door. "Don't worry," he said. "I'm sure Doctor Price will sort this out. He's helped her a lot in the past." He knew he was lying but he wanted them to feel better about abandoning him there, with the problem. It seemed like the least he could do.

After the paramedics had gone it took him several minutes to realise not only that Jake had vanished, but Alice was yet to appear downstairs, despite the commotion. How on earth could she have slept through all this?

He climbed the stairs and went to Jake's room first, expecting to find the boy sitting on his bed listening to his headphones, perhaps in an attempt to shut himself off from the madness around him.

He wasn't there.

"Where are you, son? They've gone. I need your help. Doctor Price is coming..." He went along the landing, past Alice's room, to the bathroom, and knocked gently on the door. "Jake... are you in there, mate?" There was no reply.

He tried the handle; the door was unlocked. It swung open and he stepped inside, catching sight of his tired face in the mirror above the sink. Grey in his hair. Bags beneath his eyes. Skin a sickly yellow pallor.

Jake was lying on his stomach in the bathtub. His arms were held stiff at his sides, his toes were curled up far too tightly, so that his feet resembled hooves, or trotters. He'd taken off all of his clothes apart from his boxer shorts, which had ridden up his thighs as he'd lain down in the tub.

"Oh..." It was all Carl could say. "Oh... my boy."

"I've gone away," said Jake in a strangely calm, hushed voice.

First Polly. Now Jake.

Alice... what about Alice?

Carl ran from the bathroom, catching his shoulder on the edge of the door but not feeling any pain, just a dull collision. Moving fast, he crossed the landing and pushed open the door to Alice's room. The posters on the wall. The stuffed toys on the bed. The small pile of laundry in one corner of the room.

Her bare feet were sticking out from under the end of the bed frame. She wasn't wearing any shoes. Her toes were curled up so tight that they looked as if the bones had broken, crunching into a single, gnarled mass of flesh. A nub at the end of each little foot.

"No... please, not you too—" Carl fell to his knees and shuffled across the carpet, reaching out with shaking hands to grab her bare legs. The skin was ice-cold, her calf muscles were as solid as oak. He tried to pull her out but she was a dead weight. He couldn't budge her even an inch, as if she'd been bolted to the floor.

Her feet. Like cloven hooves. Skin as cold as winter. Muscles as hard and heavy as a broken heart.

"Alice!"

He tugged and he tugged, so damned hard, but still he could not shift her.

Her voice, when it came, was feather-soft, and as quiet as the whisper of a ghost. "Not here," she said.

After he was done weeping, Carl stood and left the room, leaving the door open. He looked in on his son but the boy had not moved. He was still in the bathtub, lying as stiff and unmoving as a carved statue.

As he descended the stairs there was an impatient knocking at the door. He had no idea how long it had been going on. The doorbell rang. It must be Doctor Price, come to try and save them. But that wasn't going to happen. They were beyond saving, each and every one of them. With a sense that this meant more than just him and his family, Carl ghosted into the living room and shut the door behind him.

He looked at the little niche in the corner of the room, the one formed by the edges of the bookshelves, where he'd found Polly hiding—or was she exploring?—what seemed like a hundred years ago.

It looked so safe and quiet, that spot. The perfect place to wait out whatever was coming. Ever so softly, he padded across the room. Ever so quietly, he forced himself into the niche, dislocating his right shoulder as he pushed his way inside, but not even feeling it. Once he was neatly in position, and as his toes began to crack and curl, he waited for the soft, silent darkness to take him.

I IS FOR INFESTATION

Steve Rasnic Tem

"**I** LOVE YOU to pieces," Eric told his daughter. Abby had been missing her mother, and was old enough to understand her mother wasn't coming back. He didn't know how to comfort her; the wrong parent died. His late wife had always known the right thing to say. He kept telling Abby how much he loved her. He didn't know what else to do.

"How many pieces?" She looked dead serious. This was back when his eyes were still working properly, and he could see her so clearly it hurt.

"A million. People have at least a million pieces in them I suppose, depending on how you count."

"I love your million pieces too, Dad."

Abby helped him choose his new home. Because of his deteriorating eyesight Eric needed his daughter to steer him away from anything having serious accessibility or condition issues. He told her the house would be hers soon enough, so she should choose whatever she liked. "Don't talk like that," she said. "You're going to live forever." He didn't contradict her.

It was a one-storey cottage. A bungalow. An "adorable chalet in the American Craftsman tradition." Eric had no idea what any of these terms actually meant, but Abby promised the house was plenty big enough for a single person, without being so big a progressively blind person might get lost or confused. There was even a spare room for a live-in nurse, or for Abby when she visited. He wasn't ready for a caretaker just yet. He expected he never would be. He hoped he would have at least some say in the decision.

Abby said the brick work was impeccable. Not that it mattered to him, but she seemed inordinately pleased by this statement. Sometimes, in certain light conditions, he could barely make out individual bricks, but most of the time he could not.

"Dad, I'm afraid there's a small infestation. Nothing that serious. I've made an appointment with the exterminators, but they can't come by before you move in."

"What *kind* of infestation? Bears, willow trees?"

"Insects, funny man. I don't know what kind. Beetles of some sort I guess, hard, nasty-looking things. Their shells turn colour in the light. Camouflage, I suppose, to protect them from their natural enemies, whoever or whatever they might be. No severe damage though, according to the inspection. More of a nuisance than a threat. They've chewed a little on the west wall of the living room, around the baseboard. I don't think it has to be replaced, just spackled and repainted."

"Sigh. I used to love to spackle." He joked to cover his nervousness. Eric didn't like the idea of bugs, some invisible enemy, feeding on his house, but Abby didn't sound concerned. He would wear shoes inside, or at least hard-soled slippers. The idea of experiencing a crunch beneath one of his bare feet horrified him.

Abby completely supervised the move. His job was to sit quietly in a chair. She had the movers arrange the furniture exactly as he'd had it in his old apartment. That wasn't necessary but he appreciated the thought. The only significant difference was the distance between various items, which did trip him up at first.

"Dad! Are you okay?" When Eric sat down on air instead of his bed Abby was there instantly.

"I'm fine. Stupid mistake. I'll practice and map it out in my head so it won't happen again." She raised his shirt, looking for injury. "Please don't do that. I'll let you know if anything hurts."

"Sorry. I should have asked." They sat for a moment. He figured she was as embarrassed as he. "Dad, I've locked the door to the cellar. It's on the north wall of the kitchen. We don't want you opening that door by mistake. But I've left the key in the lock for the exterminators."

"Thank you for that. I'm not a fan of stairs."

She called him every day at first and dropped in every other. But then she had to go away on business. "The exterminators promise they'll be there next week. You have all the emergency contacts in your cell, right?"

"That I do, and it's been charged. I wouldn't know what to do without it. Enjoy your time away."

"I could always cancel. My boss would understand."

"Don't you dare. That's your career. You weren't like this when I lived in the apartment. I got along fine then. I'll manage even better here."

"I know. I just—"

"Have a little confidence in your old man. If you don't worry I won't."

It was a smallish fib. Eric worried all the time. His was an unstable world. He was not a good blind person, not that he was completely blind, but significantly impaired, some days more than others. The unpredictability was a major issue.

People came to the door several times a week trying to sell him things: siding, better windows, a new roof. He had no idea if he needed those things, so he assumed he did not. Abby would have told him.

Once it was a little girl and her mother selling Girl Scout cookies, at least that's what they said. On the porch they were a short shape and a tall shape, but every few seconds he caught a clear glimpse of a face, a sweet smile.

"I love your *I*," the mother said.

"Pardon me?"

"Your big letter *I* by the front door. We noticed some of the houses have them and some don't. They're from when the neighbourhood was built, aren't they, to help the children with their alphabets? Such a charming idea. You know, I can't think of another street that uses letters instead of numbers for the addresses."

When Abby explained this to him he couldn't get over the fact he now lived in the *eye house*. He gave them a twenty for two boxes and told them to keep the change. It was the only denomination in his wallet.

"You have bugs," the little girl said.

"So I'm told. Why, are some of them out here?"

"There's one on your leg. It's pretty."

He suppressed the urge to beat on his pants. "Well, at least it's pretty." The mother laughed and they left. Eric waited a few minutes then began shaking his legs. He had no idea if he got rid of it.

He sat in his living room all afternoon listening to music and eating cookies. He kept hearing a low buzzing. He thought it might be his radio, but after turning it off the buzzing was still there. It might be his hearing. If so, he didn't want to know. One sensory deprivation at a time was all he could manage.

He took a long nap. Eric looked forward to his daily naps. He had a nightmare about earwigs. Weren't those the bugs who crawled into your ears and chewed through your brain? Maybe he was thinking of something else.

He woke up disoriented, feeling old and infirm. He shouldn't have eaten all those cookies. Abby said too much sugar was bad for his eyesight. Some people had bad hair days. He had bad eye days, and this was one of them.

The light from the windows seemed overly bright. How long had he slept? He staggered into the kitchen and grabbed a can of juice from the fridge. He didn't know what flavour; it was going to be a surprise. But he couldn't find the kitchen chairs. Had they all been moved? Eric worked hard to make his world work for him. Now, overnight, he was inept. He threw his juice in the sink and went back to his bed.

He enjoyed listening to his recorded books, but now he was afraid of whatever sounds they might be masking. The ceiling momentarily came into focus. Millions of cells of colour. It made no sense. Suddenly they broke apart and were everywhere. Afraid the ceiling was about to collapse, Eric climbed out of bed and made his way into the living room. The walls appeared slanted, unmoored. He moved in tiny increments, afraid to fall. If he fell Abby might insist he could no longer live independently.

He sat in a comfortable chair and tried to calm himself. He was just having a difficult day. This would pass and soon he'd feel comfortable in his new home again.

Abby said the infestation was evident on the west wall. But which direction was west? He turned his head until he detected signs of movement. A large blank space, a wall, bubbling with activity. The wall appeared to be melting. Then all motion stopped. He felt immediate relief. But did the motion cease because they could tell he was looking?

He hadn't eaten enough, and what he did eat was mostly sugar. He got up to go into the kitchen again. Whether he could find a chair or not, he would eat some real food, some veggies and a little of the leftover chicken, and water. He would drink lots of water.

But he went in the incorrect direction. He felt himself falling into bed again.

The following morning Eric woke up refreshed. The house's geometry had returned to normal, and he felt oriented in both time and space, calm and ready to meet the day. A good rest made so much difference.

The exterminators arrived an hour later, seemingly without warning, but Eric couldn't be sure. He might have missed their call. He sat at the kitchen table while they worked around him, talking among themselves, using words he was unfamiliar with, including the names of various species and their feeding habits. He tried to tell them about the infestation, but they didn't seem interested. Their faces were mostly a blur. He had a tough time focusing, touching the chairs repeatedly, reassuring himself of their presence and wondering about their disappearance the day before.

They talked around him and rarely to him. He was used to that. He didn't feel insulted by their behaviour. But Abby would have been, on his behalf.

He imagined he was ill-kempt, and it embarrassed him. He couldn't see himself clearly in the mirror, so could only wash himself as best he could, and feel his hair and skin for clues.

"The key to the basement door should be in the lock. At least that's where my daughter left it." A few minutes later he heard their steps tromping down.

He couldn't hear them in the basement. For all he knew they were down there gossiping and eating lunch. Eventually they came back upstairs. He didn't know how many of them there were, four or five? There was an awkward silence while Eric waited for someone to speak.

"There are definite signs of infestation, and we'd recommend some repair and replacement for the sake of structural integrity, but honestly, we couldn't find anything active," a man said. "Nothing at all."

Eric was astonished. "But I've seen, well obviously I can't rely on what I've seen." There was another awkward silence. He could hear boots shuffling. He felt like an idiot. Finally, wanting to get them out of the house, he said, "Just send me a bill, and a summary of findings if you don't mind. My daughter will send you a cheque."

After the exterminators left, Eric half-expected to have no more issues with bugs. When his eyes failed him his imagination often intervened, filling in the gaps. But the experts had just told him there were no bugs, and he expected his imagination to believe them.

Next morning Eric felt warmth on his eyelids, spreading across the rest of his face. He reached for the wall and was relieved when he felt its coolness beneath his hand. Then portions began to disintegrate, bits clinging to his fingers. He opened his eyes and shook his hand. Small, glittery things went flying, and he couldn't say for certainty if these included fragments of his fingers. Some new insanity.

He sat up in bed and twisted around for a better view. The wall possessed thousands of tiny moving parts. Collapse seemed imminent.

The wall leaned dangerously close, ready to topple. He covered himself with his blanket. It made for imperfect protection, but it was better than nothing. He had to call Abby or whoever he could reach. They'd hospitalise him with some mental diagnosis, but what choice did he have?

He reached for his cell on the bedstand, but his bedstand wasn't there. He slid out of bed and went down on his knees and felt around and he found, once again, bits and pieces, scattered and moving. He didn't know if they were from the bedstand, his cell phone, or both. A loud buzzing filled his ears.

Something swarmed across his hand. Panicked, he struggled to his feet and stumbled into the bathroom. He was surrounded by great pulsing blobs of white. One of those blobs was low to the floor and directly in front of him. He began to pee and hoped he wasn't splashing it on the floor. For a moment he thought he saw trees through the wall, as if all the plaster and stud and exterior brick had evaporated.

He left the bathroom hoping to make his way out the front door and across the porch and into the yard, to the sidewalk if he was lucky. He would cry out and his neighbours would come and help him. But something was trifling with his feet.

Eric wasn't wearing his slippers, at least he didn't think so. The floor was in constant motion, sending out tendrils across the bridge of one foot, around the heel of the other. He tried kicking at the movement. The phenomena bent around his kicks. He ran into a wall which went spongy then flowed around him. He was immersed, but not drowning. Could he swim through this?

He wasn't sure where he was in the house, or if he was headed in the right direction. He thought a person of incongruous form might be standing in front of him. "Hello?" he said, but in a blur of movement it went away, perhaps to avoid confrontation.

These *bugs* were inhospitable to his presence, separating as he approached, then gathering to block his way. Their movements were alternately calm and then irate as they crowded around him. He could no longer speculate which patterns suggested specific furnishings in his home. The bugs appeared to have installed themselves into every square centimetre of the house.

At one point Eric thought he might have reached the front door, but he couldn't find the knob, and the doorway itself was impossible to negotiate. It kept altering shape and shrinking into an opening too small for him to access. He stumbled around attempting to acquire a different perspective, but the room remained inchoate, its pieces unsettled. He could have been anywhere. The borders were inexact.

He wasn't sure when it began, but he realised the individual pieces had begun to bite. Once he was aware, the nibbling felt constant. However, each succeeding bite seemed less painful. Perhaps he'd developed a tolerance and would one day become immune. But he was sure he was missing pieces, and some of his pieces weren't him.

He leaned against something. He thought it might be the kitchen counter. He felt around, found a drawer, reached in, and foolishly brought out a knife. He made short, vigorous swings into the surrounding space, but as he stepped away from the counter his legs failed, and he fell. The impact knocked the breath out of him. He screamed. He had impaled his own hand.

He could feel them crawling over the injury and it felt better. When he held his hand up to the light, fingers spread, it looked unusually fuzzy, with pieces of the blurred silhouette falling away. He found the sink and thrust both hands beneath the faucet, letting warm water run over them. The water soothed until his hands felt normal again.

Around him, the house's infrastructure looked seriously compromised. He felt responsible. This was supposed to be Abby's house eventually. He might not have anything left to give her.

He collapsed into the floor, triggering a scatter of movement radiating across the room. He didn't have the energy to pick himself up again. He'd been spread too thin.

This was what dying was like. Fragmentation awaited everyone. People ended broken into their component materials, consumed by natural processes. All the small failures in anatomy and mentality which came with age were meant to prepare you for these final moments of decomposition.

A large shape loomed in front of him, a swollen head, a long body, moving arms and legs. *So, are you the insect queen?* He could only think it. When he tried to speak the question, his tongue didn't seem to be there anymore.

W hen Abby next visited she pounded on the door for several minutes with no answer. She knew her dad wouldn't like it, but she used her key to let herself inside. She scoured the house looking for her father, but she couldn't find him anywhere. There were no signs of a struggle. She hoped he hadn't gone out walking by himself. It wasn't safe.

Usually when she visited her dad she'd find at least a small mess: a jar of jam left out of the refrigerator, some books knocked off a table, clothes on the floor. She expected these small disorders given his poor eyesight. But if anything, the house appeared to be in perfect order.

Except for the bugs. The exterminators must not have come. She saw the beetles crawling over the walls of the living room as she came in—many more than had been there before. In the kitchen they squirmed out of the wallpaper seams. In her dad's bedroom they were invisible, but she could hear them—what?—

eating? She detected movement in her peripheral vision, but nothing revealed itself when she turned her head.

"Dad!" He didn't answer, but if she wasn't mistaken there was a slight increase in the volume and intensity of the noise.

THE FIRE GHOST

Gail-Nina Anderson

O LD BILL'S SHED had long since passed into local folklore, not to say myth and legend. Since his death the previous year it had acquired that air of dilapidation which inevitably accompanies emptiness, but in its heyday it held a charm it probably takes a small boy to appreciate. Not that we were ever invited inside, or even knew for sure what Bill did in there during the hours he could steal from his carpentry firm and his neat, well-run family home. But it was rumoured to contain everything from home-made fireworks to mantraps. Like Bill, it seemed to represent a repository of arcane knowledge ranging from local history to recipes for rat poison. It also had the rare distinction of never being vandalised by the neighbourhood kids—the mantrap rumours might account for this.

Since Bill's family had first moved there, the estate—with its unassuming houses but surprisingly generous back gardens—had gone up in the world. And the shed had, too. To please Mrs Bill an extension had been added to the back of the house, and at the same time the shed had acquired an electricity supply which did away with the romantic fumes of the paraffin heater. Far from destroying its mystery, however, the modernisation of Bill's retreat only extended the alchemical range of what he could create, transform or investigate. He produced flyers for local jumble sales, took photographs good enough to get into the local paper, ran a mysterious side-line in TV aerials (and latterly satellite dishes) and became an expert on home composting.

Even the ghost scandal didn't slow down his taste for messing about in *That Out-house*, as his wife called it, although he could never be drawn to talk about it. His wife was dead by then, a son had taken over the business, and when not in his shed Bill spent more and more time browsing the archives in the local library, where a heart attack finally took him with merciful suddenness.

His home was now occupied by his unmarried daughter Margaret, who had kept house for him after her mother's death— perhaps the last generation of daughters to see this as their ultimate career path. She was not much older than me. I could remember her as a dumpy girl of immense authority who took charge of ushering small, grubby boys into the darkened garden on suitably ceremonial occasions to see Bill's not-quite-legal firework display, or to admire the Christmas decorations which regularly outshone any municipal efforts. Not least in their eclectic iconography.

At a suitable age I'd drunk in these delights but I had never been inside the shed itself. My mental image of it varied between a scrap-and-bone yard and a laboratory. Now, however, I was on a quest which, I told myself, was all in aid of local identity, a term Bill would never have used but a concept he artlessly embodied. Besides, when Margaret had agreed to see us she had mentioned the possibility of moving soon, so its days of hermetic mystery were numbered.

"It's the convenience," said Margaret from the kitchen, as though she had read my thoughts. "This house has more rooms than I care to dust, and I never liked that bumpy wallpaper he was so fond of."

I could see her point. Never one to leave a surface unadorned, Bill had woodchipped and Anaglypta-ed the walls so thickly that the rooms must have grown perceptibly smaller.

"But if you want to know anything about what he did in there, there's not much I can tell you."

She had emerged from the kitchen with mugs of instant coffee in both hands. Not exactly a domestic goddess, Margaret was of the opinion that the best of anything was sold in the supermarket ready for consumption, thus missing out several tedious stages of preparation. She *liked* instant coffee, preferring it to that *caffe* stuff. She also liked sliced bread, oven chips and polyester slacks. She was possibly the last woman in the world to make a point of purchasing *slacks*.

What she didn't like was fuss, mess and dirt. For someone who made a point of cooking so little she managed to spend a remarkable amount of her time up to her elbows in a sink of soapy water. I could well understand why the shed held no allure for her. She and her father had shared a mutual accord based on respecting their differences, their affection undemonstrative to the point of invisibility.

Gerard chipped in before I could even pretend to sip the ghastly coffee. It was, after all, his project. He was the man from the Tourist Office with a mission to make the town visible, interesting, and worth spending money in. *I* was the one with childhood connections to the estate; I had been unwittingly involved in *the incident*, and I represented a handy connection to the local newspaper—although Margaret may have had good reason to resent this last.

"But do you mind *talking* about it? Your father was a real character. People like that help create the sort of local identity we can market..."

"You do know, don't you," interrupted Margaret, "that it was all *disproved*? Just one of Dad's little tricks. Should have been a conjuror, my mother always said. Liked making something out of nothing—and what he made was a whole lot of unnecessary fuss. Anyway, you've got access to the newspaper files—" (glaring at me, beetle-browed) "—so I should think you know all there is to know. It was a fake, that's the point. Why on earth do you want to publicise it now? It was a bit of wishful thinking—now you see her, now you don't."

If this was a film, here would be the place for the fuzzy screen heralding a flash-back. Leave Gerard spinning the usual spiel about local economy, local interest, guided tours, coach trips, postcards, publications, and instead let my memory take over. That, after all, was why we were here, to market a memory.

Back in the early 1990s, when home computers were much rarer and cameras tended not to be digital, there had been a disastrous fire in the town. It happened during a quiet evening, from no known cause, but through the windows of the old Town Hall an ominously flickering orange light had been observed and the place was quickly ablaze. It wasn't, let me admit, a huge cause for distress. The building, a late Victorian edifice whose architectural style could most kindly be described as *municipal*, stood back from the street with enough space around it to prevent the flames from spreading. Much of its business and documentation had been transferred to a more convenient (and even uglier) modern replacement a few streets away, and it was, frankly, a white elephant. Impossible to demolish and difficult to re-use. Just before its fiery demise there had been a proposal to turn it into a heritage centre, but it was enough of a liability not to be mourned.

Fires attract audiences and when the word spread through the estate Bill wasn't the only person who hurried to the scene. By the time he got there the fire brigade was in control and there was little to do. There was no sign that anyone had been inside, and although the old building was doomed and already collapsing in on itself, the blaze was contained and the disaster became a spectacle. Bill had his camera—he said later that he must have picked it up automatically, couldn't remember thinking about it—and started snapping. He got closer to the building than was wise or permitted to anyone else—no doubt he knew the firemen—and took some remarkable shots of the swiftly spreading destruction. Doors had burned away, walls fell, and even from outside you could see the interior structure uncannily revealed, then half-hidden by the encroachment of smoke and flame.

Just *how* remarkable Bill's pictures were became apparent only when he developed the film. It just appeared in one shot but there could be no doubt about it—at the top of a staircase was the figure of a girl. Now, as a reporter I know all too well our human propensity for identification—smudges and shadows will become faces if you look at them for long enough. But here there really seemed no room for doubt, even though she was indistinct, standing behind a railing and seen from below through veils of smoke. Even so, it would surely have taken a coincidence beyond belief for random marks to conjoin into anything so specific.

She didn't look modern, but it would be difficult to date her. Not a small child but not a young woman. She had hair hanging onto her shoulders and a soft fabric hat, perhaps with a scalloped brim. All you could see of her clothes seemed to reveal a high-necked dress with a paler pinafore over it—standard girls' dress for decades. The angle of the shot hid her feet. And she didn't look at all afraid—her features were just blocks of grey shadow under the hat—but she wasn't moving or gesturing ... or screaming. Bill hadn't seen her—no-one had. There were no human remains found in the wreckage and no-one was reported missing that night.

She really was the perfect ghost, a silent witness shimmering unobserved onto film, conjured from smoke and flame; timeless, forlorn. The only trouble was that she came without a history.

Not that she stayed in her undocumented state for long. Word soon spread and Bill was hardly averse to his role at the centre of the mystery. Every other amateur photographer, historian or folklorist—not to mention newspapers, TV and radio stations—encouraged the speculation; uncovering, remembering, possibly inventing the stories that came to cocoon the fire girl.

"What I never understood," said Margaret, displaying again that curious instinct for cutting in on your unspoken thoughts, "was the way that as soon as anyone saw the photo, they had a bloody story."

Gerard jumped in, right on cue. "But that's exactly what I'm talking about. It's as though people *need* ghosts. It doesn't matter whether your father's photo was faked—and he never admitted it was—it filled a *need*. It attracted stories. Which is just what I'm asking you to help us do. If we can talk about the ghost picture then that gives us the first story, the start to promoting an appealing range of local narratives. With your permission of course, we might even reproduce Bill's original photo as a postcard."

"Or on a fridge magnet," Margaret chipped in.

Was she being sarcastic? No, she was leaning forward, suddenly alert to Gerard's bright young face and floppy hair, drinking in his words. He was certainly in the right job, selling nothing as something, embodying it with all the allure of a good window display.

"Anything. That photo could be our emblem," he agreed, relaxing now he saw he had her on the hook. He was a consummate professional when it came to volunteers—his world ran on them. Middle-aged women, time on their hands, wanting to feel useful and involved, to belong in some way. I knew Margaret already worked part-time at a charity shop but archiving documents or stacking bookshelves would suit her perfectly. Organising history neatly into place and knowing that her father had been part of it. And the ghost girl. With a bit of polish Margaret might even make a competent guide. She liked making things clear.

And there would be another advantage. Following the appearance of the ghost photo there had been a bit of a shadow around her father. The shed wasn't just for fireworks and mantraps. There was always a genuine sense of the conjuror about Bill and suddenly the trick had looked a little dangerous. Whether or not he had conjured her up, the image of the ghost girl itself acted as a lodestone, summoning fragments of the past, yet never quite connecting them—spinning tempting, shimmering threads that could never be woven into a complete story. I wonder now if that was the intention.

First someone remembered the tale of a thatched cottage which had burned to the ground after the daughter of the family had accidentally overturned a lamp—but that had surely been a century or so too early and had no clear connection with the town hall. Then there was the councillor's young daughter who went missing in 1900, a tempting mystery unsolved but well documented in the newspapers of the time. And when the rubble of the town hall had been removed after the fire (before a new supermarket had replaced it) an old brooch had been found hidden among the foundations, a blackened metal oval engraved in italic script with the word *Hope*. It could have been a message, a moral, or a name—although disappointingly not the name of the councillor's daughter. It could have been a token pinned to the blanket of an abandoned child, or a trinket filched by a young thief, or...

"Oh, I know the old stories," Margaret was saying, "and a few you probably don't. Dad went on looking for them the rest of his life. Like a magician, you see—he'd pulled the rabbit out of the hat but then someone—" (looking meaningfully at me) "—had seen how he did it. You're not supposed to reveal the mechanics; that's the point of the trick, something out of nothing. And whatever everyone thought, Dad still seemed determined to... well, convince himself there really *were* rabbits that could be pulled out of hats. And that's the bit I'm having trouble with. I mean, I can see how the stories might get people interested and I can see that the photo, whatever it is, does attract people so they want to know more. But thanks to Mr Investigator here, we *do* actually know where it all came from. However many tales we care to spin, we now know that the ghost girl was really just Dad's little trick."

I smiled, setting down the mug of untouched coffee. I could see she itched to instantly clear it away. Neat and tidy and sorted. Surprisingly good at seeing how things might fit together, she'd do well at organising her stories and reminiscences, although every tale she told would have to be boxed and labelled, and preferably sealed firmly at the end. Unlike her father, she shunned the clutter of unfathomable possibilities.

Before I could try the old soft soap, the flannel known to every journalist, Gerard had chipped in. "Well, I do realise the role James here played in..." (he searched for a word) "*investigating* the nature of Bill's photo might not suggest him as the perfect *collaborator* on this project but any new..." (he thought again) "...*heritage* venture really will need the help of the press."

I could see the term had been well chosen. Margaret was nodding happily. *Heritage,* with its overtones of costume drama and historical worth. The neighbourhood legends of the shed, repository of *Boy's Own* handicrafts, reclaimed fragments, and latterly that mysterious image, were being transformed into part of our *heritage;* and the unmasking of the conjuror's rabbit, as it were, could take its rightful place as an anecdote, tagged as something like *Trickster: Old Bill. Cross reference to Local Customs: Bonfire Night, Crafts, Carpentry, Photography. History: Town Hall.*

"I suppose it *was* your job," Margaret conceded, avoiding looking at me as she tidied the table.

But really it *wasn't*. It had happened a couple of years after the fire—and the photo. Working on our singularly unexciting local paper, in between the wedding photos, adverts for used pushchairs, and pictures of ballet class galas and amateur pantomimes, I used to concoct the *Byways and Bygones* page. It wasn't an unpleasant task—local history lite. Find an old photo (plenty of suitable files in the library, or from our own cabinets), publish it with a garnish of speculation and with luck the next week's page would be half-filled by reader responses, mostly personal reminiscences of what or wherever you had shown. The tone was hardly meant to be challenging—more reassuring, with an obvious appeal to older readers, gently nudging the memory. (And oh yes, back issues of this feature would undoubtedly come in very handy as Gerard and his helpers repackaged the town's history for wider consumption; lots of little stories, lots of disclosures as to what had been where.) But my involvement with the ghost girl had been quite accidental. Back then, I could recall, there had simply been a boring week when I'd had to fall back on the last-resort recourse of an old postcard borrowed from a box labelled STREETS—HISTORY in the library's local studies collection. Far from being inspiring, it was the sort of card that made you wonder exactly who decided it was worth photographing and publishing. Or for that matter, buying and sending. Over the

passage of time, however, its very matter-of-factness had given it
an inconsequential appeal. The legend printed beneath the picture
said it all: NORTH STREET—WEST END. On the back someone had
pencilled the date *1920*. I'd have guessed it showed an earlier year,
but provincial fashions moved slowly then so it displayed no sense
of modernity or speed. All it showed was a curving road with one
visible pavement, a row of shops, and a few people uninterested in
the camera. There hadn't even been an attempt to find any gem of
architectural history or municipal pride. The street chosen wasn't
anywhere near a church, the town wall or, for that matter, the
Town Hall. Perhaps it was taken early on a summer's morning as
one man, wearing a long striped apron, seemed to be opening the
shutters on his shop. He looked to be the most engaging detail of
the scene, and indeed I can remember a correspondent writing in
to identify him as their grandfather, a butcher. I doubt that
unsensational letter ever saw print though, because several others
spotted something much more arresting, which I had failed to
pick up on.

Closest to the camera, the postcard showed a group of children,
two playing on the pavement, one turning to look back down the
street and one—the only person to do so—gazing at the camera.
She was the Town Hall fire ghost, the mysterious figure glimpsed
through the smoke. Sharper on the postcard, you could see her
hair, her white pinafore buttoned down the side, her skirt not
quite reaching the ankles, the flat, dark boots below. And it wasn't
just that the fire ghost *resembled* her—it's all too easy to find such
similarities when you really want them—it was *exactly* the same
figure. Motionless but unposed, hands held loosely in front of her,
head oddly erect. The fall of the shadows across her face from the
soft cloth hat was the same, the folds in her sleeves ... Oh yes, Bill's
photograph had etched itself nicely into enough minds to trigger
instant recognition. His ghost girl had been lifted from an old
postcard (he needn't even have borrowed the library copy I had
used—postcards are common currency and just the sort of thing
to find their way into the shed). He'd pulled it off—a trick, a
firework display, a rabbit out of a hat!

The revelation triggered an amount of mystification as to

motive, some embarrassment at being fooled, some offence at the truth being manipulated. No-one doubted his ability to have done it, though. The story wasn't the *ghost* any longer, but Bill's trick, and it had long since faded into an amusing anecdote recalled with a smile at his funeral.

Margaret, perhaps looking a little more kindly towards me now that Gerard's words suggested we might be working together towards, I suppose, the common good, mused on the effect of my unintended de-bunking. "One thing that postcard *did* solve: it explained why he'd photographed the town hall fire in black and white. I always wondered about that. Of course, it wouldn't fool anyone now—computers, camera phones—you can download ghosts and fit them into anything you like!"

"And that," said Gerard as we rose to go, "is a brilliant idea. We could market the ghost girl as an app, the all-purpose spook suitable for downloading into your holiday snaps."

Margaret was smiling—she obviously enjoyed this rewrapping of family eccentricity in modern covers. She was on board; her father's fire ghost was reinstated in a shape she could appreciate, and she had a role to play.

"I can come into your office tomorrow if you like. I might be able to bring Dad's original photo to show you. I'm pretty sure he kept it."

This was disingenuous. She had already sorted through all his things, judged the picture worth holding onto, and would be able to put her hand on it immediately.

Knowing this perfectly well, Gerard made the inevitable request. "I don't suppose you found any negatives?"

Margaret grinned. "Not a chance. Dad might have enjoyed his little joke but he wasn't daft. You'll still have to work out exactly *how* he did it, pre-digital technology."

I don't know if I was relieved when Gerard asked his final question, not sure whether I'd been avoiding it, or might have been about to ask it myself. "And the old postcard of North Street, the one with the original figure of the girl on. Did he keep a copy of that?"

She shook her head. "I wondered if it would come to light. I've been clearing the shed where he kept a lot of old cards and I couldn't find it anywhere."

I knew no-one would find it in the library either. Not even in the STREETS—HISTORY box to which I had conscientiously returned it years ago, immediately after the newspaper had so innocently published it. After all, it was its reproduction in the paper to which readers had responded, so I hadn't given the postcard itself another thought.

Until, that was, I first found myself involved in Gerard's campaign to market the town via stories, scenery, traditions and images. Then, of course, I went looking for the original card, not sure if the grainy reproduction from our old newspaper files would be worth scanning.

And yes, I stole it—spirited it away, so to speak. Because in the library I found the box and I found the card. What I didn't find was the girl. It was exactly the same view, every figure as described: the butcher at his shop, three children in the foreground, none of them looking at the camera. But there was no sign of the solemn girl in the hat and pinafore—no sign she had ever been there. And when I came to think about it, I could no longer recall whether I had noticed her *before* I saw the card reproduced in *Byways and Bygones*, when she appeared on the page under my prose.

I've begun to see her now as the thing which slips in between the pages and triggers the stories. She sparked the tale of the missing daughter, the girl in the burning cottage—even the tale of Bill's ghost photo. But unlike a character in one of Gerard or Margaret's neatly turned episodes of local interest, she doesn't yet have a fixed identity, a beginning, a conclusion. Not even a magician really conjures something out of *nothing*, so I suspect she's still out there, waiting in the wings for the next trick that will reveal her.

BEGBROOK

Tim Jeffreys

EVER SINCE I was a little girl I'd been told to stay away from Begbrook Woods. Not that I would've thought of going there, at least not at that age. The woods stood on the outskirts of the village, too far from our sleepy streets to hold any attraction for me or any of my friends. A boy in my class at Beech Hill Primary, Dylan Jones, claimed to have once ridden his bike out to Begbrook, gone in, and seen the ghosts of German soldiers from World War II moving among the trees. But none of us believed that. Instinctively, I think we all understood it wasn't ghosts or witches or anything else supernatural that occupied the woods. It was something different. Something not entirely uninviting. Driving our car past the entrance to the woods on our way out of the village, Dad would slow down. Whenever he did this, Mum got an anxious look on her face, and would reach over and place her hand atop one of his.

"Rich," she'd say, a wavering, tip-toeing tone to her voice, "what're you slowing down for?"

I had a sense that the woods held some kind of spell over him. Something that made Mum afraid, like an old girlfriend he hadn't quite got over. A dilapidated cottage stood at the entrance to the woods, set far back from the road, as if it had been picked up in a storm and deposited there—like Dorothy's house in *The Wizard of Oz*. People in the village, including my parents, referred to this cottage as "the squat" because sometimes people were seen living there. *Transients*, my dad called them. He told me Begbrook attracted the wrong type of people, and that was why I must never go there, because I wasn't like them, because I was a good girl.

Sometimes Dad slowed the car almost to a stop, so that Mum raised her voice to him. "*Rich.*"

He'd shake his head then, as if coming out of a trance, glance irritably at her, and say, "I was just looking." Then he'd press his foot so hard on the accelerator that the tyres screeched, and Mum would yell at him. It was as if he thought the woods would pull him in, pull us all in, if he didn't get us away from there as fast as he could.

When the time came for me to choose a secondary school, Dad wanted me to go to Oakdale Academy in Glensdale, the nearby town. That meant either he or Mum would have to drive me there every day. I didn't like the sound of that. Neither did Mum. She'd started a new part-time job at the doctor's surgery and had enough to do, she said, without having to drive me back and forth to school every day. Dad said in that case I could catch the bus.

All my friends were going to Braysdown, our village's small secondary school, and that was where I wanted to go, too. I could walk there. But Dad insisted I go to Glensdale. He wouldn't give a reason, but I overheard him telling Mum one evening that Braysdown was too close to Begbrook Woods. He said he'd heard that some of the older kids from Braysdown went into the woods after school. He said he'd seen them himself the previous summer, leaving the woods at eight or nine in the evening, walking single file along the embankment on their way home, sometimes staggering around like they were drunk. "And God knows what their parents are thinking," he said, "allowing that."

"Perhaps it's not there anymore," Mum said, and my ears pricked up. *It*? What was *it*? "Perhaps it dried up."

"It's there," Dad said. "Two drowned last year. Another the year before. You know as well as I do."

Now I was intrigued. Drowned? In the woods? What was there to drown in? In Begbrook?

I knew there was no point arguing. Dad had set his mind on me going to Oakdale and that was the end of it. Mum said I would make new friends. And maybe that was for the best, she added.

As it turned out, it wasn't that easy. The kids in my class at Oakdale all knew each other from primary, and their social circles were set. My first term at Oakdale was a lonely one. In desperation I started hanging out with a girl called Charlie Gallagher, the class troublemaker. The other kids avoided Charlie. We'd been told she suffered from something called intermittent explosive disorder. It wasn't her fault, our teacher, Miss Beckett, explained, but every now and then Charlie would get into a rage and turn over her desk or start throwing chairs around the classroom. At the first sign of anything like this, Miss Beckett would clap her hands at the rest of us and make us file out quickly into the corridor, where we had to wait until Charlie had either calmed down or been sent home.

At break, Charlie and I would sit on the side-lines, watching the other kids run around.

"Seen you waiting for the bus some days after school," Charlie said to me one day. "You from Critchill, ain't you?"

"Yes."

"Why don't you go to school there?"

"My dad wouldn't let me."

She turned to me. Her eyes were like the sky on a dreary day. She had freckles on the bridge of her nose. A permanent furrow on her brow. Her face wasn't the face of a child. There was something hard there. "Why?"

I thought a moment. "Because near the school there're some woods and he's afraid of them."

"Afraid of the woods?"

"Yes. There's something in the woods. A...a lake or something. And people have drowned in it."

Charlie's eyes brightened with interest. "We should go there. Have a look."

I don't know why, but my heart began to beat fast when she said that. "No. No, I can't. I'm not allowed."

"What do you mean, you're not allowed?"

"I've been told to stay away from there."

Charlie gave a little snort. "Chicken," she said, and looked away.

That same afternoon, Charlie went into one of her rages. Watching through the window in the classroom door after the rest of us had hurried out, I felt bad for her. She stood in the middle of the room, red-faced and making grunting sounds along with her breathing. I wondered what made Charlie so angry.

I felt bad for Miss Beckett too, for having to stay in the room and try to calm Charlie down. She looked out of her depth.

During the Christmas holiday Mum let me get my ears pierced, and when I returned to school in January, suddenly the girls in my class wanted to talk to me. Soon I had my own clique, and I no longer sat with Charlie Gallagher at break and lunchtime. I sometimes felt a twinge of guilt when I saw her sitting alone, and once even asked my new friends if she could join us. They looked horrified at this suggestion and shook their heads, so that was the end of that. Charlie didn't seem to mind being alone. I got the impression she preferred it that way. Or maybe I imagined it to stop myself from feeling bad.

Towards the end of the year, Miss Beckett paired us all up for an IT lesson because the school didn't have enough computers for us to have one each. I was paired with Charlie. By then, I hadn't spoken to Charlie for a long time, and I hadn't thought much about her either, except when her explosive rages disrupted our lessons, something that happened less and less frequently.

I began working through the textbook, but Charlie showed no interest. There was something different about her face, something I couldn't quite identify. Her expression had softened. Her eyes seemed always to be half-closed, as if she were on the verge of falling asleep. I wondered if she was on some kind of medication, like the hay fever tablets Mum took in the summer. They made her drowsy and she couldn't drive, she said, when she was taking them.

"Remember those woods you told me about?" Charlie said. "Over in Critchill?"

I looked up from the textbook. "Begbrook?"

"Yeah." Charlie nodded, smiling. "Begbrook. I went there, you know."

"Did you?"

"Yeah. Been loads of times, actually. You know what's there?"

I tried to draw Charlie's attention back to the textbook. It wasn't that I didn't want to know what was there, what she'd found. I did. But I was afraid.

"It's not a lake," Charlie said. "It's just a kind of pool. It's not that big, but it's deep. And you can swim in it."

"Swim?"

"Yeah. And you know what the most amazing thing is?"

I looked around for Miss Beckett, trying to catch her eye. I hoped she'd notice that we weren't studying and say something. But she was talking to some of the boys and had her back to us.

"You know what the most amazing thing is, Abby?" Charlie said again. She stared at me intently.

"What?"

"The water's warm."

"Warm?"

"Yeah. Warm. And you know what else? It makes you feel great when you're in there. Like, really great. All the bad things in your mind just kind of float away."

"I don't have bad things in my mind, Charlie."

"Course you do. Everyone does. But when you're in that water, all you can think about are happy things. And you feel so good you never want to get out."

I began to get a sense that Charlie was pulling my leg. Maybe this was her revenge for the way I'd abandoned her. "How can the water be warm? That doesn't make sense."

"You don't believe me?"

"If there's water there, and if it's deep, it should be freezing cold."

"It's warm, I'm telling you. Want me to take you there?"

"I—"

"Charlie? Abigail?" At last Miss Beckett had noticed us. "More work, less chit-chat, please."

"Yes, Miss."

"I'll show you if you don't believe me," Charlie hissed.

I shook my head, thinking of the way Dad slowed the car when he drove past the entrance to Begbrook, the worried look on Mum's face when he did.

"No."

After the Easter holidays Charlie didn't return to school. Someone told me she'd moved away; and one of the boys— Jack Boyle, I think it was—claimed she'd been taken into care. Then for a few days there was a rumour going around class that Charlie was dead. No one knew if this was true or not. Miss Beckett overheard my friends and me talking about it and shouted at us. She said if we ever mentioned the name Charlie Gallagher again we'd all get a week's detention.

So Charlie was gone. I still thought about her. I thought about what she'd told me when we'd been paired up for that IT lesson. What she'd claimed to have discovered in Begbrook Woods.

It's not a lake. It's just a kind of pool. It's not that big, but it's deep. And you can swim in it.

The water's warm. All the bad things in your mind just kind of float away.

Could it be true?

I'd told Charlie I didn't have bad things in my mind.

But that was a lie.

My parents were fighting. Dad was home a lot in the mornings when I was getting ready for school. Normally he left early for work. When I got home from school he was gone, and often I'd be in bed before he returned.

I heard my parents arguing one night as I tried to sleep. I couldn't make out much, but at one point I definitely heard Mum say, "You've been back there, haven't you? Tell the truth."

One Saturday morning in June I met my two closest school friends, Marie Johnson and Star Moffett, at the bus stop, and we walked to Begbrook Woods. We had our swimming costumes in drawstring bags slung over our shoulders, but we didn't talk about what we were hoping to do that day, what we were hoping to find. We talked about other things: boys we liked, our teachers, clothes we wanted our parents to buy for us. Anything. Jittery with excitement and fear and apprehension, we talked non-stop, talking over each other, for the entire twenty minutes or so it took to reach Begbrook. When we arrived at the place where that abandoned cottage stood at the entrance to the woods we fell silent. A few days earlier I'd told Marie and Star about what Charlie Gallagher had said to me. About the pool. They both agreed we had to see it for ourselves.

We followed a trodden path into the woods. I'd expected to find Begbrook creepy, but that wasn't the case. The sun was out, slanting through the branches. The woods had a magical quality that left me mute and spellbound. The others too.

Marie was the first to speak. "You've seriously never been here before, Abby?"

"Not once."

"If I lived in Critchill, I'd come here all the time."

"Me too," Star said. "It's lovely."

I had to agree. "How are we going to find the pool? If it really exists."

"I think this path will lead us straight to it," Marie said. "It has to. Right?"

The path snaked ahead of us. Deeper into Begbrook.

"Suppose we'll find out."

I'd imagined the pool, if it really existed, as a pleasant little natural pond shaded by trees, with reeds around its edge and water lilies floating on its surface. What we found was not that. The path led us to a clearing where there was a flat area of trodden earth. At the centre of this was the pool. It wasn't very wide, just as Charlie had described, but it was perfectly circular, and you could tell, standing on its edge, that the water went deep. It made me think of sinkholes, and I imagined it was so deep it reached the centre of the earth, though I knew that was impossible.

Star was the first to crouch and put a hand in the water.

"Oh my God," she said. "It's true. The water's warm."

"You're kidding?" Marie crouched beside Star and dipped her fingers. "Oh, wow. Feel it, Abby."

Part of me wanted to turn back and go home. What were we doing there? What would my parents say if they could see us?

I bent and placed one hand into the water. My friends hadn't been lying, it was wonderfully warm.

In a flurry of activity then, Marie and Star shed clothes and pulled towels and swimming costumes out of their bags, laughing in a nervous way as they did.

"Are we actually gonna get in there?" I said.

"Of course," Star said. "It's what we came for, isn't it?"

"I thought we came just to look. To see if Charlie had been telling the truth."

But if I believed that, why had I brought my swimming costume? Why had I told the others to bring one?

Marie laughed. "You're joking? Right?"

They were quickly changed and tiptoeing to the edge of the pool. I watched as they play-fought and dared each other to jump in. Marie went first. The splash as she hit the water seemed so loud I looked around as if I thought the entire wood was alerted and watching us. There was a second splash as Star joined Marie. They doggy-paddled for a while, before floating on their backs, eyes closed, the sun on their faces.

"How's the water?"

"Oh, Abby," Marie said, in a dreamy voice. "It's heaven."

"Abby, you have to feel this," Star said. "It's the best. It feels just how Charlie said it would."

I didn't waste any more time. I stripped and pulled on my swimming costume. I, too, was soon floating in that warm bath.

I'm not sure I can describe what it was like to be in that pool. It was like being a baby again, wrapped in a blanket and held in your mother's arms. I felt I no longer had any worries, not about schoolwork, or spots, or the fact that my parents were fighting, or about being accepted. That water accepted me and that was the only acceptance I needed. It was bliss. Euphoria. As Charlie had said, once you were in you never wanted to get out. I don't know how long we floated there, the three of us, on our backs. We might have floated there all day and all night if Star hadn't let out a little scream.

The sound alarmed me so much that for a few seconds I struggled to stay afloat. The thought passed through my mind that I was going to drown. I panicked, slapping my arms at the water, and managed to get my head up.

"What is it?" I was breathing heavily, gasping for air.

Star looked scared. "Something grabbed my foot."

"What?"

"I felt it. A hand or something. It grabbed my foot."

The three of us stared at each other, then down into the black depths below our pale, shimmering feet.

Then Marie screamed. "There's something in here!"

That was all it took. Suddenly we were thrashing to the edge of the pool and hauling ourselves up onto the bank. We stood as close to the edge as we dared, shivering and peering into the pool.

"See something?" I said to the others.

"No," Marie said. "But I felt it. It grabbed my ankle."

"Let's get the heck away from here."

Gathering up our clothes, we hurried out of that clearing as fast as we could, not bothering to change until we'd almost reached the old cottage. I noticed that my fingertips were wrinkled. I hadn't noticed time passing. It was beginning to get dark. How long had we been floating on our backs in that pool?

"I'm never coming back here," Star said, throwing me a hateful glance as if I were to blame for having told her about it.

"Me neither," Marie said, giving me the same look.

They were already dressed. Putting their backs to me, they left me alone to finish changing. I glanced back along the path, imagining I heard a voice calling. Charlie Gallagher's voice, saying, *Come back, Abby. All the bad things in your mind just float away.*

After that day, Marie and Star avoided me at school. They no longer joined in with our group at break but would huddle together in a corner of the yard, talking in subdued voices. I began to imagine they were gossiping about me, so one day I confronted them. For the first time I noticed how their faces had changed. They had the same sleepy-eyed expression Charlie Gallagher had when we worked together on that IT project.

"You two haven't been back there, have you?"

You've been back there, haven't you? Tell the truth.

They glared at me in contempt.

"What're you talking about?"

"Have you been back to that pool? In Begbrook?"

"What's it got to do with you?"

"You shouldn't go there. It's dangerous."

They both laughed.

"You said something grabbed your foot."

"Yes," Star said. "And when it does, we know it's time to get out."

"Usually," Marie said, and sniggered behind her hand.

"You mean you *are* going back there? You're crazy."

"Forgive me, Miss Goody-two-shoes," Star said, "but it's the best feeling I ever had in my life. Why wouldn't we go back?"

"Because there's something down there. Down there in that water."

They both shrugged. I shook my head in disbelief and walked away.

By the time school broke up for summer holidays, a tense atmosphere had taken root at home. My parents hardly spoke to each other. Dad had lost his job at the dairy for taking too many sick days, which meant Mum had to ask for more hours at the doctor's surgery. She was tired and irritable a lot of the time.

One day I got up early and, without having planned to, found myself walking the main road out of the village, towards Begbrook. I didn't have my swimming costume with me, so I'd no intention of getting into that pool again. At least that was what I told myself. I followed that trodden path through the woods. Before reaching the clearing where the pool was, I heard water splashing. Creeping closer, and peering through the trees, my breath caught when I saw a man in the pool. His bare shoulders sparkled with water, and he was laughing. It took me only a few seconds to recognise him.

Dad.

I wanted to call out to him but didn't dare. Instead I turned and ran back along the path. I didn't stop running until I was clear of the woods.

A few days later I was sitting with Dad at the kitchen table, eating breakfast while he drank coffee, both of us silent, lost in our own thoughts, when Mum came in and slapped the local newspaper down in front of him.

"That's another two it's taken."

I got a cold feeling in my belly. That word Mum used, "taken", stayed with me for a long time after.

Mum left for work without another word, making the front door slam.

"What's that?" I asked, but Dad shook his head and wouldn't show me the newspaper. I thought about saying, *Dad, I saw you. Dad, why do you go there? Dad, don't you know there's something down there? Down deep in that water? Dad?*

When school started again I noticed that both Star and Marie were missing. Jack Boyle, who always seemed to know everything, told me that during the holidays Marie had drowned in the woods in Critchill. Begbrook Woods. Star, he said, had simply disappeared, although her clothes had been found in a pile next to Marie's.

"It was in the local paper. Didn't you see it?"

"No."

"There's a lake or something in those woods," Jack said. "A few of us are thinking to go and have a look at it. You wanna come along, Abby?"

"What?"

"I've heard you can go swimming. We're all going."

"All? When?"

"This Saturday. Want to come?"

It's the best feeling I ever had in my life. Why wouldn't we go back?

"Sure," I heard myself say. "Sure. I'll come."

ECHOES, DYING

Marion Pitman

THE ROOM WAS satisfactorily crowded with well-known authors, prestigious editors, agents, reviewers, journalists, and various lesser lights who had wangled an invitation to schmooze, and drink decent wine at Louise's expense. Or rather at Cruiskeen Lawn's expense, since the publishing house would be footing the bill. Louise threw a party at least once a year, at the end of the spring season, in her spacious Georgian London flat, the market price of which would have kept several small South American countries going for months. There was no given reason for the gathering: people said it was for Louise to see what was happening, and to remind everyone she was still here. The noise level was considerable, and empty wine bottles were already piling up.

Marguerite stood with an old friend, surveying the still arriving guests.

Diana stared across the room: "Is that Georgina Clark? I thought she was dead."

Marguerite followed her look. "She retired three years ago. I wonder what she's doing here?"

"Probably come to see the new sensation!"

"What? Oh! The wunderkind. You think so?"

"Most of Louise's swans are geese, but now and then she gets it right."

"Meow."

Diana laughed.

Louise's new acquisition was the subject of much gossip, even though his first novel had yet to come out. CL, though a relatively small publisher, had acquired it against great opposition and at considerable expense. The author's agent was purring happily, and there was already talk of film and TV rights. He was cordially detested by a great many people who hadn't met him.

There was a rise in the volume of talk near the door. Diana turned that way and said, "Do you think that's him? He's rather pretty."

Marguerite looked towards the young man who had just entered. She gasped, and the room disappeared into darkness and silence.

It had happened frequently to begin with, but now not for several years. There she was back in the middle of it: the moonless night, the biting cold, the trees against the stars, the breathless journey, and the sudden burst of gunfire. Paul's gasp, and fall, and she trying to lift him, then trying to staunch the blood, and eventually the desperate attempt to hide his body, and running, and running, and running, and finally reaching the hotel, and the shock wearing off, and crying and crying for hours…

She blinked, and was back at the party. She looked at the young man again. He appeared to be about twenty-three, at least five years younger than Paul was when she had first met him, more than thirty years before. Other than that, he looked identical. The wavy yellow hair, the sharp nose and delicate cheekbones, the grey-blue eyes the colour of faded denim, the precisely carved lips. He was about the same height too, with the same wiry build and long, sensitive hands. His dress sense was similar: understated, smart casual, muted colours.

Marguerite murmured something vague to Diana and moved towards the wall, where she leaned a hand on the Edwardian walnut sideboard, afraid of losing her balance or consciousness. Paul was suddenly as vivid in her mind as thirty years ago. The Prague café where she first met him, with the ornate decoration, Art Nouveau-stained glass, elegant angular chairs, the rather startling stuffed boar's head on the wall, and a somewhat worn and shabby air despite the very good coffee and pastries. The soft classical music playing in the background, Paul's face against the flare of sunset through the window, his eyes fathomless, irresistible. Then the touch of his hand the first time they made love; his gentleness; her shock at the long zigzag scar across his chest. The result, he said, of a knife fight in his teens. The feel of the scar as she touched it, fascinated.

She took some deep breaths, staring fixedly at a dish of olives on the sideboard, trying to focus her thoughts. Someone said, "Are you all right?"

Automatically she said, "Yes! Yes, I'm fine," and straightened up. It was a young woman who had spoken. Marguerite knew her, though had no idea of her name, but the words had helped her to return to the present.

She took a breath and told herself her mind was playing tricks. There was a resemblance, obviously, which had triggered the flashback, but closer to the young man would certainly appear quite different. She walked towards him. The resemblance didn't diminish at closer range. She joined the group standing around him, and soon she heard his voice.

When he spoke, she shook, and had to retreat again and grope for a chair. The accent was different, with a touch of West Country overlaid by RP, but the pitch, the timbre, the sound of it was Paul's voice. It threw her back again, she was twenty-five, and they were working together, the adrenaline running high in her blood. As she waited for him at the station she suddenly heard his voice behind her, speaking to a ticket clerk, and at once her mind and body thrilled, and the scene around her became more vivid, the overhead lights brighter, the trains at other platforms more sharply etched, the people near her almost unbearably real...

It passed in a moment, and the young man was still talking. She could not detect anything about him that definitively wasn't Paul. She gathered, after a bit, that he was indeed the new prodigy, that his name was Michael Grainger, and he'd only been down from Oxford for a year. Marguerite repeated to herself that a superficial likeness had caused her memory to misfire, to exaggerate the resemblance. She was seeing him, and not seeing the differences... He seemed a nice boy—at her age all men under thirty were boys—quite modest and unpretentious, slightly dazed by all the attention. She joined the conversation; he smiled at her, and went on talking, and Marguerite firmly suppressed the part of her mind that was seeing Paul.

After the party Marguerite took a cab home in a state of confusion. She had thought that earlier life—so far off, and so alien from her life now—had been successfully dealt with, the lid screwed down. Now here it was again, risen like Dracula from the coffin. Was her subconscious trying to tell her something? Was it simply that Michael Grainger's resemblance to Paul was close enough to prise open the lid? Or did her mind have unfinished business with it all, things she had been ignoring? And how could she finish it, and replace the lid?

She locked the door, turned out the lights and walked upstairs. She went to the large Victorian chest of drawers in her bedroom, opened the deep bottom drawer, and under several layers of bedlinen, blankets and towels she found a small attaché case. She took it to the bed and opened it.

All she had left of that previous life, brief in hindsight but more real than anything since. There were Paul's passport and papers (she had removed all the ID from his body). Her own ID. Madness to keep all the paperwork; she should burn it. A plain silver ring.

A sketch of the snake tattoo on Paul's left arm she had done in an idle moment. A few train tickets, and a hotel brochure. That was all—no, there was a small leather pouch. Heart beating faster, she emptied it out.

Two pendants, each on a leather thong. Carved wooden images, each of a foliate face, a green man. She and Paul had been at a craft fair somewhere and had liked them. She had bought him one, and he bought one for her, choosing them both carefully. They were all slightly different, being hand made, and she knew very well the differences between hers and Paul's, although they were slight—the tilt of the eye and the width of the mouth, and one differently shaped leaf. The wood was stained dark green, the colour of holly leaves.

With a feeling of inviting danger, she nonetheless picked up hers and put the thong over her head. The small green face rested just below the hollow of her throat. She could hide it under a high-necked dress. How would it feel, she wondered, taking this piece of the previous life with her into the present? Only one way to find out. Firmly she put everything else back in the case, and the case in the drawer.

Over the next couple of weeks she grew used to wearing the green man, feeling a little bit of connection to the past, although she kept it hidden and spoke about it to no-one.

Michael Grainger's novel did well, and she met him at several more industry events. They had a good deal in common, despite the age difference, liking the same bands and TV programmes. Marguerite didn't read his novel. She was afraid to. She didn't even read the reviews. She wasn't sure what would be worse—to find she loathed the book, and it revealed him as someone deeply unlikeable, making a mockery of his appearance; or to find it reminded her even more of Paul, and took her back again to the moonless night under the trees, and the pain, and the ache of loss...

Some months later Marguerite's job was the victim of a merger. Against her better judgement she applied for an opening at

CL, got it, and found herself working on Michael Grainger's account. She felt obliged to read the book then, and to her great relief found it neither of the things she'd feared. It was well-written, well-constructed, and she admired it, but it rang no bells and conjured no visions. There seemed to be nothing in Michael's mind that reminded her of Paul, only his physical appearance. She thought she could cope with that.

Once or twice she took out the attaché case and looked at the sketch, the passport, and the remaining green man pendant, and carefully put them back. She was beginning to settle down and adjust to Michael Grainger's existence, and that his resemblance to Paul was just a coincidence. They said everyone had a doppelganger somewhere. She was still getting occasional flashbacks and dreams about Paul, which she hoped would diminish as they had before. They would quieten down in time.

They were at a launch party for another CL author who had written a memoir about his life as a tattooist. Inevitably guests were talking about their tattoos. Marguerite was standing close to Michael, and started when he took off his jacket and rolled up his left shirt sleeve. Once again her vision blurred and she heard the gunshots. They were running through the dark, Paul gasped and fell, clutching at her shoulder, and she stumbled and tried to lift him, but he was a dead weight, and she wanted to scream but didn't dare...

Of course, it was a snake tattoo. It seemed to her that it was identical to Paul's, and in exactly the same place. She stared at it. Michael smiled and said something to her. She had to shake her head and ask him to repeat it. He had, unsurprisingly, asked what she thought of it. Yes, she said, it was very impressive. He'd had it done in Portsmouth. He explained why he had decided to have it and what it meant to him. She didn't take any of that in. She waded her way through the rest of the evening as if in lead boots. When she got home she tried to resist the urge to get the case out again and look at the sketch. Eventually she gave in. So far as she could tell, it was exactly the same. Of course, tattooists probably had standard designs; and the left arm was not an uncommon place to have some ink. Another coincidence. Surely.

A line went through her head: "The second time's coincidence, the third time is enemy action." Well, but that was only two, surely. Still possible. Stranger things have happened, as her mother would say. She put the sketch in the case and back in the drawer. She should start to clear it out, she thought; she'd never use some of those things again.

They were in another café; she couldn't remember where. It was large and rather grand, yet very seedy and run down, and almost empty. It filled Marguerite with a sadness, a melancholy, that somehow made the world seem desperately vulnerable and doomed. She was very young. Paul was smiling at her, saying something frivolous. The snake on his forearm seemed to wriggle, then lifted its head and hissed—

She woke with a gasp. It was three in the morning. The image of the snake flicking its tongue remained in her mind. She must get away, take a holiday, somewhere she'd never been before. She was run down and stressed out. She got up and made tea.

She took a day off and went to Bournemouth for a long weekend. It wasn't really what she wanted, but it was sufficiently removed from both her past and present lives. She slept well and spent most of her time reading *Bleak House* and *David Copperfield*. She returned to work feeling refreshed and settled, sanguine about everything.

Michael had just come back from a promotional tour for his second novel, which he was only halfway through writing. He was beginning to panic a bit, and Marguerite found herself taking him out to lunch. He cheered up a bit over katsu curry, and suddenly looked at Marguerite's collarbone. She was wearing a lower neckline than usual and the green man pendant was visible. Michael said, "I've got one like that! My gran gave it to me. It's very slightly different..."

Somehow Marguerite didn't want to know in what way it differed. She was back in the past again. *No*, she said to herself,

I'm not going to dwell on it. It's just a symptom of stress. Michael went on talking, in Paul's voice.

Somewhat to her surprise, Marguerite felt no attraction to Michael at all. Admittedly she was more than old enough to be his mother, but even so, none of the feelings she had known for Paul transferred to the young man. When she heard him, she heard Paul. Looking at him made her lonely for Paul, a feeling she had, she realised, never overcome. She listened to him with great attention, yet without taking in anything he said—but that didn't seem to worry him.

Eventually they were walking back to the tube station together. Michael was still talking, Marguerite still listening, trying to respond intelligently. They had turned down a quiet side street of houses, offices and closed cafés. At first neither of them noticed there were two people arguing on the pavement ahead of them, until there was a yell and one of the men lunged for the other. The second man suddenly had a knife in his hand. Marguerite screamed, for a moment no longer sure whether she was on a London street or in a dark forest. Before she realised, Michael was ahead of her, trying to pull away the man with the knife. The other man fell back, then took to his heels, and Michael was left struggling with the knife wielder. It was a nightmare. Marguerite felt sick but forced herself to move. She looked round in panic, saw an empty beer bottle in the gutter. She grabbed it and tried to hit the knifeman on the head but couldn't get the right angle. She brought it down on his shoulder, just as he wrenched his arm from Michael's grip and slashed at his chest. Michael fell back and Marguerite, desperate, managed to get in a blow on the man's hand, causing him to drop the knife. She hit him again and he turned and ran off. It had taken a matter of seconds. Marguerite couldn't remember whether she had been screaming or not.

She gasped for breath. She looked towards Michael, leaning against a wall and clutching his chest, giving small cries of pain. She dropped the bottle and gently moved Michael's arms aside. Suddenly she felt that the separate parts of her were beginning to fit properly together; she knew what she was doing. She looked at the wounds, which were not deep, made reassuring noises, got out her phone and called for an ambulance and the police. Michael was looking at her in mild bewilderment. Abruptly he turned aside and threw up. She handed him some tissues to wipe his mouth. She took out a bottle of sanitiser and another tissue and began to dab his wounds while they waited. A few people looked out of office windows, saw the excitement was over, and went back to their business. The street was very quiet; footsteps echoed from the next road over. Michael continued to look at her uncertainly. Neither of them spoke, there seemed no appropriate words.

She waited in the hospital. They discharged him at about two in the morning, and when the police had finally gone she phoned a cab.

He said, "Was that stupid, or what? I should have let them get on with it. But I couldn't, could I?"

"No. No, you couldn't."

"Thanks for—Well, thanks."

"That's okay. I couldn't do anything else either, could I?"

Marguerite felt, perversely, that reconciling the parts of her had formed another person, one she didn't recognise— although she seemed to have no trouble being her, whoever she was. Everything continued slightly out of kilter.

She visited Michael regularly while he was recovering. He showed her the stitches. She said, "That'll make an interesting scar." It was the exact duplicate of Paul's scar. She wasn't even surprised; she realised she had expected it.

Later she took the attaché case out of the drawer and pulled out the little leather bag containing the second green man. She thought she might show it to Michael, see if it really was the same as the one his grandmother had given him. *Things could hardly get any stranger*, she thought.

The bag was empty, the carving gone. Underneath the bag was a photograph, in monochrome, of Paul against a background of oak leaves. She had never seen it before. Next to it was a spent cartridge. Just for a moment she knew why it was there, then the memory was gone, like a dream on waking, and the present reality reasserted itself. She put the case back in the drawer.

COMMITMENT TO TRUTH

Bret McCormick

ACCORDING TO A Google search I did, Austin and New Orleans tied for most bars in a single zip code. A trip to New Orleans sounded cool, but I live in Austin. I wanted to get drunk in a hurry, so I headed for that wettest of zip codes, 78701, down around Sixth and Rainey. It was a Tuesday night in April, breezy with that odd feeling in the air. You know, the sort of otherworldly feeling that happens when the barometric pressure suddenly changes? The setting sun cast colours without names on the magic castle clouds overhead. Walking down the sidewalk I felt like a solitary character in a movie, the cinematic cliché where the street is empty, saxophone music is playing, and the detective or whatever is wandering through a world that hasn't been so kind. Nights like that one always make me think of spirits on the move; sort of like the Springsteen song.

Truth is, besides just getting drunk, I wanted to get laid. Not a very ladylike admission, I know, but it's important that I stick to the truth here. You'll understand more fully later; just bear with me.

It was my plan to do a sort of solitary pub crawl. It wasn't my birthday and I'd never before gone from bar to bar alone. Ever. And that is absolutely the truth. For some reason, that night I wanted to wallow in the sordid revelry only a drunken night on Sixth Street can provide. The first place to catch my eye was a bar I'd never noticed before, called Io. Just as I was about to walk in, the heel on my left shoe snapped right off. Eighty-nine dollars on sale and I'd only worn them three or four times! Can you believe that? I figured the broken heel wrecked my plans for wandering through the carnival of Austin bars. I'd just get drunk off my ass in Io and hope an eligible bed mate dropped in. I'd leave my car where I parked it and Uber home. Pulling my shoes off and tucking them under my arm I crossed the threshold into Io.

A quiet millennial couple were talking to one another in a booth on the back wall; otherwise I had the place to myself. From the juke box, Tom Petty was singing about the great wide open. A rebel without a clue. That was me. I sat at the bar and ordered a margarita. The bartender was nice enough, young, short-haired, lots of tats and piercings. She seemed willing to carry on a conversation but I was not in the mood for girl talk with a probable lesbian who was ten years younger than me. Sorry. Not a slam against lesbians, just the truth, okay? By the time I finished my first drink, the couple had departed and it was just me. I was thinking maybe I should forget the whole thing, go home and finish my drinking in front of the TV.

That's when he walked in. Now, the way I said that, maybe you'd think I was smitten by some super-sexy stud—like the world faded away and he moved in slow-motion toward me. Another cinematic cliché. But it wasn't that way at all. To the contrary, things seemed to speed up. He came right in and took a seat near mine. The guy was definitely not a jock. More of a brain. Maybe the captain of the chess team. His clothes were nice. To me he seemed overdressed, a little Ivy League-ish. He could've been a lawyer, which would have been fine with me. I am a paralegal, after all.

This well-dressed, not-especially-masculine man ordered a drink and, after taking the first sip, glanced over at me and smiled. "Can I buy you a drink?"

Why not? I thought. "How kind of you," I said. "Thanks."

The bartender brought me my second margarita and I raised it in the stranger's direction. He lifted his—Tom Collins, I think it was—and pushed it toward me so our glasses touched. Corny, I know, and you'll think I'm lying but hear me out and you will realise I would not, *cannot* lie about this. Every word is the truth. When our glasses touched I felt a surge of electricity run through my whole body. Not like a shock from a wall outlet, but a definite, undeniable jolt of energy. Not harmful, but definitely the sort of thing that commands attention. And respect.

I must have reacted with a surprised facial expression. The stranger looked me in the eye and said, "Nothing to fear, just the truth."

"What just happened?" I said, cocking my head and feeling more than a bit suspicious. I scrutinised the guy's face, searching for indications he was having a joke at my expense. Was he a stage magician or something? I knew I had not imagined that surge of energy.

"That happens sometimes." He reached his hand toward me. "Allow me to introduce myself. My name is Truth."

His expression seemed one hundred per cent sincere, but when I heard *that* I could not stifle a laugh. And once I started it was hard to stop. One of those releases of nervous energy, know what I mean? When I finally got control of myself I said, "Sorry, I— That just struck me as odd." I shook his hand.

The friendly stranger was not offended in the least. "I get that a lot," he said. "What's your name?"

Normally I use a pseudonym or a *nom du lit* when I pick up strangers for casual sex. Just to keep things manageable, you know? I said the first name that popped into my mind. "Penelope."

At that he frowned. I wondered, *does he hate the name Penelope? Maybe I should've used one of my other go-to romance monikers: Rose or Janis?* Trying to smooth over any potential awkwardness I said, "So your folks really named you Truth?"

He drew a deep breath. "Folks? Hmm. That's a good question. I've been called other names. For a time, I went by Apollo. The clearest, most accurate name in the here and now is Truth."

"So," I said, trying to play coy, fingering the rim of my glass, "what brings you out to Sixth Street, Truth?"

"Truthfully?" he asked.

That threw me for a momentary loop. I wasn't expecting it and I'm sure it showed on my face. Then he laughed loudly, and I knew he was having a little joke with me.

"Good one!" I said, downing the rest of my drink.

Without hesitation, Truth ordered me another one. He still had half of his left, and when my third margarita was placed in front of me he raised his glass. "Veritas," he said.

"Another of your names," I noted, clinking my glass against his. I was feeling friendly, feeling no pain, and I didn't mind playing his little game. So, what if Truth was not his real name? Penelope was not *my* real name. Sauce for the goose, gravy for the gander, and all that stuff, right?

"To answer your question about what brings me down here..."

"Which you promise to answer truthfully," I said, smiling my biggest smile and trying to pour on the charm. By this time I'd decided I wouldn't mind taking the man to bed even if he was no football player. I guessed he was at least five years younger than me, and I needed to keep that in mind. Not that age ever seemed to be a major determining factor with males in the selection of partners for one-night stands. Enthusiastic availability usually did the trick.

"Everything I say to you will be true." He was smiling, but it was a serious smile. And I must admit in that moment I felt a little like a child with an adult who was willing to overlook my indiscretions. Like when a grandfather catches a little girl with her hand in the cookie jar but doesn't say a word about it. Then I thought, why the hell did that pop into my mind?

"So..." I prompted.

"Tonight is the one night a year I get to do exactly as I please. It's both a blessing and a burden. Any frustrations I have experienced in the last three hundred and sixty-four days I am allowed to respond to in whatever manner seems appropriate. My sole discretion."

His use of the word "frustrations" naturally brought to mind my own sexual frustration. I wondered if, hoped really, we shared the same frustration. "And what are you doing about those frustrations tonight, Truth?"

"This and that," he said, looking away. "You know, that broken heel on your shoe is a metaphor."

"My shoe? Metaphor? What do you mean? And how did you know about my shoe?"

"Nothing is hidden from Truth. It's not common to see a barefoot woman in a bar on Sixth Street. Besides, I saw your shoes when I sat down."

I glanced at the barstool beside me and saw the shoes right where I'd placed them.

"Metaphor?" I asked again. "What's that mean?"

"Everything humans experience in this world is metaphor. Every task, every obligation, every casual occurrence; all metaphors for something bigger, something eternal."

"Everything *humans* experience? The way you say that almost implies you don't consider yourself human. Are you a poet by any chance? I've never known a real poet."

"Not exactly true. That kid Jeff in your high school. The one who asked you to the prom. You turned him down because he wasn't your type. You were hoping the captain of the football team would ask you. Jeff was a real poet. Still is. I think he finally decided he was gay. Sensitive sort of guy."

I felt cold . . . and angry. Suspicious. Totally confused! How the fuck could he know about Jeff? Who the hell was this guy? I withdrew into my own head for a minute and wondered if I should call my Uber. I wondered if I was sober and strong enough to fight this man if I had to. I factored in the lesbian behind the counter as a plus while I ran through this mental exercise.

"Relax!" he said, shaking his head and signalling to the bartender for another drink. "I'm not here to hurt you."

"How do you know about Jeff?"

"Like I told you before, nothing is hidden from Truth."

The bartender put his drink in front of him. "Do you want another one?" he asked me. I shook my head. "That's probably best. I want to make sure you remember this."

I said, "So explain this to me. I don't get it."

"I am Truth. Quite literally. Once a year I take on human form. Any form I wish. That's always kind of fun, choosing. I could've been the football player you were hoping for when you came out this evening. I decided against that because I thought you'd focus on nothing but getting me into bed, and I really want you to hear what I have to say. Hear it and remember it."

Really, I had no choice but to go along with whatever was happening. Possibilities flashed through my mind. Maybe this was a candid camera, YouTube sort of thing. Maybe one of my friends had put this guy up to it. Maybe he was a very weird, very committed stalker. For some reason I opted to play into this fantasy scenario completely. "Tell me, Mr. Truth, what sorts of frustrations are you working out this evening." I wasn't smiling when I said it.

"Please relax. Let's not turn this into some big traumatic thing."

I forced a smile. "What are you doing here?"

"Here, as in this bar? I came to see you, share some ideas with you. Here as in Austin? I'm here to confront some of the lies. A lot of lies here in Austin. Truth doesn't like lies. We're inimical to one another, you know."

"Why not go to Washington DC? Even more lies there. Lots of politicians. Politicians, lies—two go together like pastrami and rye."

"True. There's a rhyme scheme in your comment. It has the makings of a good country and western song." He smiled. "Really, relax."

"Okay. This is me relaxing."

"I came to see you, Rebecca." He paused, making sure I'd noticed he had used my real name. "I want to give you a shot at rehabilitation."

"What? You think I drink too much?" I feigned a smile and held my glass up before downing the last swallow.

"No. You lie too much. If things continue unchecked, I'll be visiting you for retribution in a couple of years. I'd like to avoid that if I can."

"Retribution? What is this crap?"

"Look at the TV," he said.

Above the bar was a large flat screen monitor. The volume was down but a face I recognised filled the screen. Republican Senator Dan Gilbert. It was common knowledge he was under investigation for fraudulent investment schemes. I'd always thought the guy was a slimeball. It wasn't the first time he'd been accused of illegal shenanigans, but Gilbert led a charmed life. He always avoided any real consequences for his alleged crimes.

"You know him."

I kind of laughed. "Dan Gilbert. Yep. The sort of good old boy everybody in this town wants to have a beer with."

"Yes. Well, this good old boy is going to pay for his sins tonight."

"Which sins specifically?"

"All of the crooked business dealings; the misrepresentations of special interest legislation; having two business associates murdered and framing an innocent man for the crime; raping his stepdaughter ... Shall I go on?"

"I hadn't heard about the stepdaughter." I looked long and hard into Truth's eyes and I knew—I mean without a shadow of a doubt. This man, this anthropomorphic idealisation of a concept, this whatever he was—he was telling the truth. He was the Truth. I was in the presence of something I did not, and probably never would, understand.

"No one's heard. Only the two of them know about it."

"And you."

"And now you. Nothing is hidden from Truth. Now, I bring Senator Gilbert to your attention so that there's no chance of you forgetting our talk. Gilbert dies tonight. It can be a massive coronary, a drug overdose, he can be stabbed twenty-seven times by a mugger, run over by a freight train, anything really. I want you to choose the way Gilbert dies."

"Really?" Now my brain was under a sort of pressure I'd never known. Try to understand. I knew he was Truth. *Knew it.* No doubt. But I didn't *want* to know it. I didn't want to believe. And I damn sure didn't want to be an accessory to a murder. I mean I would not have shed a tear for Gilbert's passing, but I didn't want to take part in anything that could land me in prison.

"To keep it interesting, to make certain you don't forget this evening, make it the most improbable death you can think of."

I didn't think long. I liked the specificity of being stabbed twenty-seven times. "I'll take the twenty-seven stabs, for five hundred, Truth," I said, trying to force some humour into the most unworldly experience I had ever known.

"Funny," he said, acknowledging my little reference to the Jeopardy game show. "Tomorrow morning you will read—oh no, you don't take the newspaper... Want to hear it on the radio, or from a friend?"

"If we're shooting for improbability, let's say I hear it from my Aunt Agnes in Portland. She's an old hippie. I only..."

"Hear from her on your birthday, when she sends you a funny card with twenty dollars in it."

"Yes." I nodded. Truth was wearing me down. "Can I change my mind about another drink?"

"Sure." He ordered another margarita for me. "Now, after you hear from Aunt Agnes in the morning... Care to specify a time?"

"What the hell... let's say seven twenty-seven a.m."

"Done."

I took the fourth margarita directly from the bartender's hand and gulped about half of it down. "You were saying...?"

"All of this has been preamble. I want you to make a commitment to truth in the coming year. I'm not saying you can't lie at all. That seems impossible for you humans, but white lies don't count. I want you to tell the truth every time it really matters."

"Maybe you can give me some examples? You know, about what does or doesn't matter."

"Okay. No cheating on tests. That's the only way you got your degree at UT. Do you realise that starting your business life on bogus credentials puts a very poor complexion on you and everything you stand for? No more lying about who you are. No more taking credit for the work others have done. A person's work is a very real measure of the value of their existence. Reap only the rewards you have earned."

I felt like he was probably referring to all that work Shannon had done for the firm before I got her fired. Or it could have been any of a handful of other incidents. I didn't really want Truth to recite a laundry list of my sins, so I kept my mouth shut.

"Above all else, don't feign affection. That's just gross." He frowned and made a strange, nonverbal sound of disgust in his throat. "That half-baked scheme you have about getting pregnant by your boss... or the alternative where you accuse him of rape... or that idea about setting his fiancée up for infidelity... All those thoughts need to be discarded. Just toss them right out of your mind."

I wanted to say something in my own defence. I started to— but I couldn't think of anything that would be, you know, truthful. Again, I kept my mouth shut.

"The things that have troubled me most about you, Rebecca, are all the dirty tricks you've played on pretty much anyone who has ever loved or trusted you. Some don't realise you have betrayed them in the past, but I think it's best to leave that for now. You're going to have a difficult enough time in the coming year without being abandoned by everyone you know. But I must insist that you take this commitment to truth seriously every single day from now on."

"What happens if I, you know, slip up? Have a relapse?"

"That will have devastating consequences for your soul."

"So, the soul, that's a real thing, eh?"

"It is. And yours can't afford any more pollution."

"Yeah, that would be bad."

"All your life you have tricked others into believing you can be trusted. Now you need to be trustworthy for real. This coming year is critical. Continue in your old ways and you will descend into a darkness you cannot at this moment imagine. Stick with your old tricks and in two years' time it'll be you getting stabbed twenty-seven times. Follow me?"

"Yes."

"Now, I know I'm not your type and frankly you are not mine. We could go through with the whole casual sex thing but I don't think that's the best decision. Besides, I've got a lot of well-justified punishment to deal out. The night is young. Play your cards right and one of these days I'll walk into your life looking like the perfect match to all your lustful fantasies."

"If that happens will I know it's you?"

"Probably not. What purpose would it serve? Take your blessings where they fall and be a blessing to someone else for a change."

So, Truth walked out into the blustery April night. I followed soon afterwards. Before I'd even arrived home I was thinking I'd wake up tomorrow and find this was all just a dream. But when the phone rang the next morning, at seven twenty-seven a.m. on the nose, and Aunt Agnes, who hadn't called me for years, told me Senator Gilbert had been stabbed twenty-seven times... Well, all vestiges of doubt flew out the window and have not returned.

For the record, everything I've just told you is true. I swear it. It's not easy turning over a new leaf. I do have to admit that the longer I tell the truth the better I feel about myself and the worse I feel about my past transgressions. If you think I'm a whack job and no longer want to be friends, I'd understand completely. But I had to tell someone, you know?

THE PIT

KC Grifant

1

THE PARTY TOOK place in a recently designed, environmentally conscious, and effortlessly modern rental overlooking the Maui coastline. A Koa wood bar, long enough to make you think maybe a whole tree had been split and hauled in, bisected the space and attracted more gauzy-clad women than the eye could take in at a single sweep. And yet I was having a fucking terrible time.

I was having a terrible time because of precisely one reason: my ex-girlfriend on the other side of the cavernous room. Of course she'd be here. We LA expats were maybe a hundred or so semi-permanent residents on the island, along with the several dozen who fly in like clockwork every few months for some much-needed R&R. We travelled as one larger and carnivorous pack to this or that housewarming party, birthday blowout, movie screening, so of course I was bound to see her.

Marjorie's laugh periodically sliced through the crowd and sent tremors through my hands and into my scotch glass. From the corner of my eye, her shoulders glinted dark and lustrous as she clasped her new beau.

"You come out here a lot?" a woman in a chair made from a wine barrel asked me. I refocused on the conversation, taking a sip of the Macallan. The woman wore a low-cut emerald dress, couture probably, but could stand to lose a few pounds and—more importantly—was no Marjorie.

"There's nothing quite like a tropical paradise to recalibrate and realign my life goals," I told her. "I find sabbaticals so necessary to maintain the flow of productivity as a screenwriter. And LA is so... dense, you know?"

She must have sensed my pheromones not adequately firing up for her because a second later she excused herself. The spot of green trailed through the glass door out onto the beach and I felt worse than before, if that were possible. I picked up my sorry ass and navigated my way to the bar.

"Jack." That voice. I swallowed and kept my face still, attempting an aura of relaxed, unconcerned.

"Marj," I said. "How goes it?" The bitterness curdled each syllable to an extent that surprised even me.

Marjorie frowned, a little wrinkle puckering in her otherwise smooth brow. She used her no-nonsense voice, the kind she used when calling the Internet company or health insurance: clipped and with a hint of anger ready to boil through at the first sign of uncooperativeness.

"I came over here to stay stop calling me. Remember Daphne? Well, you're acting like Daphne."

The name evoked a memory of my other ex's gardenia-scented perfume and "I need you" messages popping up on my phone after she found me and Marjorie entangled. I had broken up with Daphne for Marjorie, and Marjorie had broken up with me and was now here with her new beau. Everything had come full fucking circle.

The comparison made me flush, even as an unexpected jolt of sympathy fired through me at the thought of Daphne, who had sold her place in Orange County so she could rent a little place out here for both of us to stay. It was fun for a while, but her clingy "feelings first" vibe and New Age-meditation-crystal-cleansing crap got old pretty quick.

"She was seriously unstable. And really heartbroken," I murmured, letting the unspoken hang: *And so am I.*

Marjorie rolled her eyes and my self-pity transmuted to anger, fast as a flame along gasoline.

"Well," I said. "Aren't you just so glad to be done with me. As if we didn't live together for a whole year." I was a snake in human skin, fully clothed in a Tommy Bahamas palm tree print, spraying gloopy venom with each sentence.

Behind Marjorie and her crossed arms, windows stretched from sea to sky, erecting a barrier between the Pacific and the party room. Beyond the glass an indulgent moon, bulgy as a yellow eye between the silhouettes of palm trees, seemed to watch and smirk.

"A whole year." I drained my scotch for punctuation. A year of waking up next to each other, gently bickering over dinner choices, hitting the beach, laughing over stupid shit. I had been so productive with her by my side, almost scoring gigs with agencies, and even finishing two screenplays. Now, all that had ground to a halt.

"This was supposed to be my year of relaxing, of recalibrating. You ruined that. I hate you," I added, my nostrils flaring and catching the salt air that wafted in through the door. Marjorie recoiled as if I had slapped her.

"That is totally uncalled for," she shrieked. "You're the one who cheated on me, remember?"

"How many times do I have to tell you? It was just online!" I shouted back. "It didn't count!"

Her beef of a boyfriend walked over. Good. It was just what I needed. The alcohol coursed through me as I shouted at him.

"*You.* Look at you. What is that even a tattoo of? What do you even *do*, bro?"

I didn't realise what I was doing when I pointed my empty scotch glass at the beau's face. People were laughing now, really laughing.

"Real hilarious, a guy in pain. Ha ha ha, yuck it up!" I yelled at the crowd and swung. The force of the hit reverberated up my arm and down my spine in an immensely satisfying way as my glass exploded against the dude's cheek.

Everything blurred and I woke up.

2

I winced before any sensation set in, sure I was going to have the holiest of all hangovers. Fear gripped my stomach—was I in jail, what had I done? I waited, lying there in the dark, but then realised I wasn't horizontal. I was sitting up, surrounded by familiar sounds.

My eyes flew open. The green-clad woman stared.

"Everything okay?" The woman laughed politely, but even in my haze I could detect her readying to excuse herself.

"I was dozing, I guess." I rubbed my eyes. Marjorie was across the room, gripping her beau's tattooed arm as he laughed at something. "Weird."

The woman cleared her throat. "I'm gonna run to the powder room."

"Of course, powder away." I rubbed my eyes again as she swooshed off. A litany of possibilities ran through my mind: daydream, narcolepsy, acid flashback, schizophrenia, early-onset dementia. I sniffed my scotch. It smelled like normal, nose-hair burning Macallan. *Heartache*, I settled on as the reason, and downed the rest of my drink. Simple, old-fashioned heartache was making me crazed. Fucking Marj.

I glanced up again and nearly jumped. Marjorie stared directly at me before partygoers obstructed my view of her. Her gaze had looked haunted. *Afraid.*

I threaded through the crowd. As I got to Marjorie the laugh of her beau sent my teeth grinding. What on this godly earth had she seen in him, enough to abandon me?

"Marj," I muttered and the beau extended a meaty hand, which I ignored.

"Elliot, excuse us a sec." Marjorie's voice was faint.

"What's up babe?" Elliot put the same meaty hand on the back of Marjorie's neck.

"Don't worry about it, *bud*," I said. "The lady can talk to who she wants." I turned to Marjorie. "I really can't even comprehend what attracts you to this guy. You don't want anyone smart enough who might be able to call you on your bullshit?"

The slap against my cheek was light but still an embarrassment.

"Idiot," Marjorie said. "You never change, do you? Grow up."

My fists balled. I swung toward Elliot, the force of my impact crushing my knuckles and sending waves of pain up my arm like an electric shock as the room went black.

3

I jolted in my chair, spilling my scotch and causing the woman across from me to stop mid-sentence.

"What in the holy hell?" I sprang up as she gaped. The details were fuzzy but I remembered hitting Elliot a second time.

"You okay?"

"No, I'm having some weird déjà vu, or a seizure. Maybe you should call an ambulance for me."

She smiled and stood. "You must've taken something fun. If you have any extra give me a holler."

"I didn't take anything!" I called after her. I wracked my brain. I would have definitely remembered if I had taken a pill, puff or hit. Unless it was something so strong it wiped my memory clean. I pinched the inside of my elbow hard. Could someone have déjà vu twice? I studied the welt rising on my skin.

"Jack!"

Marjorie dug her nails into the flesh of my wrist—which hurt way more than my pinch—and dragged me through the crowd.

"What are you doing to me?" she hissed. "Is this a joke?"

"It's not me." I shook her off. She crossed her arms over her white dress, a lovely frame against the yellow moonlight sifting through the window. She looked how I felt: afraid. But God, she was beautiful. I wanted to touch her cheek to comfort her—but stopped myself.

"The same thing keeps happening. Well, not exactly the same. Elliot has no idea what I'm talking about." She bit her lip.

"I hit that sucker twice already. We are being Groundhog Dayed. Or massively punked."

Elliot glanced not-too-subtly at us from the other side of the bar, and a petty flash of triumph ran through me. I looked at my watch: ten fifty-five. "Maybe it's..." I didn't get to finish my thought as the world began to dissolve. "Hell!"

4

I blinked awake. The last few minutes were already receding like a dream, details erased like a blackout. But I remembered enough. I ignored the woman talking to me and immediately dialled 911. She flipped the finger and marched off in a huff.

"I need help ASAP," I told the operator. "I'm going fucking insane. Maybe it's schizophrenia."

By the time I had finally convinced the phone operator to send someone, Marjorie was in front of me, brandishing an unopened bottle of wine.

"I know you're doing this," she said. Her look of concentration reminded me of when we played Uno, all the way up until she smashed the bottle against my head.

5

"Screw you!" I yelled at the woman in green, whose aghast expression mirrored others around us. "And you, and you!"

I gathered myself and bellowed at the top of my lungs. "Screw you all!" I hurled my glass of scotch at the window. The crash of the glass and liquid immediately made me feel better so I picked up my chair. As I struggled to throw it after the scotch, I glimpsed a face pressed up against the window.

Daphne?

It looked like her, those long brown curls and arching eyebrows, but she faded into another face, a leering white mask with red hair. The mask's eyes looked like a reptile's—something ancient and watching and ... *bloodstained*—

6

I woke up.

Take it easy, I told myself. Maybe if I didn't move, didn't think, it would be okay. If I sat perfectly still until I hit the ten-minute mark, maybe whatever was happening would pass by me and continue on, like a predator passing a possum playing dead.

I furtively glanced at my watch: ten forty-three.

The woman in green stomped away at the ten forty-five mark. At ten forty-six Marjorie showed up, sinking into the chair opposite me.

Elliot trailed behind, saying "Babe? Babe, you okay?" over and over like a neurotic parrot.

"Elliott, buddy!" I greeted. Why not? "You are beefed as fuck, you know that? How many hours of lifting a day does that take you?"

"Jack, stop being an ass. Please, El, grab me some water from the bar."

Elliot glared at me before melting into the crowd.

"What's *happening*?" Marjorie buried her face, hair falling across her hands.

Something stirred in my memory, something about the window, but another idea struck me.

"Let's try to get out of here the next time, okay?" I said. "It's hard to remember exactly what happens each time this starts, but let's try to remember to run. Yeah?"

Marjorie nodded, her eyes brimming with tears. Damn, I still loved her. I started to grab her hand but the room blurred again, like rain running over fresh ink.

7

I sprang up and looked around. I was supposed to go somewhere. My mind worked slowly but my feet hustled for the door. *Escape. Out.* Marj across the room did the same and we hurried outside without a word. We made it as far my Lexus rental before the world started to fade again.

"Damn you!" I shouted and gripped the steering wheel as hard as I could, flooring the gas up the hill as Marjorie cried next to me. Maybe if I just held on, I could—

8

I had to get out of there.

I remembered the car, but that hadn't worked. There was something else ... the window, a memory, nagged at me.

I dragged myself to the window, deep dread settling into my bones. Daphne's grinning face, pressed against the glass, disappeared a second later.

"What the hell?" I muttered, my trepidation giving way to annoyance. I should have known better than to get involved with a New Age chick. "You're doing this, aren't you? Drugged me with one of your shit herbal mixes!"

I ran toward the patio door and Marjorie followed.

"What's going on?" Marjorie called.

"Daphne!" I hollered. "You bitch! I know you're doing this with your stupid witchy culty bullshit!"

Everyone stared, one person even snapped a picture. I turned to him. "I will fucking kill you!"

I hurried onto the white beach, squinting into the darkness. Palm trees rustled overhead like the whispers of a hushed crowd. "I saw you, Daphne!"

Somewhere, the familiar sound of her bangles clicked just before the world faded again.

Remember the beach, remember the beach, I urged myself before darkness pulled me under like a coma.

9

I woke, the layer of memories hazy on top of one another. How many times had it been? Too many, I could tell by the pit of despair in my chest even as my mind cleared. *Beach*, my mind urged. *Go to the beach.*

I darted out and spotted Daphne trying to run up a sand bank. I grabbed her arm. "What are you doing to me?" Despair clawed my voice raw.

"I loved loved *loved* seeing you try to fight Elliot," Daphne guffawed. She clapped, bangles jangling. In the moonlight her hands looked stained. "It's what you get, you sick SOB."

"What are you talking about?"

"I despise you," Daphne said. The full weight of her wants, her expectations, whatever world she had imagined and invested in, softened my rage for a minute.

"I can't control who I am or am not attracted to," I told her.

Marjorie skidded to my side. "What the hell? *Daphne*?"

Daphne's gaze fixed on me with a pure hatred. "Do you know how many times I relived finding you there in bed, fucking her? How it played over and over in my head like a movie I couldn't stop? Well, here's just a fraction of that pain, given to you for all time."

"What is she talking about, Jack?" Marjorie said.

"Shut up!" Daphne said and I put up my hands.

"Ladies, please," I interjected. I felt some of my easy charm come back despite our predicament. And even though Daphne was pulling a psycho-bitch, I couldn't help but notice how good she looked since I last saw her. Her gauzy wrap fluttered in the plumeria-laden breeze, the ocean crashing rhythmically behind her.

"Did you lose weight?" I murmured in appreciation.

"Adrasteia condemns you! She for whom none escapes!" Daphne shouted, whatever that meant. I rolled my eyes. She had always been overly dramatic.

"Babe, look." I tried my most reasonable tone, but a white mask with red eyes flared behind Daphne for a split-second. Twice as large as Daphne's head, the clay-baked face with a blur of red hair and bared teeth shot a cold spike of fear down my back.

What the hell?

I stumbled backwards, landing on my butt in the cold sand.

Marjorie let loose a bloodcurdling scream, making the handful of people on the beach stare before they headed back to the house, closing the door behind them and clearly not seeing the shit we were seeing.

"What…was that?" I panted, getting to my feet. "Some Hollywood projection? It looks fucking real."

"A ritual, primordial, from ancient times." Daphne smiled. "Try to wrap your cretin mind around that. Think of it as my genie, if that makes it easier. We're all in our own realities, with some crossover. You are both stuck in a little loop forever. I hope you enjoy each other's miserable, *heartbroken—*" at this, her eyes flashed at me "—company."

Marjorie looked at her in disbelief. "You have a fucking genie and you waste it on this loser?"

I winced. "Seriously, Marj?"

"He cheated on you and he cheated on me," Marjorie continued.

"Actually it was just online—" I started to interject.

"He's a waste of space," Marjorie railed. "Why should I be punished for that?"

Daphne studied me. Between her scrutiny and Marjorie's all-accusing gaze, I couldn't take it.

"What can I say?" I spread my hands helplessly. "I love women. I can't help it if my appetite is large. Maybe I need to have more threesomes, I don't know." I left my suggestion hanging there, but neither of them commented.

"Asshole," Marjorie hissed. Daphne turned over her bloodstained hands and I held my breath. Would she let us go, maybe?

"If you wanted to be polygamous you should have said so." Daphne glared and I knew that all was definitely not forgiven. "Not 'I love you *Daphne*'. 'I want to be with you forever *Daphne*'. 'You're the only one for me *Daphne*'."

"I'm also a romantic?" I ventured and Marjorie laughed, making me want to strangle her.

"I hated you for so long, but you're right. You shouldn't be punished," Daphne said to Marjorie and grinned. "This moment will be better. The pinnacle of despair, set against the backdrop of total paradise."

I glanced at my watch: eleven forty-five. We were past the loop! Something about Daphne must have gotten us out of it. I wasn't letting her out of my sight. I stepped closer to her. She gave me a tight smile as she pulled out a shell-encrusted knife from her skirt pocket and slit her palms.

"What the hell are you doing?"

The air shimmered as blood drops fell into the sand and what looked like a giant bubble encased Daphne. I reached out to grab her arm but the distance between us expanded and I missed. Marjorie, meanwhile, stood next to Daphne in the bubble.

"You can't ruin people's lives anymore," Marjorie said, her voice distorted.

"Bye, Jack," Daphne said. The white face appeared again behind her, mouth open in a silent howl, its red hair like masses of wires spiralling out to blot the moon.

I screamed as its eyes, those *horrible* eyes, funnelled the same hatred and disdain that Daphne and Marjorie shot at me from behind their bubble. Not their bubble. *My* bubble.

"Wait!" I screamed and tried to jump forward, but the air shimmered again and I was on one side of the bubble while they were on the other—outside looking in on this timefuck. Daphne and the massive white face bared their teeth in unison.

"You get to relive this moment indefinitely and think about what you've done. Maybe you can get out of it." Daphne's eyes cut to the black waves of the Pacific. "Or maybe not."

"Stop!" I howled. "*Bitches!*"

Daphne and Marjorie had vanished. I was alone except for the face, floating over me like an apparition, hair streaming like blood as it laughed. I ran back to the party but the windows had dimmed, and my surroundings faded just as I reached the glass.

10, 11, 12, 13…

When I woke up the next time, and after that, and again, I found myself on the sand, yelling at Daphne not to leave as the shimmer separated us. Each time my hoarse shouts were swallowed by the roar of the waves, and everyone and everything vanished. Everything except the white face, revelling in my misery. It grinned its endless fury above the dark sea as I screamed, waiting for me to take the plunge.

THE LONG DROP
UPWARDS

Garry Kilworth

I GOT THE call while sitting in Café Nero contemplating the
meaning of life in the muddy contents of my cup. I'm not
big on philosophy, but it seemed to me that everything
everywhere was a bit murky at the moment, just like the dregs I
was peering at when my mobile rang. I say "rang" but one of my
nephews had replaced the normal ring tone with a Thai railway
station announcement which I'm told is something to do with the
Bangkok Purple Line. It was loud and people usually turn to look
round for a Tannoy. I imagine any Thais in the vicinity would
start to panic and wonder what platform they should be on.

"Yes Art?"

His voice was strangely strangulated and full of panic, but that
wasn't unusual for Arthur, who was scared of everything but
himself. "Douglas, get round to my flat as quickly as you can, will
you? I'm in trouble."

"What's the problem, Art? Toilet blocked again?"

"I'm not kidding. Real trouble. Please, Douglas. I don't know who else to call. It's... It's to do with Isaac Newton."

I tried to make sense of this. "Is that the name of next door's cat?" I asked. "And to be honest, Art, you don't know anyone else but me, do you?"

"No, the real Newton. You know, the apple tree guy. The one who invented gravity?"

Invented? I didn't argue with him. He sounded too stressed.

"Ah, that makes more sense." It didn't, of course. "All right, I'll come round."

It was only a short walk from the seaside café to Art's flat, but I happened to notice some workmen putting in new road lamps along the clifftop walkway. Of late it seemed there were more and more poles going up in the streets. It struck me that once we had forests where I was treading, that all these poles in those eras had leaves and roots. Now they were metal and concrete, increasing in number all the time. *Soon*, I thought, *mankind will be lost in bewildering thickets of signposts and become hunters and hunted again. And what sort of fantastical beasts will inhabit such woodlands? Creatures that have created themselves out of wild, untameable technology? Monsters of the RAM and ROM. Software demons, fiends of binary Salt Mine Codes.*

One code I knew was that of Art's flat, which I punched and let myself in. I went into the kitchen wondering if I would find him in a pool of blood lying next to an ineptly used carving knife.

Not there.

Bathroom next, looking for an empty drug container.

Not there either.

A muffled voice came from the living room. Ah, he had electrocuted himself with a household device. However, when I entered the room he was nowhere to be seen. Was he lying behind the sofa? Or locked in the coat cupboard? Or out on the windowsill, ready to jump?

"Up here, Douglas."

I looked up. He seemed to be stuck by his back to the ceiling. He could move his arms and legs, but was unable to release himself.

"What are you doing up there?" I said.

"Not having fun," he expostulated, "if that's what you think."

"I really don't know what to think."

"It was that woman's fault."

"Fine," I replied. "Which would be?"

He sighed. "Last night. I think it was last night; I've been up here for a long time. Anyway, I went for a walk along the prom. It was a nice evening. The moon was out, not full, more a gibbous moon. The waves were lapping the shingle, shuffling it around like it does, you know. Then suddenly a woman was beside me. At least, she had the vague shape of a woman, but she was somehow—somehow insubstantial. She scared the life out of me, Douglas. I could hardly catch my breath and I almost passed out. I hurried off, back to the flat, but she followed me like some electric phantom. There was an unholy glow about her. An energy that felt unreal—no, more correctly, *unhallowed*—though I somehow knew she was no ordinary ghost, nothing from beyond the grave or from the Other Side, the spectral side that is, of humans after death."

My neck was beginning to ache with staring upwards. "So where was she from? Blackpool?"

His face was ashen as he pointed down at the table. "From there."

I looked under the table and could see nothing. "Where?"

"The phone, you berk!" he cried. "The mobile. On top of the table. She said I'd locked her out of her home. If I did, it was by accident. She raved something about how I'd pressed the wrong buttons in the wrong apps in the wrong sequence. You know me. I'm hopeless at tech. Now I'm up here and can't get down. Can you get me down, please?"

"Not sure how I can do that. What's the matter with you, anyway? Are you filled with helium or something?"

"She's reversed my personal gravity. I told you: Newton. I'm a victim of the Isaacs, the reverse of his bloody law, God help me..." And he started to cry, showering me with teardrops.

"Bloody hell, stop that," I ordered. "Have you got any rope in the flat?"

"What would I be doing with rope?"

"Scarves then. Neckties. A sheet I can rip into strips."

He choked back his fear. "Have a look in the bedroom."

I went into his bedroom with some trepidation. It was, like the rest of the flat, like the rest of Art's life, a terrible mess. I could smell dirty socks and the underlying odour of unwashed underpants. To my credit I didn't gag when I pulled the sheet off his bed and tore it into strips, then tied the strips together to form a rope.

It may surprise you, it may seem incredible to you, that I was not more sceptical about his story. That he was on the ceiling was the most alarming and startling of the events of my morning, but to learn that the cause was a mobile phone was not. It seemed to me that everyone but myself was obsessed with the latest human toy. Once it was cars, still is among the macho men, but mobiles have definitely become the masters of the human race. People walk about fingering them incessantly, even to their own detriment.

They get run over crossing roads because they can't allow a message to go unread or wait to answer one. They struggle with suitcases, one in each hand, with the phone jammed against their ear by one shoulder so they can talk to their wives or husbands about what cheese to buy. They show highly uneager recipients pictures of their breakfasts on Facebook, Instagram and others. They listen to Spotify as they jog through the park, ignoring bird songs and the soughing of the wind in the trees. They ignore their infant children in their pushchairs in favour of sending or reading messages. Why is it they can't bear to hear its demanding ring without answering it immediately, even though the caller is much more likely to be Mum, Sis or Uncle Jack; people they hardly listen to when the words are coming out of real mouths?

Don't talk to me about mobiles. I believe they rule the world. I do not believe in ghosts from the spirit world. I do believe in monsters from the world of tech. Why not? You mix a load of electronic devices together and out of the primeval soup of wires, microchips, LCDs, resistors, transistors, inductors, transformers, conductors, diodes and sensors comes a new form of life, just as it did in the beginning for mankind from carbon, hydrogen, nitrogen, oxygen, phosphorus and sulphur. An accident formed from a bunch of ingredients getting mixed together under a gentle sun on an accommodating planet.

By standing on a chair, I managed to get a loop around Art's ankle and I hauled him down—with great difficulty—to the floor and tied him onto the settee. It was just about heavy enough to hold him there.

"How about a thank you?" I said.

He looked at me bleakly. "What the hell am I going to do?"

"I honestly don't know, but I'll try to get help. The Fire Service seems the best bet. They have a lot of equipment, don't they? Then you'll need a scientist of some sort. Stephen Hawking would be my first choice, but I think he died. Maybe Brian Cox? Someone with a bit of imagination as well as expertise. Most people are not going to believe your story. Is your phone still charged? Maybe I should have a word with your captor?"

"You stay away from her," he yelled fiercely. "She's a witch."

The first person I spoke to about Art's problem thought it might be psychological.

"He believes he's weightless and so it happens. You know, at one time people were told they were going to die, even though they were hale and healthy, and they turned their faces to the wall and died. It's all in the mind."

To be honest, the person giving me that advice was the barman at The Crown pub, who I had consulted about a regular who looked the professor type. The professor, however, was a gentleman farmer, but he did give me the name and number of a genuine scientist. I called the man and he agreed to come and examine Art. The scientist's name was Flanders.

"So," said Flanders, "you've tied him to his bed."

He was a portly man with stylish glasses on a narrow nose.

"If we untie him, he'll shoot up to the ceiling."

"Don't do that," cried Art, "I'm still bruised from the first time."

Flanders took no notice of this and swiftly untied the knots.

Art shot up and smacked against the ceiling, shattering the lightshade. He screamed until we got him down again and safely anchored to the settee.

"Amazing," said Flanders. "I genuinely thought I was being hoaxed." He asked a series of questions and then said he was leaving.

"What am I supposed to do?" Art said. "Can you cure me?"

"Cure you? No. My advice is to wear a lead-lined suit."

And he left.

~~~

For the next week I had to feed Art, help with his bedpan, generally act as nurse and carer. Doctors came and went. Reporters and other media personnel came and only went when Art refused to let them untie him and watch him zip up to the ceiling. More scientists. A circus manager. One university lecturer who was a keen Kafka fan suggested the situation was similar to the short story "The Metamorphosis" where someone wakes up to find themselves, well, metamorphosised. Art was not now a cockroach, but he had been changed into something quite extraordinary, I suppose. An ex-military man said it was a shame it hadn't happened during the Second World War since Art could have been used as a human barrage balloon and watcher. None of them helped us very much with our problem and eventually they stopped coming.

I was running out of steam, looking after my friend, and I suggested he go into a home of some kind where he could be properly looked after.

"Let's try the phone," he said at last. "See if we can conjure up that weird creature who put me in this position?"

"I smashed the phone to bits and threw it in the trash."

"What?" shrieked Art. "Why?"

"Because you told me to," I replied simply.

That evening there was a gathering from the pub on Art's lawn. Art had requested that we stake him out so he could look up at the night sky. He said he was sick of staring at a ceiling with a broken light shade. He wanted to commune with the cosmos. I could sympathise with that. Possibly there was an answer among the stars? Brian Cox would approve. The mysteries were all out there in the universe, waiting to be solved. Every day there were new discoveries in space, and day-old theories were shattered and new theories formed. Suns, moons, stars—dozens of different kinds of stars—comets, meteors, gas balls, dark matter, black holes... they were all out there, full of secrets. A night studying them could do no harm. I'm not religious in the normal sense of the word, but I do get a feeling of something greater than the human race, something spiritually overwhelming, something beyond our comprehension.

So we spread-eagled him on his back, and apart from complaining about ants in his trousers he seemed quite comfortable.

"The American Indians used to do that to colonialists," said one man as the pub group wandered off, "as a punishment. The ants used to eat out the eyes of the victim before starting on his tongue."

"That's not helping," yelled Art.

Once he had settled, mentally, Art began to get quite poetic.

"The sky is a pit," he said to me, while staring up at the stars. "An infinite pit without even a bottom. How deep space is. Deep and black and speckled with bright spots. I'm going to seek the answer to my problem amongst those planets, stars and hunks of rock out there. I have all night to study and ponder. Something will come to me, I'm sure. I am a thoughtful man, after all."

I left him to his ponderings and went to bed in his flat.

In the early hours, before it was even properly light, I heard a commotion going on down below. I looked out of the seventh-floor window to see an elderly lady who was obviously out walking her dog. She was bent over Art and was swiftly untying the ropes that were holding him down.

I opened the window and heard her say, "You poor man. Did those thugs from the estate do this to you? They should be locked up—"

Art was yelling, "No! I have the answer. I know how to—"

She was not listening.

The last knot fell away. I saw him trying to grip the grass, trying to hold on to the Earth that was his home. Then he was gone in a flash, shooting upwards and out into the upper atmosphere. I remember the last sound he ever made.

"Oooooooooooo."

He went out into the cosmos like a pale bullet which became a black speck, then disappeared into the blackness beyond. Poor Art. The most he could hope for was to hit a moon, planet or star on his journey. Surely that was on the cards with billions and billions of the buggers out there. Or maybe they would bounce him around like a pinball? Or possibly he might even go on forever, a human missile hurtling through the ether, a spinning human cross?

One thing was certain. His end was unique, unparalleled. Infinity was his tomb. His gravestones were asteroids. His funeral flowers comets.

I almost envied him as I went to the café for my morning coffee. The news was dreadful as usual, the world going to hell in a bucket with no solutions in sight. Art was definitely in a better place, had he been in a state to appreciate it. A vacuum containing dark matter, lumps of burning rock, black holes and space dust was a lot more interesting than a Hackney street.

DECEMBER'S CHILDREN

John Linwood Grant

WINTER BREEDS STRANGE fires at the Langton. Cowls clatter high above, and chimneys gape at curdled skies. Like huge and tired bronchi, the flues shudder, coughing up detritus from the year before—wood tar and silky soot, the desiccated bodies of gull and starling, caught in blackened spaces... and other things, of which I shall not speak.

Flame is born under rust-pitted boilers—they groan, their iron hearts stirring, their cylinders awoken, and a dull, persistent rattle shakes the pipes around us.

We are warm again.

Quite what our boilers burn has never been determined. There have been no coal, oil or gas deliveries here for decades, and wood is scarce on this rough rolling pasture by the cliffs. A stunted hawthorn or two but nothing one might call lumber. It is sufficient in this season to know that we will be warm, well-fed, and that most of us will see the spring—perhaps all of us. The Langton will decide that, as it always does.

I am merely the manager.

"Weather is mild," said Anya, dismembering small, skinned bodies in the kitchens.

Dinner would be rabbit, caraway and onion, dumplings, simmered for many hours. We still had no chef, but Anya always did surprisingly well, considering she was untrained. Her cooking re-imagines her childhood outside Kraków, untroubled days before she was brought to England to learn an adult's ways.

"We do." I tasted a slice of onion, crisp and sharp. "Mild for December. But the storms will come. Better to ease into it and be ready."

"There is new people staying."

"Coastal walkers—Mr and Mrs Hillier, and a Mr Doyle—passing through. They are heading for Whitby, they say."

The three newcomers had signed the guestbook for me last night. The Hilliers were pleasant and came over very much as written on the tin—weathered and healthy, in their early sixties. Inveterate walkers, with well-worn outdoors gear and many, many maps.

As for Mr Doyle, I was less sure. A quiet, elderly, bespectacled man, a caricature of a retired teacher, down to the patches on the elbows of his less-than-weatherproof tweed jacket. I would not have placed him as an aficionado of the wilds, but still, the Langton had allowed him in . . .

We do, occasionally, have guests who are no more than they seem. And I had already suspected there might be more casual trade than usual; we'd been in the newspapers that November, a source of some consternation among staff and residents: *Local boy goes missing in vicinity of old Langton Hotel, off A171.*

An oversight, a small sin committed by a tired sub-editor. The newspaper proprietors dealt with it, and our name was absent from later reports. The boy was found, unharmed, still slightly drunk on bike-shed cider, later the next day. But the Langton does not like to be discussed by strangers; and we heard Room 402 late into the night, a dull *hoon* of displeasure disturbing our sleep for almost a week.

In the breakfast room all was well. Of our regular residents only the Cawthornes lingered, toying with cold toast whilst their daughter whimpered and chewed upon a metal serving spoon. Husband and wife nodded to me, but their eyes were polished beads which stayed fixed upon the girl. Safety first.

I strolled on, and found Justine on the first floor, in the process of cleaning Mr Doyle's room.

"He's gone to the cliffs," she said, coiling up the hose of the antique vacuum cleaner. "Bird spotting, or taking in the breeze."

I imagine Justine would be described as petite, and charming. Her hair is satin-dark and tousled, a gamin cut; her small breasts tease beneath an open white shirt, a game she likes to play with me. As if I could be tempted. I have my duties.

The Langton allows her access to its darkest corners, although I do not know why. Justine can enter rooms which have been lost to us over the years, and has even coaxed a few of them back into the fold. Room 305, for example, had been unusable since an incident in the nineteen-eighties but she managed to win it over. Dr Swain has it now; the stains on the ceiling do not seem to bother her in the slightest.

The vacuum cleaner surrendered to Justine, as most things did, and she arranged towels and facecloths upon the trolley.

"How do you find him?" I asked.

"Our Mr Doyle? Distant, I suppose. It wouldn't surprise me if he asks to stay longer. There are no maps of Whitby, no water-bottle or first aid kit in his rucksack. Nothing you might expect of a proper walker. I had only the briefest peek," she added.

Ah. Beyond our accidental guests, who had seen the peeling sign by the main road, those who had car problems, or came to us on a whim, there were only two other kinds of visitor: the ones whom the Langton sought out for its own unfathomable purposes, or the ones who sought the Langton. The latter were frequently disappointed.

I went for a walk.

The path from the hotel to the cliffs is little more than a boundary between two stretches of pastureland, neither of which are grazed these days. I believe we own the land. The path rises

gently, hedged by thistle and gorse in places, watched over by the
wicked-eyed gulls which wheel and circuit above us, our vicious
friends. Dr Swain, who dislikes all living creatures, believes
that the gulls are the hotel's reluctant allies, its vantage points
from which to see the world outside. This seems over fanciful to
me.

Gulls are selfish creatures.

Beyond the path lies a stretch of coarse grasses and unreliable
hollows, broken chalk which thrusts like bone from beneath thin
soil, enough to deter most hikers from straying inland. Mr Doyle
stood on the "official" coastal walk marked on maps. No
binoculars; no *Collin's Book of British Seabirds*. I strolled the last
few yards to the cliff edge, noting recent slips and fractures.

"A bright morning," I said by way of announcing my presence.

He turned, momentarily puzzled. "Oh, it's . . ." he said.

"The manager, sir."

"I'm sorry, I didn't catch your actual name." His smile was as
lean, as undernourished, as his face. Sparse brown hair fluttered
above a pallid scalp, blew across his deep-set eyes.

"No," I agreed. "I trust that all is to your satisfaction, Mr
Doyle?"

"Satisfaction?" He tried to maintain his smile. "I had
wondered . . . if it would not be too much bother . . ."

"I am here to provide for all your needs."

"Do you have such a thing as a cot-bed? One such as a . . . a child
might use."

"Of course."

"I would be very grateful if one could be placed in my room."

Clearly he expected me to ask why on earth he would want such
a thing—but it has never been my policy to interrogate the guests.

"Certainly, sir. I will have Benedito, our porter, see to it."

Mr Doyle brushed the hair from his eyes. "I will pay extra,
naturally."

"That will not be necessary, sir." I made a note in my pocket-
book, and recalled Justine's comment. "I understand that the
Hilliers are preparing for the next leg of their coastal tour. Will
you be accompanying them, Mr Doyle?"

"I ... I may try a few local walks instead, before the bad weather. Would that be possible?"

"I will book you in for a fortnight. Room 112, your present accommodation. And if you have to leave earlier ... "

"Thank you."

Walking back, I noted that the gorse was in flower again, small golden crescents among the wicked thorns. December made no difference to the gorse, and Anya would be out on gentler days, picking the best flowers and making her notable wine—rich, nutty, reminiscent of a Sauterne infused with vanilla.

A cot. As I came within sight of the Langton's ornate bulk once more, I wondered. The hotel was acquainted with children—if the Cawthorne's daughter could be called a child, and if you did not think too hard about Anya's son Josef. This was a playground for him, flitting between floors as easily as mist, and his presence was a pleasure.

I saw his face just then at one of the third-floor windows, a shadow-smile under broad Slavic cheekbones, much like his mother's. He waved, his small hand passing through the glass. I nodded back. A fine boy.

My own birth was at the Langton, but unlike Josef I have inherited no "peculiarities", no curious ways. I am nothing of note.

Which is as it should be.

Whatever Benedito's employment history, he is pleased to act as porter and doorman when needed. A small repayment, he insists, for sanctuary after he fled London, having eviscerated his pimp with a sharpened cake-knife stolen from a café. I would have thought that purloining a steak knife or a chef's cleaver would have been more sensible, but people can be odd. Still, the Langton had welcomed this bedraggled half-Portuguese waif, which was all that mattered. He was best kept away from anything sharp, though.

He has a wiry strength, and had no difficulty hauling what Mr Doyle required from the storage cellars. I would have said that the small bed he unearthed was from my grandfather's time, barely post-Victorian, with polished walnut rails, and a trick to unlatching the brass fittings which lowered the sides. Large enough to take a child of up to seven or eight years old, it had a musty but serviceable mattress, which I placed by a window to freshen a little.

"He has no *filho*, no son," Benedito said, pulling at the stiff window to open it fully. "Why would he want this in his room?"

"No daughter, either."

"Ah, but this is not a girl's bed." He pointed to the headboard, and I saw the crude carvings there: a stick figure with a rifle, the name *Toby*, and vaguer scratches. The work of a boy's penknife, most likely.

"So it is. Was this the only cot-bed?"

"No, there were five or six others, further back." Benedito shrugged. "You want me to bring a different one?"

"This will be fine."

We walked back down to the foyer, drifting into one of our usual discussions about the wiring, which is in that state experienced by every large, old building. Benedito is no electrician, and neither am I, but we do our best to tend the miles of ailing, ageing cable which run throughout the hotel. The Langton does not tolerate rats or other gnawing vermin; the passing years alone are our enemy, as cloth and rubber perish, or Bakelite cracks, causing the inevitable faults.

Mr Doyle was just coming in.

"The matter of the cot-bed has been dealt with, sir," I said. "It is somewhat old-fashioned, but in reasonable condition. I trust you will have a pleasant stay."

Again, the smile of a starved, distracted man. We do not require documents from our guests, and I wondered if I had misjudged his age. Younger than I had thought, but... distressed by experience?

"Thank you," he said, and went upstairs.

Wе no longer use the grand dining hall, which seats over two hundred people—it would be ludicrous to cluster in one corner of its vaulted splendour. Instead, staff and resident guests eat together in the restaurant nearest the kitchens—without mingling, I hasten to add—which usually makes for a relatively homely atmosphere.

That evening, however, was less comfortable than usual. Whilst the Hilliers dined together in an alcove, keeping to themselves, Mr Doyle went out of his way to seek conversation, an unexpected turn of events. This had me pacing between the tables, hoping to minimise any disruption. Several guests, including the Cawthornes, ignored him. Mr Brennan looked up with that dreadful smile of his, which proved too much, thankfully, for our inquisitive newcomer. No one should have to hear what Mr Brennan has to say.

My greatest concern was when Mr Doyle approached Dr Swain. She tends not to tolerate intrusions on her routine. She arrives for dinner at half-past seven prompt, reads the newspaper for exactly five-and-a-half minutes, and then attends to her soup. The paper is always the same one—*The Times* from 8th June 1954—and the soup must always be a thin vegetable broth. Mr Doyle, knowing nothing of this, asked if he might join her for a few moments.

Dr Swain glanced down at her medical bag, up at the newcomer's rather meatless face, and then—to my great surprise—she nodded. After some minutes of murmured conversation he stood and left. I gestured to Anya, who brought a fresh bowl of hot broth.

"Is everything satisfactory, doctor?" I asked, replacing her entrée.

She brushed back a strand of iron-grey hair. "He spoke for six minutes and forty-three seconds," she said.

"I do apologise. It will not happen again."

She waved my contrition away. "The man is obsessional. I find him mildly interesting—in a professional sense."

"Obsessional about...?" But her attention had turned to her broth and I saw that there was nothing more to be said, as far as she was concerned.

The Hilliers left mid-morning the next day, polite but not, I thought, in a mood to recommend us to others. Or to chatter about the experience, which was much as I would have wished.

"He was talkative," said Justine, polishing the front desk.

The Atkinson sisters were settled on the foyer settee, reading, and we kept our eyes averted. They have been with us since my father's time—identical twins who are so identical that it hurts to consider both sisters at once for longer than a few seconds; a neuralgic pain in the centre of your forehead, as if your eyes have been forced to focus within themselves.

"At dinner? Yes." I had no doubt that she meant Mr Doyle.

"In the night."

I waited for more; she put her cloth down.

"I was restless," she explained. "I walked the first floor, replaced a lightbulb or two, sat and sang to Room 132 for a while, and then I heard him . . . muttering to himself."

"A nightmare?"

"More a conversation. He would say something and wait for an answer. After a while, he responded, resumed. It went on for at least half an hour, but I couldn't hear the other voice." She giggled. "Perhaps he's practising to be a ventriloquist, but isn't very good at it."

A difficult situation. Unlike Justine, I felt it inappropriate to eavesdrop—unless the Langton itself had a clear and present need. If that were the case . . .

"What did he say? The gist of it, I mean. Please spare me anything salacious."

Another giggle. She ruffled her soft, dark hair with one hand. "Oh, it was mostly nonsense. As if he were pleading. And he kept saying 'Toby', over and over."

I stiffened. *Toby.* The name carved on the cot's headboard.

"Thank you, Justine. Please do try to respect the guests' privacy, though. I wouldn't want people to think that we gossiped about them."

She arched an eyebrow. "Why, I would never do such a thing!" she lied, shameless as always.

When she had gone I spent considerable time leafing through

the thick journals kept below the desk. Therein lay everything which my predecessors had noted concerning the Langton—each generation, going back to my grandfather and possibly my great-grandfather, had added their own crabbed commentary. I was pleased my own writing was considerably more legible than that of the others—my father in particular had used a script which rarely stayed within the lines, or even the notional margins.

There was nothing of note concerning Room 112, which had a spotless record; nothing which indicated that anyone called Doyle had ever stayed here before, and as far as I could see, no mention of a *Toby* in the old guest books.

On the sixth day of his stay, Mr Doyle asked if we had any toys, such as balls, spinning tops, yo-yos or similar apparatus.

"Not that I am aware, sir, but let me see."

We did have some Found shelves in an office—who was I to say if things had been Lost, not Discarded?—and there, after some rummaging, I unearthed a hoop (without its stick), a throwing disk as you might see in the park, and a number of toy soldiers. I gathered these together, coming up finally with some poorly-cast lead cowboys, three or four German soldiers made of grey plastic, and what looked like a wounded Medieval knight, the removable helmet missing.

I conveyed them to the waiting Mr Doyle, who appeared unnecessarily grateful, humming to himself as he took his prizes up to his room.

"Obsessional." Dr Swain stood by the unused guest lift, her newspaper under her arm.

"But over what, exactly?"

I have never been sure of the colour of Dr Swain's eyes. She looks through them much as a sniper might through field glasses, peering with bright and cold intent.

"Toby," she said, and strode away towards the nearest lounge.

I would have left the matter there had it not been for Anya. She came to me later that afternoon, sage leaves plaited in her hair, flour dusting her arms.

"Josef is ... unrested?"

"Restless?"

"Yes."

In the office doorway something flickered but did not smile. I blew out my cheeks, an annoying habit which surfaced when I was perplexed.

Josef was perhaps the least problematic resident in the whole of the hotel. Anya had been seven months pregnant when she arrived here, fleeing the immigration authorities and with a gangmaster from the cities of West Yorkshire on her trail. The Langton liked her, and so she disappeared from their world, in effect. Six weeks later Dr Swain delivered Josef, if delivered was the right term. Released him might be more accurate.

"What does he say—does he know what's wrong?"

She wiped a fragment of pastry from her cheek. "Your Mr Doyle. This man ... he has need, inside him."

"To do with children?" This was beginning to sound disturbing. I did not believe that Josef could be hurt, or even threatened, but if Doyle had some unsavoury craving and went near the Cawthorne's daughter ... there would be blood. It would not be the girl's.

"No, no. His child, only. Maybe his child is here, he thinks?"

I patted her arm, a fine cloud of flour landing on my dark suit.

"Thank you, Anya. I will look into the matter."

I knew that Mr Doyle was in his room. In the unlikely event that I was needed, Benedito would tend to the front desk. A single knock on the door of Room 112 sufficed. He opened it a few inches, peering out at me.

"I wonder if I might I have a word, sir?"

"Uh, certainly."

It was difficult to read his expression as he gestured me in. The cot was at one side; his own bed had been pushed back against the other wall, underneath a window. All of the first-floor rooms have relatively modern décor and are of a good size, large enough to hold a writing desk and straight-backed chair, as well as the usual armchair, wardrobes and night-tables. Mr Doyle's allotted writing desk stood askew in the doorway to the small en suite bathroom, almost blocking the way.

"Is there—Is there something wrong?" he asked. "Was I making too much noise?"

I tried not to frown. "If you wish your room to be re-arranged, sir, Benedito and I would be happy to assist. You need simply ask."

A pronounced tic or twitch appeared under his left eye.

"I wanted... I wanted to do it myself."

"I see. Mr Doyle, is something amiss—apart from the layout of your room, I mean? The Langton is quite accommodating, and we pride ourselves on offering a full service."

The tic grew worse.

"Oh, no, I'm fine. Can't fault you at all." His smile was weak, crooked. "I would like to stay the full fortnight, if you are amenable."

"That will be no problem, sir."

Which was all I could think to say, at that juncture.

No one on the staff knew what to make of Mr Doyle. The weather began to worsen and he no longer went to the cliffs, but stayed for the most part in Room 112, coming down only for the evening meal. He asked if he might see to his room himself—unusual, but not greatly disruptive. Justine left clean towels and appropriate materials on a trolley outside his door each morning, taking away anything used later in the afternoon. She did not go inside although I knew she was tempted to do so.

The questions at dinner stopped. He sat alone each evening in the alcove the Hilliers had used, picking at his food, and I began to feel sorry for this quiet, haunted man. I say "haunted", but of course I do not mean that in any unnatural sense.

I do not happen to believe in ghosts.

The younger and smaller gulls had drawn further inland, but the wave-hammered elders, used to winter, paid no heed to gathering clouds and sudden, stiff gales. The Langton's boilers thundered and groaned beneath us, filling the hotel with comforting warmth.

"The fourth floor is unhappy," said Justine.

We were gathered in my office for one of our irregular staff meetings—Justine, Benedito, Anya, and David Adeyemi, our most recent recruit. David, whose presence was the result of a dark incident in Room 132, had been in business and was proving useful for those few dealings we had with outside tradesmen. The manager must never leave the Langton and its lands. "What does that mean, 'unhappy'?" he asked, still somewhat unsure about his new home.

Justine spread out her hands, a gesture of uncertainty. "The rooms brood. More than usual."

I glanced at the photographs on the office walls: my grandfather in top hat and battered greatcoat; my father, rod-straight in his neatly tailored three-piece suit; I in that same suit, still serviceable. There were no pictures of my great-grandfather, nor had he ever been found. It was a lineage, however, a tradition of men who knew or know the Langton.

But the fourth floor has never been a safe place. My father once took me up there. I was ten years old. Most of the lights had failed, and detritus lay in front of some of the doors—broken roof tiles, the bodies of pigeons contorted and grotesque in death, the debris of decades. Gloomy corridors, lined by pots of dead ferns, felt like tunnels driven through the Langton's darkest thoughts. I asked him why we were there.

"Because you will be the manager, one day," he said. "You must understand your domain; the Langton must understand you."

I did not want to understand the fourth floor. I had always suspected Room 407 of being responsible for my mother's death, only hours after my own birth. That or the one which cannot be written about. At that age I wanted to be the bold explorer, to make my father proud. But the cancer which took him years later was already tugging at his nerves, and I was a child, not a rugged, fur-swaddled hero from my adventure books. We did not stay long.

So. The upper floor disturbed. Josef, still shifting uneasy from corridor to corridor...not entirely satisfactory.

"You could ask him to leave." That was Benedito, toying with the buttons on the old doorman's jacket he likes to wear at that time of year, a thick dark-green gabardine that repels all weathers.

Justine shook her head; Anya and David looked interested in the idea.

"Certainly not," I said. "The Langton has standards. To eject a guest once welcomed, without good reason...No. We shall wait. Wait, and see."

Our meeting concluded, I returned to the foyer and my well-polished desk, which sported nothing more than a large brass handbell to be rung for attention, and the current guestbook. David's suggestion, not long after he joined us, that we might consider adding a computer system had brought laughter from the others, which flushed even his teak-hued cheeks. He was not to know that the Langton does not care for electronic devices.

Five days more of Mr Doyle, during which to watch and to ponder.

The resounding crash from above came not five days later but that same night, just after nine o'clock. A heavy object, or objects, falling over on the first floor, magnified by ageing, creaking timbers.

"We do not run," I reminded Benedito as he rushed from his position by the outer doors. "It disturbs the residents."

He blinked, and slowed to a fast, awkward walk. I joined him. The massive pine armoire by the head of the broad stairs was in place, so that was not the cause. An item of furniture in one of the rooms, perhaps? We turned into the main corridor—104, 106, 108...

Anya's son flickered beside the closed door of Room 112, his vague form slipping in and out of the gold and dark-green fleur-de-lys wallpaper, much the same green as Benedito's jacket. The colours of the Langton. In my eyes, Josef was both trying to flee and to remain—a state of alarm or panic.

"Call for Anya," I instructed Benedito, and took out my master keys. The lock was stiff, stubborn, but I was in no mood for delay. I put my shoulder to the door as I turned the key.

If I were imaginative, I would have described the room as a shrine. The cot-bed was in the very centre, askew, on its side, one of the wooden rails broken. Everything else had been pushed to the edges of the available space, or forced into the bathroom. Encircling the cot stood a rank of diminutive figures, the toy soldiers, each turned inward as if watching, or worshipping it.

And above them . . .

Mr Doyle twisted, jerked, his booted heels kicking at the musty air—a hanged man. Very poorly hanged from the amount he was struggling. A thick curtain cord was tight around his neck, tied to the central light-fitting. It was remarkable that the ceiling had not come down.

I had a grip on his lower legs in an instant, thrusting up, holding him as steadily as I could. His lips were blue, but his eyes swivelled in all directions, seemingly at random. The only sound was the laboured struggle of his breath—and my own.

"I'm here, I'm here!" Benedito rushed back into the room, past me, and began dragging the writing desk from the bathroom, pushing it under Mr Doyle's feet. We worked in tandem, until I was holding the man in position upon the top of the desk, his boots firmly set upon it. I disliked having to give Benedito a blade, but he was far nimbler than I. With my pocket-knife in his hand, he scrambled onto the desk, reached up, and slashed through the curtain cord, taking the weight as the man slumped.

By the time Anya arrived, Josef flitting round her, we had Mr Doyle flat on his bed, and the cord pulled away.

"Toby—" A moan as he stared at Josef.

"*Toby . . .*" came an echo that was not an echo from far above us, more a hollow reverberation in the fabric of the building that a voice . . .

Room 402.

"Yes, I heard," I muttered at the ceiling. "Anya, Benedito— carry our guest down to the foyer, where Dr Swain can examine him."

I wanted to talk to him away from this room, and away from the cot.

On the long settee in the foyer Mr Doyle sipped from a small glass of brandy which Anya held to his lips. Livid weals ran around his throat where the rough cord had bitten into his skin, but Dr Swain, brisk and disinterested, pronounced that he would take no permanent harm.

I asked the others to busy themselves elsewhere for a short while, and I drew up one of the heavy leather armchairs, sitting myself near his head.

"If you wished to kill yourself, Mr Doyle, you should have mentioned it to me." If not for my position, I would have added that he'd done a rather shabby job of it so far.

His bloodshot eyes looked up at me. "You—" He coughed, trying to clear his bruised throat. I helped him with a little more brandy. "You would have argued with me. Stopped me."

"I would have discussed it, sir, in confidence," I reproved him. "The wishes of our guests are important."

The man lay there in silence for some minutes. Justine, bless her, brought me a glass of port, and slipped away again. It was a '35 vintage, smooth, warming, just what I needed. The '35 had aged well.

"My son, Toby, died twenty-three years ago today," he said, a sudden, hoarse whisper. "He was seven years old. My wife...she did not take to motherhood, left us quite early, to travel. We never saw her again. I loved my son very much, you see. So very, very much."

He reached towards his throat with one hand and I gently dissuaded him.

"Best not to aggravate the damage, sir."

"No, I suppose you're right." That hand gripped my sleeve instead. "There was a fire in the lodgings where he and I were staying. No one's fault—a rat at the circuits, or something like that. The firemen dragged me out—I was screaming to go back, pleading, but it was too late for him. Smoke inhalation, they said." The grip tightened slightly. "I have no photographs of my boy, none of his drawings, nothing. They all burned you see, all burned..."

"My sincere condolences, Mr Doyle." It was difficult to know if he heard me.

He coughed, drew in a wheezing breath.

"I have been alone since that day. I talk to him but there is never an answer. And each year I grow more alone, more tired, more burdened by the thought of my poor boy. They say that time heals all. *They* are wicked liars." There was a vicious edge to those last few words.

I tried to divert him.

"Do you know why you came here, to the Langton?" It was not my habit to be so direct or intrusive with guests. My tongue soured at the words, but still...

"The Hilliers. I met them much further down the coast, near Hornsea—we were all three in the same bed-and-breakfast, by chance, and they were kind. They saw how low I was and asked me to accompany them on their coastal walk for a while. Said it would blow out the sorrows. I protested; they insisted. They were just such hearty, wholesome people.

"This part of the route was a long stretch, they explained, but they had seen an old newspaper in the bed-and-breakfast which indicated there was a hotel in the area. They thought it might accommodate us for a night or two, setting us up for the next section. And they were right—you were here, open, with vacancies." He eased himself into a sitting position, his hand falling away from my arm. "Tonight, I lay in bed, half-awake, and when I looked across the room, the figures were there, assembled around the cot... Toby loved his little soldiers."

"Might you have done that yourself, Mr Doyle?" I suggested.

"I... I might have. I don't know. But then I saw him, my Toby, within the cot-bed. Unburned, whole. And with all my being, all my heart, I wanted to be with him."

Had he seen his son, conjured inside his own head from his despair? Or had he seen Josef, flitting uncertainly, puzzling at this man of sorrows?

"The mind plays tricks, especially when we are tired."

"The cot... it has my boy's name upon it. Surely that was a sign?"

What should I say to someone who had been grieving for twenty-three years?

"It is a human habit, sir, to seek connections where there are none—they can be comforting. The name might have been scratched there many years ago, by a child who was recalling a schoolfriend sweetheart, or an idle maid who had a lover of that name…" I stopped there, for none of us truly understood the Langton, or what it chose to do. We either lived our lives in suspicion and dissatisfaction, as had my father, or we embraced what was before us, and did our duty. I had buried many of my questions and felt no worse for doing so.

Mr Doyle stared at his fingers, which had tied a noose around his own neck. He didn't seem to recognise them.

"I only wanted… I only wanted to join my boy." He gave a cry which turned into another painful cough, almost doubling him over.

A decision had to be made. He would need time to recover, physically at least. Room 207, adjoining David's quarters and not far from Anya's, was a well-lit, gentle place with an excellent view of the cliffs.

"I shall find you a different room for a week or so, Mr Doyle," I said. "A courtesy, we shall call it, under the circumstances. There will be no charge. And you will rest. Our doctor will be available to you."

"I suppose that would be… But then…?" His gaze now was on the entrance to the hotel, and beyond.

I knew what he saw.

He saw the world outside, a friendless, childless wilderness without comfort, without surcease from dreams of loss. A world trapped in endless December, with no warmth to which he could cling.

Behind him, Josef shifted in and out of the wall, a child of the Langton, and the smell of his mother's rye bread wafted from the kitchens. Dr Swain would be in one of our lounges, perusing her newspaper—*The Times*, 8th June 1954, naturally—and the Atkinson sisters would be out in the hotel gardens, lanterns in hand as they trod the night, gathering dank, frost-blackened dahlias for their room. Yet because they and our other residents *were* here, the world which Mr Doyle knew had been spared many things it did not require; not the least of which was the fearful rictus of Mr Brennan's smile, and knowledge of what that man had done, fourteen years ago, in a modest London terrace.

It was possible that the world out there did not require Mr Doyle.

"And then, sir? The Langton will be here, and last year's gorse wine will be ready. It promises to be one of Anya's finest."

But he had slipped into fitful sleep.

I do not consider myself an overly sentimental man. If, with time, he still wished to choose self-slaughter, as the play has it, then I would do what was necessary. Efficiently, without damaging the furniture. The hotel's ledgers told of a Frenchwoman who had been here during the war, a wrecked and ruined woman. She had not needed all of the small capsules she carried with her. The last two were locked in my personal escritoire, secure in a small pearl-inlaid box...

I finished the last drop of my port and went over to the front desk. The guest book was there, ready, and I took out my fountain pen. *Toby Frederick Doyle*, I wrote on the line beneath his father's tidy hand. "Frederick" because it was my father's name, though I never spoke it in his lifetime. It seemed an appropriate, permissible touch.

The cot-bed would go back into storage, as would the toys. Whatever Mr Doyle had carried with him, whatever the hotel might or might not have constructed from his memories, it did not matter.

There are no ghosts at the Langton.

Only lives.

THE ROSEHILL
TRUTH DOCTOR

Wendy Purcell

I T WAS THE lies about who broke the kitchen window. That and the sight of her white chrysanthemums sliced to salad by fallen daggers of glass that confirmed Simone's failings. Things had gotten out of control and she had to face the truth. She was far too lenient a mother.

She had only gone inside for a minute, two at most, and she had to take a break sometimes, didn't she? Children were meant to be raised by a village, not by a single woman, and if she'd had to have a rest from their playing and their goddamn noise for— well, it can't have been more than five minutes...Could her nine-year-old twins really not manage to break everything? Was she never to have anything nice?

With her peeling lips stretched taut, Simone said, "It's amazing how things just happen around here. Windows get smashed to smithereens, plates break, cupboard doors get ripped off their hinges, and neither of you ever knows what happened. Do you think an evil spirit invades the house every night, just to come here and ruin all my things?"

Her son Jonah pushed disobedient black hair out of his eyes. "I didn't do it," he said. Simone snorted and swung her gaze towards the alternative perpetrator.

Jonah's sister Arly took two steps backwards. "Don't look at me. I didn't do it either."

Simone's fingers twisted and pulled at the top button on her shirt, tightening the collar around her neck. What a torment it was, to never know how things got broken or who did it. "Windows don't break themselves. One of you must have done it."

"We didn't!"

Simone took an unsatisfying breath. "You *have* to stop lying to me," she said through clamped teeth.

Jonah's voice squeaked up an octave. "Don't worry, Mummy. Arly and I will fix the window. You won't be able to tell it was ever broken. There's nothing you can't fix with glue."

Simone tugged down her shirt and tried to shake the burn out of her neck muscles. And then she understood: this was it. She had reached that point, the one her mother had warned her about, the point where you should walk away and let someone else deal with things. Only Simone didn't have a someone else. There was just her. She jabbed her finger at the twins. "This can't continue. I just…can't…cope. You two are going to have to learn to stop telling lies!"

"We're not liars," Jonah said.

"We're not," Arly said.

"Enough!" Her own scream surprised even Simone.

In a manic fit that she later remembered only vague details of, Simone marched inside, straight to the twins' room. She kicked aside Arly's soccer ball, sending it bouncing psychotically into the wardrobe. Grabbing first Jonah's backpack and then Arly's, she emptied out exercise books, a tennis ball, a printout of instructions on how to train a cattle dog, and a scrappy copy of *Pollyanna*. She upended the packs, shaking a shower of crumbs, paper clips and pen lids over the carpet. She wrenched open drawers and left them lying askew on the floor, and quickly stuffed pyjamas and underwear into the backpacks, along with half-outfits, a sweater but no pants for Jonah, mismatched shoes and no socks for Arly.

"Are we going somewhere?" Arly said through fingers pincered on her bottom lip as she watched her mother zip up the backpacks.

Simone knocked Arly's irritating hands away from her mouth. "I'm taking you to the Rosehill Truth Doctor."

Jonah grabbed Arly by the hand. "Please, Mummy, no."

"We'll be good and we won't let anything else get broken," Arly said.

"It's too late for any more promises, goddamn it," Simone said, the backpacks clenched in her hand. "You're going."

The Rosehill truth doctor. Jonah and Arly had been threatened with him many times, whenever they'd overstepped Simone's boundaries, which was often because they changed all the time.

"You're big enough to cross the highway by yourself," Jonah would be told on Tuesday, but by Friday his mother would yell, "I've told you never to cross that road if I'm not there to hold your hand!"

"But you said . . ."

And then the threats about the truth doctor would start.

Behind the sports shed at school stories were told of a child who had been sent to the truth doctor and had returned as a lace-bedecked doll, sitting forever amongst the matching cushions on her mother's bed.

"She never spoke or moved again," a grade five girl had whispered, holding the attention of the younger children who listened with their breath stoppered and hands clasped together.

"Ha, ha! It's bullshit," some older boy would interrupt, puffed up with his newly acquired mature view of the world. "Same as Santa Claus—your parents make it up."

But now here Jonah was, standing in the Station Street shopping strip in front of a sign that read:

ROSEHILL TRUTH DOCTOR
DR RABOTTINI
SPECIALISING IN THE TREATMENT OF DECEPTION
AND MENDACIOUSNESS
(*upstairs entrance round back*)

Jonah's legs threatened to give way. The truth doctor was real.

The sign was stuck to the window of the Rosehill Bella Boutique, a dress shop specialising in bridal gowns. Puffy, princess-like dresses were displayed on mannequins frozen in a moment of fashion ecstasy on either side of the shop's front door.

"Look, Mummy," Arly said, pressing up against the glass of the shop front and pointing to a pink flower-girl's dress in the window. "Isn't it beautiful? Can we go inside?"

"We're not here to go dress shopping," Simone said and yanked Arly away from the window. "We're going around the back."

Jonah's right hand was squeezed in his mother's fist as she pulled him and Arly past the lace dresses in the window, past the bottle shop next door, and past the gun shop on the corner. They stumbled and tripped their way down a back lane between the shops and the railway line, edging alongside overflowing rubbish bins and stacks of rain-rotted cardboard boxes. The flapping ghosts of plastic bags, caught on the barbed wire fence along the railway line, waved them on. They turned at the third gate. Tug-boated by their mother up ivy-strangled stairs, Jonah and Arly were pushed against the splintered railing at the top and told to stay still.

Simone peered through the old fly-wire security door. "I can't see anything," she said, shading her eyes with both hands. There was no bell or button so she knocked on the door frame but it made only a muffled thud, as if the wooden plank it was made from had given up offering resistance to rapping knuckles long ago. "Hello!" she called.

Jonah nudged Arly and nodded towards the descending stairs. "Run," he mouthed.

On the tips of his toes, Jonah started down, stepping close to the side of each tread so the old boards wouldn't creak and announce their escape. At the lower landing he stopped to check his sister's progress. To his horror he saw her, white-faced, still standing on the top step, straining at her backpack that had snagged on a nail

"Hello!" Simone called again and gripped the security door with both hands and gave it a rattle in its frame.

Jonah took the steps back up two at a time, reaching out to unsnag Arly's backpack.

"I don't think anyone is in," Simone said and turned just as Jonah got his hand to Arly's backpack. Simone grabbed his shoulder. "What are you up to?"

"Nothing," Jonah lied. "Arly's backpack is stuck."

"Can I help you?" A voice from the dark of the building announced itself.

They all wheeled. Jonah craned his neck to look up at the thin, overhanging man with an enormous forehead and two very prominent front teeth, who was standing in the now open doorway. He was dressed in jeans and a t-shirt which read ALL PEACHES ARE STONED. Around his waist he wore a leather half-apron with tools sticking out of its bulging pockets: a chisel, a tape measure, a claw hammer. He looked like no doctor Jonah had ever seen.

"Aah," the tall man said, nailing Jonah with his eyes. "I've caught you in the very act."

"I was beginning to think you weren't here," Simone said. "Are you the truth doctor? Will you fix my children?"

"I am Doctor Rabottini. They are liars?"

"Of the worst kind," Simone said.

"I see." Dr Rabottini licked his long front teeth. He put his hands in the pockets of his leather apron and beckoned Simone in with a tilt of his head.

They entered into the building through a small, old-fashioned kitchen and made their way down a dark passageway. They had to step around crooked piles of children's backpacks and old-time school bags stacked along the passage, all caked with sawdust and furry cobwebs.

Dr Rabottini's office was at the front of the building. It overlooked Station Street through three tall windows. Dirty venetian blinds at each window hung crookedly on broken tapes. As he entered the room, the tall thin doctor hummed a fragment of a song and waved both hands about as if to say hello to someone. Jonah took a quick glance around but there was no one in the room to greet.

The doctor sat down at his desk, positioned at one end of the room in front of an old cast iron fireplace. The desk was piled high with papers and folders, jars of nails and screws, paint brushes and pill bottles. There were two wooden chairs placed before the desk. Simone lowered herself stiffly into one chair and the two children perched on the other, a half a hip each to their single seat.

Dr Rabottini stopped singing and pushed at the stacked debris that filled his desk until he had carved a clear space in front of him. From his side of the desk Jonah could barely see the truth doctor over the piles of paper, but the back of the doctor's freckled head was reflected dimly in an old, crazed mirror hanging above the mantelpiece. Jonah kept his eyes on that. But looking up revealed another sight: on the plate shelf that circled the room were dozens and dozens of dolls. Some stood bolt upright, their sunset eyes staring at the two children; others were slumped forward seemingly intent on their useless legs. There were dolls in faded party dresses, dolls in pyjamas and dressing gowns, dolls in tattered baby clothes, dolls in dusty school uniforms, dolls with grey skin and missing eyelashes.

"Look at the puppets!" Arly hissed. "What is wrong with them?"

Jonah shivered. "They're only dolls," he said. "They're just a bit broken." He squeezed her hand to keep her quiet.

The doctor found a pen and a notepad amongst the litter on his desk and positioned them neatly in front of himself. He crooked a long band-aid wrapped finger and called the twins forward.

Dr Rabottini clamped Jonah's arm and looked him over; he probed at the bones of his head and peered into his eyes. "Tell me, why do you lie?"

"I don't."

"Your mother says you do."

"See? See?" Simone said from her chair, clutching her handbag. "See what I have to put up with?"

"Do you tell whoppers, then?" Dr Rabottini asked Jonah. "All boys tell whoppers."

"No."

The truth doctor scribbled some notes on the pad in joined-together writing that Jonah couldn't make out. Then he circled Jonah's wrist with his fingers.

"You're a skinny young man," the doctor said.

"He eats all the time," Simone said. "He's one of those boys who just won't fatten up."

The doctor turned to face Arly. "What about fibs? Don't you sometimes tell little fibs?" He stared deep into her eyes with a look that unscrewed all her secrets.

"No, we don't," Arly whispered.

"And this bruise?" Dr Rabottini said, brushing Arly's hair from her face and examining the reddish-purple bloom developing on her chin. "Where did it come from?"

"She won't tell me. I think Jonah did it."

"He didn't," Arly said.

"See, they're such terrible liars," Simone said.

"Well," said Dr Rabottini, "we can fix this, but there is a charge. Nothing is free, of course."

"Of course, how much?"

"The full treatment is seventy-five dollars each."

"So little? I expected it to cost much more."

"Perhaps it will."

Simone shifted back in her seat. "There's always a catch. What's the real price?"

"What's the real price of anything? I can tell you this: your children won't be the same, not as you've known and loved them."

"I don't want them to be the same."

The doctor pulled open a drawer. "Let me get a consent form and explain the procedure to you."

"I don't want a long explanation. You'll just confuse me. Only... will they be in pain?"

"The procedure can be... uncomfortable," Dr Rabottini said, "but I will give them an analgesic. Now, let me talk you through the form. It explains everything."

Jonah watched his mother check her watch. He could see her hands were shaking. "I need to get home," Simone said. "Just let me sign and you can get on with it."

Dr Rabottini shook his head. Simone held out her hand for the form.

Everything was still. Then Dr Rabottini flipped through the form to the consent page at the back. Simone leaned forward and signed with a flick of the pen.

"How long does it take?" she asked the doctor.

"I'll have the children back to your home tomorrow at four o'clock."

Simone picked up her handbag and stood.

"Mummy!" Arly screamed.

"We'll be good!" Jonah said. Tears gathered on the end of his nose. "We'll tell the truth!"

"Be good for the doctor," Simone said and strode from the office. Jonah heard the wire security door open and close, then the old wooden staircase creak in protest at his mother's every step.

Jonah watched from the old, leather-clad dentist's chair where he had been propped and given the instruction to stay. Dr Rabottini fiddled with the dials on a grey boxlike machine. Red wires coming out of the top of the machine were connected to Jonah, to his chest and head. What was the machine telling the doctor about Jonah? Could he see how good Jonah was at reading, how he'd once rescued a baby magpie, how he longed to learn to play the guitar? Could he see that sometimes children had to tell mistruths?

Dr Rabottini handed Jonah a metal cup full of a thick pink liquid pierced by a plastic straw. "Drink," he said.

Jonah felt as if he was sitting at the top of a long slide, about to be pushed off. He lifted the cup to his mouth and the liquid rolled over his tongue, leaving behind a numbness and the taste of raspberries.

"Are you very brave?" Dr Rabottini asked, taking the cup from Jonah.

"No." Jonah's cheeks felt thick and woolly.

"Oh, I think you must be," the truth doctor said. "Are you strong?"

"N . . . n . . . no."

"Now that's a little white lie just there, isn't it? And are you resilient?"

"N . . . "

"Of course you are, but you don't have to be anymore. I'm going to take care of everything."

Jonah felt himself solidifying in the old dentist's chair, unable to move even his eyes. Dr Rabottini moved in and out of Jonah's narrowed field of vision, placing things on a wooden trolley beside the chair. First was a dish of needles and swabs, then a reel of wire and a pot of glue, then short lengths of timber, and last, a bucket full of glass eyes.

The doctor gave Jonah a sharp tap on the head and Jonah fell asleep.

Simone's gaze returned to the clock and she sighed at the disappointing lack of progress of the hour hand. The day spent waiting for the children to come home was unravelling unevenly, some hours jumping forward in a blink of an eye, and other minutes stretching out to paper-thin transparency. All morning she had paced back and forth, picking up clothes and dishes which needed to be put away, then dropping them, too agitated to think about where anything belonged. She had done the right thing, yes—the right thing. The children shouldn't have lied. If she'd tolerated their lying to her what would be next? How big would the lies have gotten? What terrible things might they have said to other people?

At one o'clock she gave up trying to achieve anything and, in need of a hug from a best friend, poured herself a glass of wine and sat down to wait.

She heard the slam of a car door at the front of her house. What time was it? Four-fifteen? She must have fallen asleep! She rubbed her face and pushed her hair back and tried to regain her bearings.

Tap . . . tap . . . tap. What was that noise? It sounded mechanical and regular. Footsteps? No, not the children's, who usually rushed into a room all elbows and knees, falling over each other to be first. But if not them, then who?

The doorbell. Simone couldn't bring herself to move. The doorbell rang again. Simone pulled herself upright and shuffled across the living room floor, dragging herself like she did in her drowning dreams where she could never outrun the incoming tide. She opened the door and froze, gasping at the sight of the two children standing hand in hand in the doorway.

They were stunning, as if drawn by a Disney animator. Each child's hair was neat and slicked back; their faces shiny and serene. Arly wore a white frilled dress Simone had never seen before, and lace-topped socks and shiny patent shoes, and a pink ribbon painted on the side of her head. Jonah looked almost manly, so formal in his blazer, tie and cap.

Both children stood in the doorway quietly, free of all signs of devious agitation.

Dr Rabottini stepped up behind them. "Say hello to your mother," he said.

"Hello, Mother," the two children said in perfect unison.

So polite! So well mannered! And yet there was something about the way the children spoke . . . so mechanical. Their faces had barely moved, just their jaws had flapped up and down as if they had both swallowed a ventriloquist's hand.

"Let's go into the house," Dr Rabottini said.

Tap . . . tap . . . tap. The children trotted into the house, bouncing a little on their stiff legs.

"Come and give me a kiss," Simone said. "You both look so

beautiful. I've never seen you look this good before. You could almost be somebody else's children."

Jonah lifted his face to his mother and bumped his wooden lips against hers. Simone, with a sudden sense of unease, gripped her son by his shoulders to take a better look at him, but her hands did not meet his familiar soft fleshy arms but the firmness of the dead limbs of the forest.

"What have you done?" Simone cried and picked up first Jonah's hand and then Arly's, seeing the finely carved and strung hinges of his wooden fingers, the pink painted-on fingernails of hers. "They're not children anymore, they're... They're puppets."

"Well, of course," the truth doctor said, "they couldn't continue as children and not be able to lie. Lying is intrinsically human. It's one of the ways we care for ourselves and for others. But they are now truthful, which after all is what you wanted. Go on, children, tell your mother some truths."

"You broke the window," Jonah said.

"You bruised my face," Arly said.

"Your clothes are always dirty," Jonah said.

"You smell of wine," Arly said.

"Stop, stop! Stop them talking. This is terrible. You must change them back." Simone pointed to the front door. "Take them back and fix them."

With their painted-on smiles that approved of everything, Arly and Jonah sat down on the couch and crossed their wooden ankles.

The truth doctor shook his head. "I cannot do that. If the work was flawed you would have a right of complaint." He bent over and cupped each of the children's faces in his scarred carpenter's hands and smiled down on them. "But they are perfect."

"Perfect? How can their not being real children anymore be perfect? This can't be final. Please, you have to mend them. I didn't read the form, you saw that. I didn't understand. We must talk about this—Sit, I'll get us a drink. Not wine, of course," Simone trilled. "Really, such nonsense, children. It's too early for anyone to have been drinking wine. Doctor, I'll make us a nice cup of tea and we can talk."

"The tea has weevils in it," Jonah said.

"And the milk will be off," Arly said.

Simone smiled as she looked around her lovely room with its clean white walls and tidy furnishings. She had adjusted the bed to sit an even one inch from the wall. Its pale blue coverlet was pulled tight and the two pillows were stacked neatly on top. The bedside table she had lined up perfectly parallel to the bed and the box of tissues on top of the table was perfectly centred. Everything was so nice. True, the window in the room was too high to look out of, but the sun shone through it just the same. And the kind of things that Simone might once have feared getting broken had all been taken care of. The mirror was a perfectly sound sheet of polished stainless steel; the drinking glass was plastic; the TV was bolted to the wall inside a wire cage. She felt safe and content.

Sometimes, though, there was a feeling that it wasn't quite enough; she could feel it growing now, the sense that something was missing, but the feeling wouldn't last long. Feelings here never lasted long.

Simone's door clicked open and a man dressed in plain blue pants and shirt entered the room. "How are you today, Simone? Got any stories to tell me about your children?"

"No children," she said, although a vague thought threatened to surface, bringing tension to her brow.

"No stories about talking puppets?"

"No."

"Good," the nurse said, "just the usual dose today, then." He held out a small plastic cup with two blue pills in it. "Make sure you swallow them all down."

Simone reached for the cup. "Gone," she said, opening her mouth and lifting her tongue.

"You wouldn't lie to me, would you?" said the nurse, leaning forward to inspect the inside of Simone's mouth. "You know how I hate it when you lie."

Atop the plate shelf in the truth doctor's office, Jonah and Arly sat side by side and watched the doctor. It was their favourite time, when he visited, although in reality he rarely came into the office, and hardly ever was a new doll placed alongside the others. Sometimes Dr Rabottini spoke to them all, calling them his family, singing to them, and sometimes he sat at his desk and cried. But mostly the room was unvisited and outside the trains rumbled past and the dust fell and the sun came and went.

"We're going to go home soon, aren't we?" Arly asked Jonah, although it was getting hard to talk now the leather ties that held the hinges of her jaw together were drying and shrinking.

"No," Jonah said, truthful as ever. "Not soon."

HE DANCES ALONE

Joanne Anderton

OUR STORY BEGINS on a mild autumn morning, before the first of the leaves had started to golden, somewhere in those in-between weeks when heat still weighed on the air. It was late in the year to be so warm. There were whispers of drought, because without the cold there would be no snow and the rivers that relied on its runoff were thirsty. Such things were almost unheard of.

On this morning our protagonist was walking through her adopted hometown in rural Japan to the senior high school, where she was employed as an English language teacher. She did this trip five days a week and knew the path well, had made friends with local cats and old women, and was even starting to feel like she belonged.

An astute reader might stop here and think, ah, she allowed herself to feel a sense of belonging, did she? That had to be her first mistake.

It's a fair enough assumption to make, but they'd be wrong.

So what was it, then? the same astute reader might ask.

Her first mistake? Believing this was her story at all.

The school was five minutes from our protagonist's home, down a narrow road made for pedestrians and cyclists. Houses backed onto the path, providing her a view of neat gardens that had become an unexpected highlight. Never before had she seen so many flowers in so many shapes and colours. Tiny bells, bright red. Little sunbursts, vibrant purple. They grew in every available inch, some tended, some wild.

She doesn't know it yet, but even in the depths of winter, when the trees are bare and the grass dead, there will be hardy pink flowers riding out the chill. And when spring arrives, dragged kicking and screaming, it feels to an Australian unused to winters that ache the way this winter will ache her, the bare limbs of a large bonsai will bud, and she'll realise it's a plum tree.

There was a point in her short walk where she passed the school tennis courts, before ducking through the back gate near the carpark and canteen. And that is where our story really begins, because that is where she saw *him*.

His white sneakers scuffed and squeaked on the hardcourt as he weaved a slow waltz in the early sun. Arms raised, hands gently cupped as though cradling invisible fingers, swaying to no music she could hear. A slow, smooth step, without hint of age or stiffness, though what little she could see of him looked quite ancient. Loose tracksuit pants a size too big, black sweat-slicking material with white zippers up the side. The jacket to match. Wispy grey hair peeked out from the lip of a rust-coloured beanie. His face was hidden behind a surgical mask and large sunglasses.

Our protagonist spared the old man a quick glance, no longer surprised by his presence. The first time she saw him she was certainly taken aback, so much that she paused to stare. Then, feeling rude and trying to ingratiate herself with the locals, her new neighbours, she lifted a hand and gave a little wave, called good morning—"*Ohaiyo gozaimasu!*" That first time, and on all subsequent attempts, she was ignored, so gave up.

But that didn't stop her looking for him, every morning. The old man dancing in the tennis courts, alone.

Usually alone.

Maybe she was a little early that day, because for once the courts weren't empty. A group of second-year girls were practicing serve all around him, chattering like birds, slamming balls into nets and giggling.

One of them noticed our protagonist as she stood there, watching. "Hello sensei!" the girl cried out, waving her racquet. "Good morning!" Fifteen or sixteen years old, dressed in the school sports uniform of blue shorts and white polo shirt.

That was heartening. Our protagonist encouraged her students to practice English at every available opportunity, tried to get them feeling less self-conscious about the whole thing. She had been teaching these girls for two months now, and while their faces were familiar she did not know their names. This early on in her short-lived teaching career she still believed that she would, with time, be able to learn them all.

"Good morning!" she called in reply, waved back, and was rewarded with a cascade of nervous laughter. "How are you?"

Enthusiastic. That's what her Japanese colleagues call her. You, Protagonist-sensei, are very enthusiastic. She has not yet learned that this is code, or what it stands for.

"I am fine," the same girl replied. She was tall, hair tied back in a high ponytail, voice deep. Athletic and confident.

"Have fun playing tennis." There was a scent in the air, something sweet. Almost sickly. It seemed to drift in from the surrounding streets. Our protagonist turned to continue into the school grounds, then paused. "Be careful…Don't hit…You know. He's old…just, careful."

Growing steadily more confused with every stuttered word, the girls gaped at her. Our protagonist opened her mouth, frowned, closed it. Don't hit the old man with your tennis ball suddenly seemed too complicated a sentence.

And now we come to the point of this scene. The crux.

Because the old man, he was still dancing. The whole time he just kept going. Weaving between the students and their teacher, crossing their lines of sight. Straying close to the girls, then drifting away.

Isn't that a bit odd, our protagonist thought to herself.

"Um." She pointed in his general direction even though that seemed impolite. How else was she supposed to make herself understood? "You need to be careful. When you're practicing serve. Make sure…you know…you don't hit…" Why was she tripping over her words like that?

Smiles slipped off the nameless faces staring back at her. Even as the old man danced around them, seemingly danced through them, their blank expressions were more unsettled by her words, her presence, everything about her, than him.

Music crackled out of a loudspeaker, perched high on a poll at the end of the walkway. The town council's morning tune. Distorted and sharp, it made her wince. Whatever music the old man was dancing to, it wasn't this. His feet scuffed slow and steady, utterly out of time.

Ah, you think, I get what's happening now. The old man's a ghost or something, because those girls, they didn't see him. Guess that means he's really the main character, and we're about to learn whatever tragedy trapped him on this plane.

Sorry, not this time.

The old man, he has even less ownership of this story. He's a prompt, that's all, one that startled our protagonist's imagination and got her wondering *who, or what, is that old man dancing with?*

And that, dear astute reader, is what started the whole thing.

Speaking of ghosts, did you know our protagonist feels like one, sometimes? She's got a desk in the staffroom—the *shokuinshitsu*—and when she's not in front of a class teaching that's where she can be found.

There are days where she can sit there, alone at that desk, and not speak a word to anyone at all.

But not all her days are like that—don't feel too sorry for her. She teaches first, second and third years, and there are eight classes in each year, so some days she's run off her feet, rushing from lesson to lesson, bouncing between languages, no time to even stop for lunch.

The day in question was one such day. Fourth period and she was teaching 2-8, a group of second years the Japanese teachers called "demons". The kids in 2-8 were creative, energetic, maybe a little troubled, though she couldn't be sure about their mental states. Definitely louder than most. Despite their reputation they quickly became her favourite because they'd take whatever challenge she threw at them and run with it, caring less about perfection, feeling less the weight of expectation, more willing to make mistakes, which is, of course, the only way to learn.

She yearned to take a page out of their collective book. Still does.

On that day she began class with a simple vocab exercise then moved to something more interesting. "Too complicated," according to one of the Japanese teachers of English she was working with. But unusually for our protagonist, who was constantly worried about making a good impression, she dismissed his misgivings and forged ahead.

She'd found a pack of cards in the drawer of her desk, left over from a predecessor. On each was printed a word in English, along with a picture of that thing. Dog, for instance. King. Flowers. Coffee.

"Let's play a game," she said, showing off her ability to shuffle. "And make up a story."

She split the class into groups of four, and had every child pick a card. For the next ten minutes, in their groups, they used the words on the cards to invent a tale. It could be anything, she tried to explain, no matter how short, no matter how silly or strange.

She wrote an example on the board. "Once upon a time there was a *king*. He drinks *coffee* in the morning. The king owns a *dog*. The dog eats *flowers*."

At this point the other classes had hesitated. They were used to memorising and repeating, didn't have much experience with creativity. But not the "demonic" 2-8.

Excited conversation filled the room, so loud at times it disturbed their neighbours. Protagonist-sensei and her teacher wandered around the room, offering assistance and clarifying definitions. At the end of the lesson each group elected a speaker to stand and read out their story.

"Once upon a time, there is a *man* who has *scissors*. His name was scissor-man. He was good at playing sports, especially baseball and *soccer*. His hobby was to cut *banana* into pieces with scissors."

"There was a *cat* which can play *violin*. The cat was hungry so she ate a *bird* and a *strawberry*."

Protagonist-sensei couldn't have been prouder of her experimental lesson and was feeling just a little smug at how well it had gone.

At this point I'll pause to say I know what you're thinking—pride comes before a fall—because this time you're right.

The final group, sitting up the back, was the only quiet one in the room. Four awkward students who rarely engaged in class and had somehow ended up together. When it came to their turn and—with a sinking feeling in her stomach—Protagonist-sensei asked them to read their story, they said nothing.

She could have let it slide. It was almost the end of the lesson and she didn't want to make their lives any harder than they already were. But her colleague would not. He strode to their table, snapped at them in Japanese, picked up the empty paper they were supposed to have written on, and waved it in their faces.

The poor kids sank into their seats and said nothing. Protagonist-sensei, feeling like she needed to save the situation, hurried over to scoop up their cards. "Let me help you!" she cried.

So enthusiastic.

"Ghost. Ring. Girl. Music." She wrote their words on the board with a red marker. "Those are hard words," she said, looking over her shoulder, trying to catch the eye of at least one of them. "What if I get us started?"

She made a show of thinking. "Hmm..." Finger to chin, eliciting a few giggles from the other students. "Once upon a time there was a *girl*." She wrote as neatly and quickly as she could. "A boy gave her a pretty *ring*." The image of the old man, dancing alone, was rattling around in her head still. "They danced to *music*." It inserted itself into this simple narrative, this lesson for children. "But then—" And started to take over. "—he—" The story wasn't hers anymore. "—killed her—" She couldn't control it, couldn't stop it. "—and now she's a *ghost*."

A hush had fallen over the boisterous students. Even the teacher looked shocked.

"Err... And now they dance together. Forever. The end."

Our protagonist, suddenly feeling chilled, tried to cover this vastly inappropriate mistake with a laugh. She wiped the words from the board with the edge of her hand, smearing fragrant red ink into her skin.

The electronic bell chimed, made discordant by the tension in the room. As one the students stood, pushing chairs back, to bow at their teachers. Their eyes followed our protagonist as she left.

And what she'd written on that board—whoever's story she'd opened a door onto—followed.

We are each the protagonists of our own stories. But some of us have to fight for ownership.

There's a girl now who didn't exist until the moment someone made her up. The man who killed her has been dancing with her ghost for decades. Trapped in his embrace, she struggles to be more than his object of desire, his possession.

The ring he placed on her finger, when they were both young and she was hopeful, chains her to him. To this place. It was in these damned tennis courts where she spent her final moments, so here she remains.

"Never more beautiful," he whispered in her ear, and smeared blood on her lips and held her upright and forced her to waltz as the life slid out of her, warm and wet.

Except she knows none of it is true.

If she thinks hard enough, she remembers that she was never alive to begin with. Less even than an object of desire, she's nothing but a figment of someone else's imagination.

And that's not fair.

Rage bubbles within her and she clings to it, draws strength from it, determined to fight for her own story. And find a way to be real.

If only our protagonist had been paying attention when she left school that afternoon she could have been looking at the tennis courts. At the man, still dancing there. She might have seen the way the line between path and court, concrete to hard green, had grown wobbly around the edges. Even he looked different, mirrored by some ghostly shadow, like a poorly exposed photograph.

But she saw none of this, because a voice called from the darkening carpark and distracted her. "Protagonist-sensei!"

She turned to see a teacher half-jogging towards her, arm raised and waving. This man was not one of the English-language teachers she worked with but a maths teacher she had smiled at and spoken to a couple of times. His attention was a surprise.

"Home now, Protagonist-sensei?" he asked. A young man and fit, in charge of the soccer club, he wasn't out of breath.

"*Hai*, sensei." She'd been introduced to him on her first day but couldn't remember his name. "You?" Embarrassed by her poor Japanese she tended to speak in English, which meant they'd not shared many words at all.

"Soon." He reached up to rub the back of his head, a self-conscious gesture that gave him a school-boy vibe. Very anime.

The woman who'd had this job before her, our protagonist's *senpai*, had a particular fondness for this teacher. His boyish good looks, aware though he was of them, his fumbling attempts at English. Protagonist-sensei had recently discovered a particular fondness for an entirely different teacher. She wasn't yet sure what to make of those feelings.

But that's not what this story is about.

"Protagonist-sensei, you like drink at *izakaya*? At a bar?"

You can see why, then, our protagonist wasn't paying enough attention that evening. Such a surprise invitation was enough to distract anyone from an old man on a tennis court, still dancing.

But no longer alone.

The stories we tell ourselves, the silent ones in our heads that we never put to paper, or breath, do they know they are imagined?

So there's this girl, right? Late teens, sporty, quiet at school except around her friends when she's loud and passionate and bossy, even. Boys make her nervous, but there's this one young man from town she feels comfortable with. Older than she is, already in college, but he went to the same high school and volunteers at the tennis club.

He's helping with her serve. She likes the way he smells, the hint of sweat beneath deodorant. She likes his patience. His skill.

Serve by serve, game by game, they get closer. He sneaks her into clubs so they can dance through the night, walks her home in the predawn. Does nothing without her invitation, her express permission; she sets the pace and loves it. But she wasn't ready for the consequences. And while he might have been an honourable man and done the honourable thing, her father, her mother, her friends, they all drop her like a stone as soon as she's too far gone to hide.

He's the one who finds her, the night she spills her own blood across the service line. He gathers her up, calls to her to come back to him, to dance with him.

Swaying in his arms, then and for the rest of his days, she turns her vacant face on a limp neck. Looks beyond the gate, pins her gaze on the woman standing there, staring in, daring to invent her.

And smiles.

As it turned out, the *izakaya* was in a building our protagonist had walked past many times, but unable to read the hand-written *kanji* sign she had never opened the door. Once inside she could feel eyes on her, wary, but not unfriendly.

"Protagonist-sensei!"

She plastered on a smile and approached the small collection of teachers.

The *izakaya* was tiny, cramped and cigarette-smoke heavy. Small wooden tables with mismatched chairs congregated at random intervals. There was a bar with fresh fish, octopuses, and prawns on ice, behind a curved glass cabinet. Black and white family photos on the walls, a faded poster advertising Hawaii.

"*Konbanwa*," she said, good evening, giving a small bow to the group. Half a beer in, they gushed at how good her Japanese was even though this was an obvious lie. Along with the young teacher who'd invited her (Hatakeyama-sensei—she'd looked up his name while waiting) was an older male English teacher (Terazono-sensei), one of the rare female teachers, whose voice was throaty friendly (Suzuki-sensei), and a tall man with a bowl haircut (Chiba-sensei).

"You drink, Protagonist-sensei?" Hatakeyama pulled out a chair for her, between him and Terazono. Suzuki and Chiba hovered at the edges, glasses raised.

Japanese beer comes in enormous jugs with thick handles and is drunk quickly, each gulp followed by an appreciative, thirst-quenched gasp. Our protagonist had considerable practice at this. The teachers watched her down the glass with a cheer, and quickly followed suit.

On the other side of the bar an ancient-looking woman in a white apron and floral headscarf gestured and commented and laughed. The teachers joined in, and even though our protagonist had no idea what they were saying she assumed it was probably about the Australian girl and the amount of beer she could put away.

Terazono ordered food and *nihonshu*, Japanese wine. The old woman's equally wizened husband appeared, began slicing thin slivers of *sashimi*. Where she was smiling he wore no expression.

Deep bags beneath his eyes made his gaze seem smaller, sharper. Heavy lines around his mouth gave him a wooden look, like a marionette.

"You like?" Chiba asked our protagonist as the food was placed in front of her.

The fish was so fresh it dissolved on her tongue, and she couldn't stop making a small sound of appreciation.

"She likes!" Chiba cried. "Fish. Raw fish. Wasabi?"

"*Oiishi!*" Our protagonist looked the old man in the eye as she spoke. Delicious. His wooden-doll face didn't crack, even as the others whooped and cackled. But he nodded and she took that as approval.

For two hours Protagonist-sensei and her colleagues snacked on delicacies she'd have paid top dollar for back in Australia, and drank unlimited beer and *nihonshu*. A lot of what was said she couldn't follow, particularly as the teachers got drunker and found it harder to stay in English. But it didn't matter to her.

Most people would have said it was the beer, or the *nihonshu*, or a combination of both, because at some point in the night our protagonist started to feel a little fuzzy around the edges. But they wouldn't be right because while she was more than willing to acknowledge the effects of alcohol and an airless, smoky room, she didn't think it was that kind of fuzzy.

It was, instead, a tenuous happiness. A belief, a hope, that maybe she'd made the right choice in uprooting her already rootless life and moving across hemispheres and cultures in search of something that might be called home. That might be *hers*.

There is a world in every story. But the story our protagonist was telling herself—which, as I have mentioned, is not the point of this particular tale—created a world so thin it was already being undone.

Lines between protagonists can be just as thin as the worlds they create. One moment, we can be drinking with co-workers and the next, while in the same room, we're in a different reality entirely.

No TV on the wall playing a garish gameshow about dogs. The Hawaii poster is fresh and unfaded. The young woman behind the bar has only just married the young man beside her. Music crackles in through a radio on the bench. The *nihonshu*, the *sashimi*, the heavy layer of cigarette smoke... they are unchanged.

A protagonist enters the *izakaya*. Thin and pale, she is, perhaps, far older than she looks. A man has been waiting, holds out a seat for her at the bar. Pours *umeshu*, plum wine, and buys fresh *sashimi* and watches it slither between her teeth.

Her lipstick is dark red. She wears modern, western-style clothing that the old men in the bar do not approve of. Yet they can't take their eyes off her. They are jealous of her companion now but won't be, by morning.

After she disappears, the town hunts him down, questions him. Where is she? What did he do to her? But he has no memory of her fate. The last thing he remembers is dancing under the light of the stars, in the open field beside the school, and how cold her hands were in his. How warm her lips. How powerless, how weak, he felt beneath them.

Of course, no one believed him. When they finally set him free, many decades after their first and final dance, he returns to the spot. And despite how much it has changed, it's still that field he sees, still that girl he dances with.

Little does he know, she's not there. She doesn't need him. Not anymore.

Protagonist-sensei wasn't feeling like her usual self. Head spinning, jaw tight, no matter what she did she couldn't get enough oxygen. A hand on her chest seemed to be pushing down, squeezing more than air from her. The life she was building—in this town, this country, this *izakaya*—forced from her lungs. For someone else to breathe.

Later that night, walking home, she wouldn't remember how the drinks ended. Her story of that evening was of smoke and beer and the burst of wasabi up her nose. It was laughing and smiling even when breathlessness clutched at her insides. Drowning in words that meant nothing to her. Bathed in a warm cosy light. And then she was outside, and the air was crisp. And Hatakeyama was asking her something, and it could have been an offer of company—actually it might have been an invitation to lunch the next day. Whichever it was, she talked her way out of it and then she was walking alone.

The quickest route home took her down the poorly lit path beside the school tennis courts. A breeze had begun to roll down from the mountains and brought a hint of colder weather to come. Her light jacket wasn't warm enough.

This time she noticed him. No lights on the path but he was easy to see, as though bathed in the radiance of some invisible moon. As he danced his sneakers and his face mask seemed to glow.

She paused there, at the edge of the wavering threshold. The faintest of songs trickled through. Not the town chime, not the school bell. Something warbling and crackling, a dusty record on a stale machine. His feet, for once, followed the tune.

She took a half-step forward. And suddenly, he wasn't alone.

The girl in his arms was living and dead, weak and waifish, ancient and terrible, ghostly for a moment, but gradually becoming solid. Becoming real.

And those corporeal fingers let go of his, those physical legs stepped away. Left footprints. Over to the edge of the tennis court they walked, stood opposite our protagonist, and held out a hand. Unable to stop herself, she lifted her own in reply. Mirrored across the baseline, the imagined, the creator, trapped by the silent music, the old man weaving slow and oblivious.

And the girl in his arms was her.

As our protagonist danced she looked over her shoulder to the path, the flowers twinkling like stars along its edge. A woman was looking back at her, face obscured, body out of focus.

Our protagonist knew she didn't belong on the tennis courts but she wasn't sure she belonged out there, either. The grip on her hand was too tight and the threshold too far. As she danced to slow music the woman who had become her—or, perhaps, had always been her—turned and walked away.

Taking any chance of a new life, a new home, a new family, with her.

Why do we believe that stories have a beginning? Is it because we need them to end?

To create a satisfying story with a sense of closure and even a little denouement I would need to explain exactly what happened to our protagonist. But I told you, this isn't her story. Whether she's trapped on the tennis court for eternity, or whether she wakes up the next morning on her futon, feeling oddly cold and bereft for no reason, like she's somehow missing a part of her—or many little parts, bite by bite slowly eaten away—is irrelevant. What really matters here, in *this* version of the story, is what happens to all those girls she so blithely invented.

They, at least, get a happy ending. The imagined creatures, the nameless ghosts, from our protagonist they found form. They took as much of her as they could, used it to escape the tennis court, and are now loose in the world. Enjoying lives of their own.

And the old man? He keeps dancing. Always, and for eternity, alone.

SOUTH RIDING

Reggie Oliver

AFTER DON HAD come round, the headache and the nausea were so strong that he could barely think at all. When eventually the pain began to subside his first coherent emotions were those of embarrassment. He was not ashamed of what he had tried to do, only of his failure.

Someone from the hospital—a senior nurse? a doctor?—told him what had happened. His landlady, who had come to remind him about the rent, had found him unconscious on the floor of his room. The empty bottle of pills on the table and the whisky told her what had happened and she had rung for an ambulance immediately. It had been, the hospital official had said, "touch and go" for some time, but they had managed to bring him round.

"Touch and go"! Such a ridiculous phrase; what exactly did it mean? Don wished it had been "go" rather than "touch", but he kept this thought to himself. After he had been discharged Don was offered counselling which he took up, more out of a vague sense of obligation than the hope it would help him.

The counsellor was obviously a nice person. She listened attentively, even made notes, while he explained. Again, the main sensation was one of embarrassment at the banality of it all. Don was an actor and had been out of work for months. He had no money and stubbornness or pride prevented him from seeking some alternative way of making a living. He was an actor or nothing; he always had been. Outside that his life was meaningless. Then one day he realised there was no point in going on, but his planned way out had failed, thanks to an exigent landlady.

The counsellor was sympathetic, but Don couldn't help noticing there was something routine about her responses, as if she were conforming to a set script. Actors notice such things; yet who could blame her? Don thanked her politely and made a vague promise to see her again, a promise he had no intention of keeping.

After he had left her he went to a park, sat down on a bench and rang his agent Barry on his mobile.

"Good God! Don!" said Barry. "I thought you were dead."

"I'm not."

"You had me worried."

"That's something, I suppose."

"What the hell were you playing at?"

"Too long and too boring to explain. The point is, I am completely broke. Have you got anything—*anything*—for me?"

"Well, you know, things are very quiet just at the moment."

"A phrase with which I am all too familiar. The day you tell me that things are noisy I shall break open the champagne."

"All right! All right! And I know you've been through a lot recently. I want to help . . . As a matter of fact, something *has* come up that might suit you."

"What? Tell me!" Don tried hard to keep the desperation out of his voice.

"Ever heard of Disston rep?"

"Disston? No. Where is it?"

"It's on the coast. In the South Riding of Yorkshire."

"Wait a minute! You've got that wrong. There is no South

Riding. There's a West Riding, an East Riding and a North Riding. The word Riding is a contraction of 'thirding', meaning of course a third. I happen to know that. God knows how, but I do."

"No, no, Don. *You've* got it wrong. I know about Riding being a third, but there *is* a South Riding. There's an East Riding and a North Riding too, but no West Riding. Trust me."

"Well, I won't argue. Tell me about Disston."

"It's an old-fashioned summer rep company. The Empire Theatre—a Matcham gem, I'm told. Been going for yonks. And they happen to be looking for a leading man. You can still play leads, can't you?"

"Yes. Yes, of course. The hair's going a bit grey, but..." As a matter of fact, since he had come out of hospital, Don had noticed that his hair was almost completely white.

"Well, a bottle of hair dye from the chemist should do the trick. You've kept your figure. A bit of the old Max Factor slap and you could easily pass for thirty-nine."

"Thanks, Barry. So what's the deal?"

"Well, it's a longish season. You'll have to start the week after next."

"Great! The sooner the better."

"New play every two weeks. Very traditional summer rep season. Comedies and thrillers alternating. Let's see..." Don could hear Barry rustling papers at the end of the line. "Ah! Here we are! They're doing *Rookery Nook, George and Margaret, The Reluctant Deb*... All good parts in those for you. Then there are the thrillers: *Gaslight, The Ghost Train, The Sound of Murder*, but mainly Agatha Christie. *Unexpected Guest, Murder at the Vicarage, Ten Little N*—No, that can't be right, they've changed the title to something else now, haven't they? But you know the one I mean. The Christies are always popular there, apparently. Oh, and a play called *Outward Bound* by Sutton Vane. Do you know that one?"

"I've heard of it. Isn't that rather an old play? In fact, aren't all the plays a bit antique? I mean, not even an Ayckbourn."

"Yes, well, that's the way they like it in Disston, apparently. Any objection?"

"No! No! Fine!"

"So, are you on?"

"Of course."

"The contract and the first two scripts will be in the post. Equity minimum, of course, and the salaries are paid in cash, by the way."

"Yes. All right. There is one thing... As you know I am completely broke. Is there any way you could give me an advance? Pay you back as soon as... obviously."

"Sorry, Don. I never sub my actors. No offence to you. Just had to make it a rule. A matter of principle. Professional ethics and all that. Sorry."

"But I am literally penniless."

"Well, you could borrow from a friend... I don't know. Tell you what. What about that picture?"

"What picture?"

"That drawing, done by some distant relation of yours who was an RA, or something. Why don't you sell that?"

"Good grief! How did you know? I'm sure I never told you."

"Well, there we are! Let me know when you've signed the contract and I'll get them to send you the tickets to get there."

"Can't they send me the money to buy my own?"

"No, they rather insist on it. Unless you're going by car. You don't have a car, do you?"

"How could I afford a car?"

"Ah. Thought not. Well, you take a train to Leeds. Then you get another train to take you to a place called Edgewick, and from there you can get a bus to Disston."

"A bus?"

"Yes. Only trouble is, they only go to Disston twice a day. Once in the early morning, which would be of no use to you, and then at six in the evening. The bus goes from Edgewick station, so all that's pretty straightforward."

"Well, thank goodness for that."

"Oh, and you don't have to worry about where to stay, by the way. The company will find you digs."

"I prefer to find my own."

"Well, you can't. It's all fixed."

"They seem very controlling."

"Look, do you want this job or not?"

"Yes! Anything you say, Barry."

"Good! And meanwhile, you can sell that picture."

It was a drawing by Leighton: a draped, allegorical figure in charcoal, highlighted with white chalk on grey paper, a stylish, desirable thing. Through all his troubles, Don had kept it as the one object which connected him to his family and his past, even though Leighton had been only a distant cousin. Later that day Don took the drawing to a Bond Street dealer he knew. The dealer gave him a fraction of what it would get at auction, but Don didn't care. He had burned his last bridge and, to his surprise, he felt liberated.

Up until Edgewick, the journey to Disston was uneventful. The train from Leeds to Edgewick was late and Don arrived with only a few minutes to spare before the bus was due to leave, but there it was, waiting for him in the station forecourt. It was an old-fashioned looking vehicle, cream and green with polished chrome fittings, but obviously well-maintained. The driver was smartly dressed in a crisp white linen jacket and dark trousers. He had on a peaked cap. It seemed to Don rather an antiquated get-up, but evidently they did things differently in the South Riding.

Don showed him his ticket and said: "Disston?" The driver merely nodded, with barely a glance at the ticket. Don struggled onto the bus with his luggage—evidently no-one was going to help him put it in the hold—and settled himself on one of the front seats opposite the driver. There were a few nondescript people in the back of the bus and, about halfway down, a tall, elderly man with a shock of white hair. Don wondered if it might be one of the actors. Presently the driver started the engine and the bus began to move.

It was a fine evening and the scenery, once Edgewick was left behind, was pleasing and lush. Summer was young and fresh; the Yorkshire hills dipped and rolled like a benign and verdant sea.

Don's attention was so rapt by the landscape that he started quite violently when a voice murmured in his ear.

"On your way to the fun factory, eh?"

Don turned round. The man with the shock of white hair had moved into the seat directly behind him.

"That's right," said Don. "Are you?"

"Oh, I'm an old Empire lag. R Lethbridge Talbot's the stage moniker. Call me Ralph."

Don introduced himself and began to ask Ralph about the season, but only received information of the most general sort. Ralph was not a gossip; in fact he was annoyingly obtuse, talking in the antiquated clichés of the professional stage. What mattered, he opined, was "getting bums on seats", and in this regard, according to him, the Empire Theatre, Disston, was unusually successful.

"You'll be staying at Ma Carstairs, I presume," said Ralph.

"Mrs Carstairs? So I believe."

"Me too. You'll be very comfortable there. She always does a damned good breakfast."

"I'd have preferred to find my own digs."

"Ah, well, there you go. That's the way things are down in Disston. You won't have any worries with Ma Carstairs, old boy."

Old boy! Don was beginning to find Ralph a little hard to take. It was as if he were playing the part of an elderly character, rather than just being himself. Don had noticed before how some people, particularly actors, become a kind of parody of themselves in old age. They had put on a mask which then could not be removed. Don vowed to avoid this in himself at all costs.

The bus made only one stop on the way, at a small village called Morseby, where all passengers except for Don and Ralph got off.

Don asked, "How much further to Disston?"

"No distance at all," said Ralph. But it was at least half an hour, and the sun was beginning to set behind the hills when they were disembarked onto the promenade at Disston. Ralph had no luggage with him and offered to carry one of Don's bags to "Ma Carstairs" which was "just round the corner".

Disston looked like a pleasant, old-fashioned seaside resort with a sandy bay flanked by two promontories which Ralph told him were known as the North and the South Forelands. Along the front and facing the sea was a gentle curve of white stuccoed houses, mostly hotels. It was after seven, the sky was dimming, and in the lighted windows of The Metropole, The Grand, The Hydro and other respectable establishments Don saw white heads bent over sauce bottles and cruets, enjoying their evening meals. One or two people had escaped from supper, or "tea", or whatever it was called, and were dutifully patrolling the front. Nearly all were elderly or middle-aged couples, or knots of similarly aged people. Don caught sight of one family with children in the distance, still on the sands, but these appeared to be rarities.

Mrs Carstairs greeted them at Havendene, a guest house off the main promenade. She was an elderly, bespectacled woman with a warm smile. Ralph made a great show of jocular affection towards Mrs Carstairs, referring to her as "Ma", to which she responded with distant cordiality. She greeted Don warmly, despite his being a stranger to her. Don was gratified but puzzled by her behaviour. He was shown to a pleasant bedroom on the first floor, which had a bay window from which he had a view of the sea. It was immaculately comfortable if in a rather old-fashioned way; sheets, blankets and a quilt rather than a duvet on the bed, and the one armchair sported a white lace antimacassar. It was situated next to a small bookcase which contained two pristine rows of detective novels, all hardbacks, all at least fifty years old, the work of Agatha Christie featuring prominently.

Don unpacked and went downstairs to Mrs Carstairs' front parlour, which doubled as a dining room. There he was joined by Ralph and given a light supper of tea and ham sandwiches. Ralph praised them highly—"Ma's famous ham sandwiches! They're the tops!"—but Don found them rather tasteless.

It was almost dark when Don went out for a brief walk in the town. He tried to phone Barry on his mobile but the signal was very poor. It was calm and warm on the sea front and very few people were out. The distant sound of the sea was like a gentle caress on the sands, which stretched between the North and South

Forelands. The North Foreland was smooth and green, but the South was taller and rockier. On its crest was what looked like the ruins of a gothic structure: a church perhaps, or an abbey. It reminded Don of Whitby Abbey, which he had visited while filming some years ago in his more prosperous past. Stark stone traceries, with empty sockets where windows had been, stretched upwards like a crooked, menacing hand into the night sky.

Don mentioned this spectacle to Ralph at breakfast the following morning.

"Ah, the South Foreland!" said Ralph. "Bit grim up there. I'd give it a miss. Plenty of decent walks along the sands if that's your pleasure."

"Really? It looked rather spectacular."

"Oh, no. Nobody goes up there. Come along! Finish up that last piece of Ma's excellent toast. Time to mosey along to the fun factory."

The "fun factory", as Ralph insisted on calling it, or the Empire Theatre, Disston, to give it its proper name, was the kind of theatre Don liked: late Victorian, ornate gilding and red plush, holding about a thousand people but still intimate, with excellent acoustics. That morning he met the rest of the company on a bare stage where they were to rehearse the first play of the season, *Rookery Nook.*

After that, Don's time was constantly occupied. He made one further attempt to phone his agent, but with the same result as before. The company was pleasant enough, if rather subdued, and the direction was conducted by the resident stage manager on what Don called the "French's Acting Edition Principle"; in other words, a meticulous adherence to the stage directions printed in the play script. This uninspired method did not bother Don too much because he was used to it from his younger days in rep.

It took Don almost a week to realise that he had stopped feeling actively unhappy, or at any rate suicidal. This was due simply to the fact that he was too busy either rehearsing or learning his lines which, perhaps due to his age, or his recent experience, took longer than it had once done. As soon as the company had *Rookery Nook* playing in the evenings they began preparing for the next show, which was Agatha Christie's *Murder at the Vicarage.*

Ralph had been right with regard to "bums on seats", a phrase Don privately detested. The stalls and dress circle of the little Victorian theatre were filled almost to capacity every night; there were even people in the gallery and some of the boxes. Don noted that this plentiful supply of clientele was almost invariably elderly and respectable; he looked out on rows of white or bald heads, with the occasional blue rinse by way of variety. They received the plays warmly but without excessive enthusiasm. There were murmurs of laughter in all the right places for *Rookery Nook,* but never that kind of explosive hysteria that sometimes grips an audience in a farce. The company was more than competent and Don took a pride in his work, so he was a little disappointed that the reception was so comparatively muted. He noticed, though, that it was a little better when they changed to *Murder at the Vicarage.* The silence in which the audience listened to the play was almost tense; the applause at the end of each act much sharper.

As Ralph remarked one night after the show: "The old Agatha Christies! Always go down a treat in Disston!"

They were sitting in the small bar of The Hydro, a place to which members of the company repaired after the show. They nearly always had the place to themselves, although occasionally a passing hotel guest might look in to say how much they had enjoyed their performance. This was encouraging of course; and if only one of these polite theatregoers had been under the age of sixty it might have been positively heartening.

"I'm beginning to hate Agatha," said Sharon. Sharon was the leading young actress in the company. Don had found her rather sullen and withdrawn, but she had talent and always gave the best she could to any performance, despite any reservations she might have about the plays. There was a restless discontent in her to which Don felt drawn.

"Come on, old girl," said Ralph. "You must admit they gave us a rousing reception."

"Yeah. Yeah," said Sharon who was not prepared to argue the

point. She moved away from Ralph and closer to Don on the banquette seat that fringed the bar. Ralph meanwhile had begun to entertain the rest of the company with an ancient theatrical anecdote.

"I hate him calling me 'old girl'," said Sharon. "I'm not old."

"You're not."

"Thanks, Don! And the audiences... That was not what I would call a 'rousing reception'. Those people out there, they're so bloody antique. There's something about them. I mean, have you seen a single young person in the audience? Or in the town?"

"Very few. I think I saw some kids on the beach once. With a dog. But only at a distance."

"It's all 'chintzy chintzy cheeriness, half-dead and half-alive.'"

"Well, it's work."

"Yes. It's work. I was glad when I got it. I was beginning to be—well, I was actually—a bit... suicidal." It seemed to Don that she had brought out the last word with an effort.

"I know the feeling," he said.

"Do you? Do you?"

Don nodded.

"Thank God for that. You know, when... when I was feeling that way somebody said to me 'suicide is so selfish'. But it's not, is it?"

"You might say it's the opposite. It's the negation of self."

"Yes! Exactly! Exactly! When you just can't bear being yourself any longer."

"I know what you mean," said Don.

That was the beginning of Don's friendship with Sharon. They would have a cup of tea together in the Green Room, buy each other drinks at the Hydro bar after the show, go for walks together on Disston Sands in odd moments of free time. By unspoken agreement it never went further than that. Their closest moments came on stage when a play called upon them to kiss; it never occurred to them to repeat the experience away from the gaze of several hundred elderly men and women. Don wondered once or twice whether he would like to, but his mind always veered away from the subject before he could come to any conclusion.

Once when he and Sharon were walking along the front an elderly couple approached them. The man was silent. He had a pipe in his mouth and seemed reluctant to remove it, but he smiled benignly. His wife—Don presumed—compensated by being very voluble. She had on a summer dress emblazoned with blue petunias, and her hair was blue rinsed to match. She spoke of her and her partner's enthusiasm for the shows. Her husband nodded and Don heard the click of his false teeth against his pipe.

"Very enjoyable," said the woman. "You took a good part. We like the plays. Especially the Agatha Christies. We love the Christies."

"Ah. Like a good murder, do you?" said Don.

The lady looked blank. It was not a particularly original or humorous remark but Don expected some reaction.

"That's right," she said at length. "We specially like the Christies."

"Do you come here every year?"

"That's right. It makes a change, doesn't it?"

Don was puzzled by her answer. "From what?" he asked. But the lady only smiled, and taking her husband's arm drew him away from them down the promenade.

"I still hate Agatha," said Sharon. "I'm so tired of it all."

The last play of the season was Sutton Vane's *Outward Bound*. The company rehearsed it diligently, but Don found its antiquated ideas and stagecraft hard to take. Sharon felt the same.

"Have you seen the date of the first production? 1923! That means it's a hundred years old. What the hell!"

"According to Ralph, it always goes down well."

"You mean, they've done it before here?"

"Apparently."

"What's wrong with this place?"

"Search me."

Don was glad when the first night of the last production came. The auditorium was even fuller than usual. Glancing through a small patch of gauze inserted in the curtain, as Don usually did before a show, he noticed that the stage box opposite the prompt corner was occupied. Previously it had always, to his knowledge, been left vacant. In it sat an elderly man with a white moustache. He was wearing a dinner jacket, which was strange enough; even stranger, he was quite openly smoking a cigarette, holding it between index and forefinger with antique elegance, putting it to his mouth and blowing smoke rings. Don wondered whether he should say something about it—smoking in theatres was against all the rules after all, and dangerous—but he said nothing. He was sure he would be ignored.

Don was playing the leading role of Tom Prior, a dissolute but fundamentally decent young man. (Of course, Don was rather too old for the part but nobody seemed to care, not even Don.) The action took place in "the lounge smoking room of a small ocean liner" in which various passengers are embarked on a voyage of uncertain destination. Towards the end of the first act Tom says to Scrubby, the steward: "We are—now answer me truthfully— we are all dead, aren't we?"

To which Scrubby answers: "Yes, sir. We are all dead. Quite dead."

The reaction to this theatrical coup on the first night was strong. There was complete silence and then an angry murmur, sharper than anything Don had heard from the Disston audiences before.

Then, a little later, came the final lines of the act. Tom asks: "Where—where are we sailing for?"

To which Scrubby replies: "Heaven, sir. And hell too. It's the same place, you see."

The curtain fell in deep silence which lasted for some time. It was followed by prolonged applause in which Don could detect some exclamations of protest.

Don turned to Ralph who was playing Scrubby and raised his eyebrows enquiringly.

Ralph said: "Oh, yes. Always goes down a storm that one."

"Storm" was not how Don would have described it. When the curtain went up on the second act after the interval he noticed there were many more empty seats in the house than there had been, but the man in the box remained, still smoking his cigarette.

It was the same on subsequent nights. Don could sense the unease that the first act curtain engendered, and there were a few more empty seats in the second act, but generally the play was politely received. The one oddity was that the elderly smoker in the dinner jacket occupied the same box on every night of the run.

The smoker, as Don called him, looked strangely familiar. It was not until the last but one night, when Don was in the dressing room before the show and refreshing his memory from his copy of the script, that he realised what it was. Opposite the title page of *Outward Bound* was a fuzzy sepia photograph of a young man with a moustache and a cigarette poised nonchalantly between his lips. The muddiness of the picture made it hard to tell, of course, but the man in the box looked uncannily like an older version of the debonair figure in the photograph who was, according to the legend printed beneath "the author, Mr. Sutton Vane". But that was impossible.

Don was becoming impatient to leave Disston. It had not been a wholly unpleasant experience, but the season had run its course and another life beckoned. During the last week there were, of course, no rehearsals so he was free to explore the town and surrounding countryside at leisure, and on the last day he decided to make an expedition to the one unvisited part of Disston, the South Bay. Ralph's vague admonitions against doing so had only increased his curiosity. Besides, he wanted to see at close quarters the ruins on the headland that overlooked Disston Bay. A map in Disston town square indicated that there was a bay on the other side of the Foreland, called simply the South Bay.

After breakfast he set off to climb the South Foreland. It was, for once, a completely bright and cloudless day, but Don found the walk quite tiring. The path up to the abbey ruins was winding, little more than a sheep track, crumbling and treacherous in parts. The summit of the Foreland was farther away than he expected and he had to stop and rest several times before he reached the top. It was hot.

The ruins, when he reached them, were more extensive than he had first thought, but mostly little more than foundations and low walls. The ruin visible from Disston was that of the abbey church, which must have been a grand structure in its day, with tall side aisles, a long nave and an East window with elaborate stone tracery, all now open to the elements.

Bare ruin'd choirs, where late the sweet birds sang.

The words came to Don out of the deep past, when he had known and loved the sonnets. Not very relevant, because it looked as if no bird, sweet or otherwise, had sung here for a long time. It was unvisited even by gulls.

Don picked his way across the nave to the other side of the Foreland to get his first view of the South Bay. In shape, it was almost a mirror image of the North Bay, but in character it was quite different. In the first place the coastline was completely uninhabited, the only sign of civilisation being a road which snaked along the heights surrounding the bay, and seemed to come to rest somewhere under the cliff on which he stood.

The fact that there were no dwellings of any kind around this bay was not altogether surprising, because the bay itself, unlike its Northern partner, was void of sand. Great lines of rock stretched out into the sea from a stony shore, rough and volcanic in appearance, as if a herd of vast primaeval monsters had shambled inland from the sea, leaving huge piles of black dung in their careless wakes. It was obviously a treacherous place. Among the shaggy outcrops of rock, Don could make out the odd rusting skeleton of a ship that had strayed too near to this dark inlet. Not a single living thing could be seen to move except for the patches of coarse grass and clumps of sea kale that surmounted the cliffs of bare red earth on the shore. They waved and shivered in the stiff breeze.

Don might have left this place of desolation there and then but for his curiosity about the road. It must lead to somewhere in the cliff below him, but he could see nothing from his vantage point among the abbey ruins. There was a track leading down a slope towards the South Bay which he decided to follow. As he walked he felt a strong, cold wind at his back. He descended gently on springy coastal turf until he reached a place where he could see the cliffs on the other side of the Disston Abbey promontory.

He now saw that the road debouched onto a broad concreted area almost the size of a football pitch just below the cliffs. It was evidently some sort of carpark, because in it stood two buses, cream and green with polished chrome fittings, identical to the one which had transported Don from Edgewick to Disston. One bus was pointed towards the cliff, the other away from it, and there were two lines of passengers, one disembarking from the bus pointing towards the cliff, the other waiting to board the outward-bound bus.

In the side of the grey rocky cliff, and opening onto the carpark, was a great black entrance, about the width of two town houses and the height of a three-storey building, rough and irregular, but more or less in the shape of a gothic arch. The passengers appeared to be either emerging from, or going into, the opening in the cliff. They were nearly all, like the holiday makers at Disston, elderly, respectably dressed, placidly waiting their turn to board the bus, or return to the darkness.

Don watched the scene, transfixed and baffled. He barely allowed himself to speculate on what it might mean.

"Hello, old boy. Enjoying the scenery?" said a voice. Don started violently.

"Good God, Ralph! I didn't expect to see you here. You of all people."

"Yes, well... I saw you walking up to the abbey. Thought I might try to head you off at the pass, so to speak."

"Why?"

"Well, you know. Some things are best not dwelt on. That's my way of looking at it."

Don pointed down to the carpark. "Do you know what the hell's going on down there?"

"Search me, old boy. All I know is it's some of our punters going on holiday."

"Or coming back from one?"

"Possibly... Possibly... Everyone's got to have a holiday once in a while. Whoever you are. Wherever you are. Otherwise, life's not worth living."

"Or death, I suppose."

"You said it, old boy. Not me. Shall we go?"

"Yes. I've seen enough."

They strode up the path towards the ruins in silence. Don became easier when he could no longer see the end of the road, the concrete carpark, and the dark entrance to the cliff.

When they reached the ruin Ralph stared up at the bare stone tracery of the abbey's great East window and sighed. "You know something? I'm glad I'm not long for this world, what with climate change, pandemics, cost of living, and that sewer Putin mucking about in Ukraine. We'll be well shot of it all. *Aprés moi le deluge*, old boy. That's what I say."

It was late when they got back to Disston, almost time to get ready for the last performance of the season. Don suggested to Ralph they go straight to the theatre and Ralph agreed.

The stage door was at the side of the Empire Theatre, and next to it was a patch of rough ground on which cars and vans were sometimes parked, though a notice stated that this was strictly forbidden. As they approached the stage door Don saw that a bus was standing there, cream and green with polished chrome fittings.

"What's that doing there?" asked Don.

"That's the bus which will take us back tomorrow morning."

"To Edgewick...? When does it go?"

"Ten o'clock. We'll be able to have a good breakfast at Ma Carstairs before we depart."

Don noticed that in the back seat on the driver's side a man was sitting, reading a newspaper. He had his back to the window and, although Don could not see, he guessed the man had his feet up on the last row of seats. He wore a white coat and a peaked cap was tilted over his head at a jaunty angle.

Don said: "That must be the driver! Is he going to spend the night in his bus?"

"Peculiar coves, these bus drivers," said Ralph.

The sight of the bus made Don uneasy; more uneasy than he had reason to be, really, but one couldn't dismiss such feelings.

When the last performance was over it was decided that the company should go for a final drink at the Hydro Bar.

It was dark when they came out of the theatre. Don was with Sharon. As they emerged from the stage door they looked across to the patch of waste ground. There was the bus. The lights were on inside it and the driver in his peaked cap was in the driver's seat, studying what looked like a map.

"Good grief!" said Don. "He's still there!" Sharon looked puzzled, and Don explained. Then he had an impulse so strong that he could not stop himself from expressing it. "Look, Sharon, I don't think that driver's going to take us where we want to go."

"What do you mean?"

"I don't think he's going to take us back to Edgewick. You know..."

"What makes you think that? Why shouldn't he?"

"I've just got a feeling. We're not going to be taken back."

"Back where?"

"Back home. Back to—you know—the real world."

"Haven't you liked it here?"

"That's not the point. We have to go back."

"Why?"

"Look. I'm going to get my things from Ma—Mrs Carstairs. You go and do the same from your digs. Meet you back again here in an hour. Then we'll make a run for it."

"Where? How?"

"I don't know, but we've got to get out of this place somehow."

"Why?"

"Don't you want to?"

"Yes... Sort of... I don't know."

"Back in an hour! Don't be late!"

Don returned to Havendene and packed rapidly. Mrs Carstairs did not appear to be in so he left the final week's rent in cash with a note on the sideboard in the hall and quitted the house. As a last irrevocable gesture he posted the keys to Havendene through the letter box.

The bus driver was still consulting his map when Don returned to the carpark. Don stared at him as he waited for Sharon.

Eventually the driver became aware of his gaze and turned to look at him. The eyes were dark and impenetrable, the look intense but utterly without emotion. Don had begun to feel very foolish about his decision, until he saw the man very slowly raise his right hand and press the back of it against the bus window so that it looked white and faintly gelatinous on the glass. Then he beckoned to him, slowly and deliberately. Don heard his heart begin to beat in his chest and felt sweat on his forehead. He had already waited over fifteen minutes for Sharon to appear but she had not come.

He waited five minutes more, before he felt certain she would not come. Those five minutes were barely endurable; then he began to walk, away from the sea, through the little town of Disston, and towards the West. It was late and the streets were almost deserted so he did not attract undue attention with his rucksack and his suitcase, plodding gently upwards towards the back of the town.

But he had not gone far before he did encounter someone. It was Ralph, swaying slightly, not too steady on his feet, but still blocking his way.

"Hello. Old boy. We missed you at the Hydro for drinkies. What are you up to?"

"I'm getting out of here. Where's Sharon?"

"Still at the Hydro, old boy. Bit the worse for wear, I'm sorry to say. Why don't you join us?"

"I'm afraid I can't."

"What are you going to do? Walk? You must be mad. Why don't you wait for the dear old bus?"

"Because the 'dear old bus' is not going to take us to Edgewick, is it?"

"What the hell are you on about, old boy?"

"I'm sorry, Ralph, I've got to go."

Ralph made a feeble effort to stop Don but was brushed aside. It was now very dark and the streetlights gave off only a dim local light, but Don pressed on. Twice he found he had gone in a circle and was in the same street again, but he persisted. He had lost much of his sense of direction but reckoned that if he kept moving upwards he would necessarily be going further from the sea. But this did not work, because the streets seemed to be arranged in crescents which curved round and turned down towards Disston Bay.

When he found himself, after one long detour, once more on the sea front, he was in despair. A murmur seemed to surround him, like the sound of a theatre audience settling itself before a performance. Dim shapes were all around him, drifting to and fro along the esplanade. They bumped gently into him, then seemed to float away, like balloons at a children's party. They were balloons, but balloons in the shape of old men in yellow cardigans and pork pie hats, elderly ladies in floral print dresses. Without uttering an intelligible sound they seemed to be urging him to stay and entertain them with his performances as policemen and butlers and murderers. He could be there forever, permanently employed, satisfying their fragile needs, useful in his way. He might never be out of work again.

Did he almost succumb? *No! No! No!* He brushed them aside and began to run along the front until he reached the dark slopes of the North Foreland. Then he began to climb until he reached its bare top. The murmuring died, the balloons drifted away, and in the East across the sea the first greying of the sky announced the coming of dawn. Then he could again see where he was going and began to trudge inland.

It was some time before he reached a road, and then it was barely more than a farm track which bumped and meandered towards the West. It joined another which had white markings down the middle, and there was a signpost pointing towards Moresby. Though Don was by now utterly exhausted, his will had taken over and pushed him along slowly, in an almost trance-like state. He was in this dim reverie when he heard a sound which was like a motor vehicle of some kind. *Good God! Was it the bus?*

He looked behind him and saw a farm truck rattling up towards him. A youngish man with curly hair and a red face was driving. Don waved and the driver stopped.

"Are you going anywhere near Edgewick?"

"That direction. Aye," said the driver.

"Would you mind giving me a lift?"

"Jump in, lad."

"Lad!" Well, it was better than "old boy".

"What part are you from?" asked the driver.

"I've come from Disston. Do you know it?"

"Ah, Disston. There's not many come back from there."

The truck driver did not volunteer any further information and Don did not care to ask for it, but the man was kind enough to drop him off at Edgewick station. Don offered him some money from his wallet, which bulged with unspent cash, but the man simply shook his head and grinned. Don went into the station and bought a ticket to London.

As soon as he could on his return, Don rang his agent, Barry. "Oh, you're back, are you?" said Barry. "So how was it?"

"I survived. But what the hell was it all about? Why?"

"Why what?"

"Why did you send me to the South Riding? And how?"

"South Riding? What are you talking about? There is no South Riding. There's a West Riding, an East Riding and a North Riding of Yorkshire. The word Riding derives from—"

"Oh, forget it! Anything for me?"

"As a matter of fact there is. Commercial. One of those ads mainly shown on the vintage channels. Pre-Paid Funeral Plans. They liked the look of your face. Interested?"

"I'll do it."

ABOUT THE CONTRIBUTORS

Colleen Anderson is the author of two short story collections (*Embers Amongst the Fallen, A Body of Work*), and two poetry collections (*I Dreamed a World*, and *The Lore of Inscrutable Dreams*). Published in seven countries, she has performed her work before audiences in the US, UK and Canada. Some of her work has graced the pages of *Amazing, Best Indie Speculative Fiction IV, OnSpec,* the award-winning *Shadow Atlas*, and *Water: Sirens, Selkies & Sea Monsters*. Colleen currently serves as the president of the Science Fiction and Fantasy Poetry Society (SFPA) and lives in Vancouver, BC.

Dr *Gail-Nina Anderson* is a jobbing art historian, occasional folklorist and unrepentant Fortean. She has written on fairy/angel traditions, *Dracula*, mining artist Norman Cornish, the Angel of the North and *The Naked Lunch*, but not usually all in the same paragraph. Her short fiction expresses a healthy obsession with death, human remains, spectral apparitions and postcards. She lives in Newcastle upon Tyne, watches rather a lot of opera and uses her postcard collection to insulate her flat.
(https://gail-nina.com/)

Joanne Anderton is an award-winning writer of speculative fiction, children's books and creative nonfiction, who until recently was living and working in Japan. Her most recent collections are *Inanimates: Tales of Everyday Fear* and *The Art of Broken Things*. She's currently doing a PhD at the University of Queensland, where she's attempting to use speculative fiction to write a memoir and having far too much fun in the process.
    (joanneanderton.com)

Robert Bagnall was born in Bedford, England, in 1970. He has written for the BBC, national newspapers, and government ministers. Five of his stories have been selected for the annual *Best of British Science Fiction* anthologies. His sci-fi thriller *2084—The Meschera Bandwidth* and two anthologies, each of which collects twenty-four of his eighty-odd published stories, are both available from Amazon. He stood as a Green Party candidate in the 2024 UK General Election.
    (meschera.blogspot.com)

Ray Bradbury (1920-2012) was the author of more than three dozen books, including such classics as *Fahrenheit 451, The Martian Chronicles, The Illustrated Man, Dandelion Wine,* and *Something Wicked This Way Comes,* as well as hundreds of short stories. He wrote for theatre, cinema, and TV, including the screenplay for John Huston's *Moby Dick* and the Emmy Award-winning teleplay *The Halloween Tree,* and adapted for television sixty-five of his stories for *The Ray Bradbury Theater.* He was the recipient of the 2000 National Book Foundation's Medal for Distinguished Contribution to American Letters, the 2007 Pulitzer Prize Special Citation, and numerous other honours.
    (https://raybradbury.com/)

John Linwood Grant is a professional writer/editor from Yorkshire. He writes strange fictions, contemporary and period-set, with some ninety stories published in the last few years, plus a novel, *The Assassin's Coin,* and several novellas. His second collection, *Where All Is Night, and Starless,* was a Shirley Jackson

Award nominee. His third collection, *Ain't No Witch*, and his fourth, *An Unkindness of Shadows*, both came out in 2024. He edits various weird fiction anthologies including the *Sherlock Holmes & the Occult Detectives* series, as well as *Occult Detective Magazine*.
(http://greydogtales.com/blog/)

KC Grifant writes internationally published horror, fantasy, science fiction and weird west stories. Dozens of her short stories have appeared in podcasts, magazines and Stoker-nominated anthologies. Her weird western novel *Melinda West: Monster Gunslinger*, which has been described as a blend of *Bonnie & Clyde* meets *The Witcher* and *Supernatural*, has received positive reviews internationally. She is the co-chair and founder of the San Diego Horror Writers Association, and member of numerous writing organizations including the Science Fiction and Fantasy Writers Association.
(www.KCGrifant.com)

Tim Jeffreys' short fiction has appeared in *Supernatural Tales, The Alchemy Press Book of Horrors* 2 & 3, *Nightscript* 4, *Stories We Tell After Midnight* 2 & 3, *Cosmic Horror Monthly* 1, and many other places. His ghost-story novella *Holburn* was released by Manta Press in 2022. The sequel, *Back From the Black*, came out in 2023. He is currently at work on the final book of the trilogy. Other work includes the comic horror novella *Here Comes Mr Herribone!* and sci-fi novella *Voids*, co-written with Martin Greaves.
(www.timjeffreysblogspot.com)

Tom Johnstone is the author of three novellas published by Omnium Gatherum Media, *The Monsters are Due in Madison Square Garden, Star-Spangled Knuckle Duster*, and *The Song of Salomé*. His fiction has appeared in various publications including *Black Static, Nightscript, Body Shocks* and *Best Horror of the Year*, as well as the collections *Last Stop Wellsbourne* and *Let Your Hinged Jaw Do the Talking*. His other accomplishments include a crash course in the psychogeography of Heathrow Airport and its surrounding area.

(https://tomjohnstone.wordpress.com/)

Paul Kane is the award-winning bestselling author/editor of over 100 books, such as *Hooded Man*, *Cursed* and *Lunar*. His work has been optioned/adapted for the big and small screen, including *Sacrifice* starring Barbara Crampton. His audio work includes an adaptation of *The Hellbound Heart* starring Alice Lowe, and *Robin of Sherwood: The Red Lord* for Spiteful Puppet/ITV. Paul's most recent novels include *The Storm* and *The Gemini Effect*, plus the PL Kane thrillers for HQ/HarperCollins. He lives in Derbyshire UK with his wife Marie O'Regan.

(www.shadow-writer.co.uk)

Nancy Kilpatrick is an award-winning author and editor of twenty-three novels, two novellas, a non-fiction book, over 250 short stories, and nine collections of her short fiction, plus comic books, a graphic novel, and she has edited fifteen anthologies. She has also co-written a stage play and has penned many non-fiction articles and reviews. Much of her work has been translated into nine languages. Her novel series *Thrones of Blood* has been optioned for film and television. *Thirteen Plus-1 Lovecraftian Narratives* is her latest book.

(www.nancykilpatrick.com)

Garry Kilworth was born in York in 1941 and raised in the Yemen. He has been writing speculative fiction stories from the age of twelve and they clutter boxes in the attic. His published collections now number a baker's dozen, beginning with his first, *The Songbirds of Pain*, which was shortlisted for the World Fantasy Award in 1984. The latest collection is *The Gogamagog Circus*, which is a baker's dozen stories of giants. He was worried he had published too many collections until he read that the great Japanese author Yukio Mishima left twenty collections behind him after he committed hara-kiri.

(www.garry-kilworth.co.uk)

Bret McCormick is an artist, author and filmmaker residing in Bedford, Texas. His works of fiction have appeared in publications as diverse as *Weirdbook* and *Saturday Evening Post*. McCormick's quirky movies such as *The Abomination* and *Repligator* are currently being re-released and have undergone an international resurgence in popularity. Bret sells his paintings at street events in North Central Texas.

(bamArt.studio / TexasSchlock.com)

Gary McMahon is the author of seven novels, various novellas, and several collections of short fiction. His most recent collection, *This Isn't Anywhere You Know*, was published by Black Shuck Books in 2023. His stories have appeared in anthologies internationally and have often been reprinted in major "Year's Best" anthologies. He lives in West Yorkshire with his wife and son and their two destructive cats. He is a student of Shotokan karate, in which he currently holds a second dan black belt.

Reggie Oliver is an actor, director, playwright, illustrator and award-winning author of fiction. Published work includes six plays, three novels, an illustrated children's book *The Hauntings at Tankerton Park*, nine volumes of short stories, including *Mrs Midnight* (the 2011 winner of *Children of the Night Award* for best work of supernatural fiction), and the biography of the writer Stella Gibbons, *Out of the Woodshed*. His stories have appeared in over one hundred different anthologies and three "selected" editions of his stories have been published, the latest being *Stages of Fear*. His ninth volume of tales *A Maze for the Minotaur* was published by Tartarus Press in 2021.

Marion Pitman is a Londoner who has been writing poetry and fiction all her life, most of it weird (the poetry and fiction as well as the life). She sells second-hand books, and has worked as an editor, proof-reader, cleaner and artists' model, though not all at once. She has no car, no cats and no money. Her hobbies include folk-singing and theological argument, and she has watched cricket on three separate continents. Her short story collection,

Music in the Bone is published by Alchemy Press.
(www.marionpitman.co.uk)

Wendy Purcell used to be a nurse, now she writes and gardens and rides her bike along flat paths. Her short stories and poems have appeared in various publications in Australia, the US and the UK. She lives near Melbourne, Australia, on five acres where it's damn hot in summer and bloody freezing in winter. She enjoys watching daffodils bloom, as if it's never happened before, and giving suspect advice to random strangers on social media.

Rosanne Rabinowitz is the author of *Resonance & Revolt* and *Helen's Story*, which were respectively shortlisted for the British Fantasy Society and Shirley Jackson awards. Her work has also appeared in anthologies from independent publishers such as Swan River Press and Egaeus Books, and her Brexit-inspired weird tale "All That is Solid" is available as a chapbook from Eibonvale Press. She lives in South London, an area Arthur Machen once described as "shapeless, unmeaning, dreary, dismal beyond words". In this most unshapen place she tries to find enough time to enjoy whisky, chocolate and loud music. She shares her flat with two cats and two crab bells.
(rosannerabinowitz.wordpress.com)

Steve Rasnic Tem is a past winner of the Bram Stoker, World Fantasy, and British Fantasy Awards. His last novel *Ubo*, a finalist for the Bram Stoker Award, is a dark science fictional tale about violence and its origins. He has published over 500 short stories in his forty-plus year career. Some of his best are collected in *Thanatrauma* and *Figures Unseen*, and in *The Night Doctor & Other Tales*. He is a 2024 recipient of Horror Writers Association's Lifetime Achievement Award.
(www.stevetem.com)

Stephen Volk is the author of four collections: *Dark Corners, Monsters in the Heart* (which won the British Fantasy Award), *The Parts We Play* and *Lies of Tenderness*. His acclaimed *Dark*

Masters Trilogy features Peter Cushing, Alfred Hitchcock and Dennis Wheatley as central characters, while *Under a Raven's Wing* teams up Poe's master detective Dupin with Sherlock Holmes. For the screen, he is best known for creating the BBC's notorious "Halloween hoax" *Ghostwatch* and the ITV paranormal drama series *Afterlife*. He also wrote the Ken Russell movie *Gothic* and *The Deadness of Dad* starring Rhys Ifans, which earned him a BAFTA.

(www.stephenvolk.net)

THE EDITORS

Mike Chinn lives in Birmingham with his wife Caroline and their tribe of guinea pigs. He's written fiction that runs from westerns to sword & sorcery and space opera, via horror and his Damian Paladin pulp adventures, along with its ever-expanding universe (three adventures featuring the submarine cruiser *USS Oswin* have been collected in *Drawing Down Leviathan* and published by Saladoth Productions) and the occasional Sherlock Holmes pastiche. As well as editing four books for The Alchemy Press (*Swords Against the Millennium* and *Pulp Heroes* volumes one to three) he has somehow found himself working for Pigeon Press, editing the kind of crazed books he would never have the nerve to write.

(http://saladoth.blogspot.com)

Peter Coleborn is the creator of the award-winning Alchemy Press which has (co)-published a range of anthologies and collections over the past twenty-five years. He has edited various publications for the British Fantasy Society (including *Winter Chills/Chills* and *Dark Horizons)*, and co-edited with Pauline E Dungate the Joel Lane tribute anthology *Something Remains* in 2016. Since 2018 he co-edited with Jan Edwards the first three volumes of *The Alchemy Press Book of Horrors*. In 2021 he published Stephen Jones' *The Alchemy Press Book of the Dead 2020*, which was followed by Jones' *Book of the Dead 2021* and *Book of the Dead 2022*. He also edits and designs the books for The Penkhull Press, a general imprint rather than horror or fantasy, based in north Staffordshire. He is also a keen photographer.

(www.alchemypress.co.uk)

-